Other books by Sheila Hardy:

The Diary of a Suffolk Farmer's Wife, 1854–69
The Story of Anne Candler
1804. That Was the Year . . .
The Village School
Pages from the Past
On Audio Tapes – Stories of Edwardian Childhood

In the 1950s, the author left her native Suffolk to read English at the University of Nottingham. Teaching posts followed in various parts of the country, and it was while she was living in Dorset that she met and married her Captain Hardy. She feels that it is the 'kismet' associated with both Nelson's captain and the writer Thomas Hardy, that eventually brought her back full circle to live in Suffolk.

When teaching she always placed great emphasis on the contemporary background of the literature her pupils were studying and from this has grown her fascination with 'real history' – the everyday lives of the people who never made it into the history books. Fortunate to have in Ipswich 'the best Record Office in the country', it is there that she carries out much of the background research for her books. Newspapers of the C18 and C19 provide a treasure house of information, some of which she uses in the talks she gives both to groups around the county and in her regular monthly broadcasts for BBC Radio Suffolk.

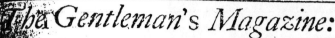

The Gentleman's Magazine:

ST 'JOHN's GATE.

For JUNE 1763.

CONTAINING,

In Quantity and greater Variety than any Book of the Kind and Price.

By SYLVANUS URBAN, Gent.

LONDON: Printed by D. HENRY, at St JOHN's GATE. May be had Compleat Sets, in 32 Volumes, beginning with 1731.

THE
GENUINE TRIAL

OF

MARGERY BEDDINGFIELD

AND

RICHARD RINGE,

FOR

Petty Treafon and Murder, committed on *John Beddingfield*, late of *Sternfield*, in the County of *Suffolk*, Farmer.

THURSDAY, MARCH 24, 1763.

THE prifoners being fet to the bar, were arraigned as follows.

Clerk of Arraigns.] Richard Ringe, hold up your hand.

Margery Beddingfield, hold up your hand.

Richard Ringe, you ftand indicted by the name Richard Ringe, late of the parifh of *Sternfield*, county of *Suffolk*, Labourer, late fervant of

A 2

<figure>
⎯⎯⎯⎯⎯⎯ ◆ ⎯⎯⎯⎯⎯⎯
</figure>

IPSWICH, *March* 25.

At the Affizes held at Bury Yefterday, Marg. Beddingfield, Widow, and R. Ring, Hufbandman, were found guilty of the Murder of John Beddingfield, late of Sternfield, Farmer. The Woman was fentenced to be burnt, and the Man to be hanged and his Body anatomized.

TREASON'S

FLAME

With my very good wishes,

Sheila Hardy

Sheila Hardy

A SQUARE ONE PUBLICATION

First Published in 1995 by
Square One Publications
The Tudor House
Upton-on-Severn, Worcestershire WR8 2HT

© Sheila Hardy 1995

British Library Cataloguing in Publication Data
is available for this title

Hardy, Sheila M.
   TREASON'S FLAME
   I.Title
   823 [F]

   ISBN 1 899955 00 3

Typeset in 11 on 13pt Palatino by
Avon Dataset Ltd, The Studio, Bidford on Avon B50 4JH

Printed in Great Britain by
Antony Rowe Ltd of Chippenham, England

Author's Note

Four very brief newspaper reports, 'An Account of the Trial at Bury St. Edmunds' (SRO) and an article entitled 'Some Account of the Murder of Farmer Beddingfield' in the Gentleman's magazine, May 1763, inspired what follows. Most of the characters mentioned were real people who were involved in the short lives of Margery Beddingfield and Richard Ringe.

While I have used the evidence given at the trial to support my own theory as to what actually occurred at the farm at Sternfield, I must emphasise that this is an imaginative attempt to explain what might have led up to the trial and its hideous outcome.

'Burning to death – an ancient punishment of women for petty treason or high treason. Included murder of a husband by his wife, murder of a master or mistress by a servant and several coinage offences.

This punishment was last inflicted for murder of a husband in 1726 and was abolished by the Treason Act in 1790; in practice it had rarely been actually inflicted, the custom being to strangle the woman before she was burned.'

'Treason Act 1351
Petty treason – servant killing master, wife killing husband, an ecclesiastic killing a superior – abolished in 1828. Replaced by Offences Against Person Act of 1861 when the crime became murder.

Dramatis Personae

The Family

Cornelius Beddingfield	Yeoman of Sternfield	b.1663	d.1755+
Margaret (neé Poles)	his second wife	m.1732	d.1783
Anne *(Margaret)	their daughter	b.1736	
John	their son	b.1737	d.1762
Margery (neé Rowe)	of Peasenhall	b.1743	d.1763
Pleasance	b.1760 – married at Felixstowe		
Elizabeth Burnham	b.1723 daughter of Cornelius and his first wife		
Richard Burnham	m.1743 – of Felixstowe		

Servants

Chandler Cobb — Farm bailiff – dismissed

Betty *(Elizabeth) Riches	Dairymaid
Liddy *(Elizabeth) Clebold	Nursemaid
Richard Ringe	Farm Bailiff
John *(William) Mastertown	Cowboy
William *(John) Nunn	Farm boy

At Parham

Robert Rowe	Margery's father	d. August 1762
Mrs Jollye	His housekeeper	

Others

William Starkey	Friend of John Beddingfield
James Scarlett	Butcher of Saxmundham
Dr Sparham	
Dr Edgar	

* Indicates the baptismal name – changed in this account to avoid confusion, e.g. Margery or Margaret were considered to be too similar. In the 18th Century the same few names enjoyed great popularity.

+ In the story this date has been ignored.

For Sue Kerswell whose
encouragement meant so much

One

DECEMBER 1758

'The burning question is, how are we amuse ourselves in the short time we have been granted?'

The question rebounded from the walls of the inn surrounding the courtyard where the two young women stood alone except for the elderly ostler who shuffled towards them from beneath the archway where he had seen off the departing coach on the next stage of its journey.

'Won't you step inside and take something warm, Miss Anne, while you wait for Master Beddingfield's carriage?' He addressed his remarks to the taller of the two girls.

'No, thank you, William. We will wait here – or perhaps take a turn in the street to stretch our legs.'

'You may be in for a tidy wait, m'dear. You be somewhat forward of the time expected.'

'Never mind us, William. I am sure you have much to do, so please don't let us detain you.'

The old man left them, mumbling as he went of the chill in the day and how things ought not to be changed without folks being given proper warning.

There had been a mix-up over the girls' travelling arrangements. It had been expected they would arrive upon the regular coach but such were the numbers wishing to make their way to London and the towns which lay upon the route, that an earlier coach had been brought into service. Without thinking of the consequences, places had been taken for the young ladies on that one.

So now, they stood waiting beside their boxes.

'I say again, what shall we do? Where shall we go? Let us live a little while we can!'

'I don't think it would be proper for us to go anywhere. We were told to wait here for your father's carriage. Suppose that it should come and the man not find us here?'

'Then he would most certainly wait for us. My dear, you really must not be so anxious. Life should be exciting, full of new experiences – and I certainly intend to make the most of the freedom we have gained at long last.'

The taller girl looked at her friend and smiled reassuringly.

'If it will make you feel easier, I will leave a message with the ostler to tell father's man where we have gone.'

'But,' the other insisted, 'it is not seemly for us to walk alone in the town. What would Mrs Clarkson say?'

'My dear Margery, we shall not be alone!' She laughed as she caught the look of bemused fear that crossed the girl's face. 'We shall be together, so it cannot be said that we are alone! And as for Mother Clarkson, she, I am delighted to say, is no longer responsible for us. The moment we left her house this morning, we left school and all its rigours and drawbacks, like these fearfully dull clothes, behind us. It is all very well for you, my pet, your pink cheeks and chestnut curls look splendid against this sombre grey gown and cloak, but it does absolutely nothing for me. I need bright colours to look my best. Why, I sometimes think when I tie on my bonnet that I can hardly tell where my face begins and the straw ends!'

'Anne, you are incorrigible.' Margery laughed though she thought, as she so often did when she was with her friend that she really ought not to encourage her in her worldly ways.

'Indeed I am – if that means what I think it does. So, let us seize this opportunity and go in search of some diversion. And we will start with the delights being offered in this.'

She pointed to the large printed advertisement displayed on the wall behind them.

'I've never seen waxworks, have you?'

'No, Anne! We shouldn't. I'm not sure that it is not wicked to look at images . . .'

'How can it be wicked, pray? It's, um, it's . . .' inspiration struck her, 'it's educational! For look, we are to see,' she read from the advertisement, 'a full sized model of the King of Prussia himself in full uniform. With two from the regiment of the Death-heads standing guard over prisoners, two grenadiers of the second battalion of Footguards armed for duty and four prisoners of war representing the different nations the illustrious king has encountered. Well, my child, I think even your papa would own that you will learn much from a view of this exhibition. And, as dear Mrs Clarkson was so fond of telling us, "a practical demonstration can often teach more than study of the book!"'

Margery often found herself swept along by her friend's glib tongue and quick reasoning, and on this occasion as before, she felt she should resist but could find no convincing argument as to why they should not take a few minutes to view the waxworks. Provided, of course, that it was not too far away, for they really should not walk unaccompanied through the streets.

Anne left word with the ostler and then they set off across the main square in Saxmundham to the inn where the exhibition was housed.

They were halfway across the carriage way when a troop of foot soldiers came bearing down upon them, followed by a dozen or so on horseback. The girls scuttled to the raised sidewalk and Anne made Margery stop to watch as the group came to a halt in the market place. The officer in charge took his place in front of them and issued orders which were indistinct to the bystanders.

'There is something very dashing about a man in uniform – and on horseback he's even more . . .'

Anne's words were lost in the sudden clamour as the armed troops broke ranks and swiftly began to search the premises on either side of the street.

Fear overtook Margery. Here, already, was retribution for their daring to leave the safety of the inn courtyard. She whispered as much to Anne who roundly pointed out that it was quite to the

3

contrary, now they were with other respectable townspeople but had they remained waiting alone in the courtyard, they would probably be facing the stares and possibly impertinent remarks of the soldiers who had just poured in through the archway.

When those troops who had searched the Three Tuns had returned to the street, the girls slipped through the doorway marked by a handwritten sign that read 'Exhibition'. The room was dimly lit and deserted except for the life size models. After the animation of the uniformed figures they had just witnessed outside, the stillness of the tableau before them was most striking.

Both girls were awed by the impressive detail of the Prussian sovereign. Even Anne found herself speaking in hushed tones as they moved from one group to the next.

'You could almost fancy that they are alive,' Margery whispered.

'Indeed, I could swear that this one breathed.' Anne was looking closely into the face of one of the group of five closely packed prisoners, kneeling before their Prussian captors.

'I admire the care that has been taken with the detail.' Margery said softly. 'That one's clothes look as if he has slept in them for days on end.' She was about to put out her hand to touch the figure when a voice from the doorway made them jump. The elderly woman in charge of the show demanded their entry fee.

'Such a to-do,' the woman said, 'and I've lost several good customers just because there's a Frenchie prisoner on the run.'

She sensed the girls would be willing listeners so folding her arms across her chest she imparted what had been gleaned from the search party.

'Seems a gang of them broke out from Yarmouth Jail a couple of nights ago. Our lads have got 'em all back except for this one that's given them the slip. But he's hardly likely to be around here, is he?'

She laughed at the implausibility of such an idea. 'And if he is, silly . . .' The expletive was totally foreign to the girls, 'Well, good luck to him, I say. It's not the weather to be without shelter at nights and him clad only in breeches and shirt, by all accounts.'

As they went out through the door, Margery turned for one last look at the figures. The room was even darker now, but just for a moment she fancied that the floor-length curtain at the far end billowed slightly and that the composition of the tableau of the group of prisoners differed from how it had looked a few minutes before.

'And are you young ladies going to see the other wonders on display in the square?'

Margery grabbed Anne's elbow in entreaty that they should return to wait for the carriage, but the other girl was all agog as the woman regaled them with a summary of the entertainers likely to be seen at the annual Midwinter Fair.

As they stepped out into the street, the early afternoon had already turned into the darkness of the shortest days of the year. Lamps had been lit in shops and those on the stalls twinkled and shimmered. Here and there a brazier glowed and the air was filled with the smell of roasting food. The tinny notes of a pipe band heralded a group of Mummers. A stilt walker passed beside them, so high in the air that they could barely see his head in the fading light. A troupe of acrobats spun their way among the crowd causing people to move quickly to one side to avoid colliding with the gyrating bodies.

On the far side of the square, quite close to the entrance to the inn courtyard where the girls ought to return, a large crowd had gathered. From the bursts of applause and the sudden gasps of amazement, it was clear that something out of the ordinary was happening. As they reached the edge of the crowd, the area above their heads was suddenly illuminated as great tongues of fire leapt upwards.

Anne pushed Margery ahead of her through the ring of mainly male spectators. In the centre of the clearing was a man naked but for the rough animal skin slung across one shoulder, which when secured about the waist barely covered his buttocks. The girls took up their place just in time to see the man take up a set of red-hot tobacco pipes flaring with brimstone and put them into his mouth, licking his lips with relish as he did so. Next he placed a bundle of matches between his lips, lighted them all at once and held them in his mouth until they were all extinguished.

Anne was entranced by the spectacle, craning forward to watch every move the man made. She almost held her breath as he put his hand into the brazier and took out a handful of live coals, slowly and sensuously licking them in turn. Then with a quick movement, he replaced those with a handful of glowing charcoal which he piled upon his tongue. Throwing back his head as if in laughter, he turned to his assistant who handed him a slice of raw beef which he placed on top of the coals in his mouth. He moved slowly round the circle, mouth ajar so that all could see for themselves. He stopped in front of Margery, removed the slice of charred meat from his mouth and held it towards her.

In stark terror she stared into the fiery cavern of his mouth. The colour drained from her face, her eyes, stinging with the smoke, filled with tears. Inside her head she could hear the sound of drums beating, faster and faster. Somewhere, a long way off it seemed, she could hear a voice saying something about singeing hair. There was a sickening smell. All about her she could see flames, feel their heat searing her body. She was desperate to escape but yet she was held there as if by unseen bonds . . . she fell to the ground at the feet of the fire-eater.

The noise of the crowd was deafening. Those at the back were oblivious of the small drama which had been played out at the front, seeing only the head of the entertainer. He, for his part, was quite used to having young women faint during the course of his performance, in fact, he would have been disappointed had there not been one at least each time. Showman that he was, he selected the female most likely to react and made a play for her attention. Most, he had discovered, were likely to be entranced by his prowess and he would hold them captive, their eyes watching his every move, their bodies swaying in time with his until eventually the growing fervour was too much and they would collapse – usually at his feet. It gave him an added sense of power that he could walk away from the prone figure, giving a look that would send the rest of the spectators wild with applause. There was usually someone in the crowd, a kindly older woman or a respectable farm labourer, who would help the victim to her feet and convey her to comparative safety at the edge of the throng. The fire-eater was not above taking his share of the contents of the pocket purse which the 'good Samaritan' managed to lift while helping the lady. Sometimes, the young woman when fully recovered might linger until he had finished performing and offer him supper and other delights of the night. He did not think that was likely to happen in this case. In truth, he was a trifle disconcerted for it was not this girl that he had been watching at all. He had hardly noticed her, it was the other one he had his eye on. He had seen how flushed the taller one had become as she watched; he had sensed her excitement and it was to her that he had made the offering, not realising that to do so, he would come so very close to the other who had let out that bloodcurdling scream before she dropped down.

Anne knelt beside Margery who showed no sign of regaining consciousness. Panic overtook her. No one seemed to care. What should she do? She tried to raise the insensible body but was hampered by the press around her.

'Will no one help?' she cried.

As if in answer to her plea, the crowd parted to allow a young man passage. He took a startled look at Anne and then scooped Margery up into his arms and carried her off.

'Now,' said the young man when he had propped Margery up in the corner of the carriage and Anne had returned from the inn carrying smelling salts, 'perhaps you will be good enough to explain just what you were about, Miss Anne.'

Before she could reply, he went on, 'I come here to have my dinner with some friends to find my father's carriage parked in the way and the man beside himself because Miss and her little friend cannot be found anywhere. So, knowing that my sister has still to find her brains in spite of having been at school all these years, I forego my dinner to go in search of you. And just as well I did, it seems.'

Anne had regained some of her spirit now that the worst

7

danger was over and would have chided her brother for treating her still as a child but she was concerned that Margery was only just beginning to show signs of life. She held the strong smelling salts to the girl's nose and was gratified to note the sudden inhalation they caused. She sat on the edge of the seat opposite and chafed Margery's icy hands in her own.

'She is thoroughly chilled, I fear,' Anne whispered to her brother.

He left his place immediately muttering that he would see what could be done and she heard him giving some order to their driver who was hovering close by.

Margery's now open eyes stared about her. As consciousness returned, so too, did the horror of what had led to her present state. Anne's worried face and the close confines of the carriage were, for the moment, both reassuring yet baffling. The sudden appearance of a young man bearing rugs and warmers for feet and hands added to the mystery.

'What . . .where . . .?'

'Say nothing, Miss Margery, until you have drunk this.'

He handed her a glass of negus.

'Go on. It will do you good. And I suppose you could do with one too, young Madam?' he enquired of Anne. To her surprise she saw that the porter who had followed her brother out had a tray containing glasses for all of them as well as a platter holding slices of cold meat, small pies and bread.

'I've missed my dinner and I don't suppose you have eaten either since breakfast, have you?'

The girls confessed that this was so, adding that in their excitement to be leaving Mrs Clarkson's Academy, neither had eaten more than the usual bowl of porridge, foregoing the thick slices of stale bread which it was customary to soften in their cups of chocolate. The mundane memory made both girls smile, thus relieving the tension of the past hour.

All three attacked the food with vigour and as they ate, brother and sister talked of trivial matters in an attempt to take Margery's mind off what she had witnessed. For herself, Anne could not think what had made her friend react in such a milk-sop fashion to so exciting a spectacle. Margery might look fragile but never before had she shown such weakness. Anne knew that her friend had been strictly brought up by a father who was said to be very conscious of the lurking presence of the Devil. Perhaps Margery had seen Hell's fire and Lucifer himself in the market square. The idea made the irreligious Anne giggle.

'What's caught your fancy, Miss?'

The girlish half suppressed noise cut across the thoughts of the young man who was gazing at Margery with keen interest. He could hardly believe that this striking looking young woman was the rather mousey little creature who had spent at least two weeks twice a year for the past three or so at his home. Of course, he had not spent much time there himself recently and when he did, there were other things to do than take notice of schoolgirls.

John Beddingfield had always been quite fond of his sister Anne who, unlike his older step-sisters, had idolised him. Anne, three years his junior, had graduated from the baby trailing after him, to being quite useful in his games. She had, for example, developed an unusual but powerful overarm bowling technique which had allowed him to practise his batting stroke; she climbed trees as well as he did and was almost as proficient with a catapult.

However, being away at school, as well as growing up, had inevitably changed their relationship, so that now the only pursuit they had in common was a love of riding. This they still did together whenever the chance arose but then, three years ago, John had been annoyed to find that Anne's time was taken up with the quiet, doll-like creature who had become her bosom companion at school.

That was three years ago, when the young man of seventeen's interest in females looked out – towards the unobtainable – young married women, young unmarried women of superior rank, even mysterious older women – and the obtainable who were to be had for a price.

Now, by his own estimation, an experienced man of the world, he was forced to admit that maybe having Miss Margery in the house for the Christmas period might prove more interesting than he had previously thought possible.

He shook his head severely at his sister. 'Almost seventeen you may be, Miss, but you still behave like a foolish child. Giggling is definitely not ladylike.'

His gift for mimicry, in this case a passable imitation of Mrs Clarkson, set both girls laughing.

'Well, my dear ladies, I am going to send you off home. I would come with you except that I have some business here to attend to.'

At Anne's snort of disbelief, he added. 'Since our parents do not look for my return for a day or so, you will oblige me by not saying anything of our meeting here.'

He looked at Margery's wide-eyed puzzled expression.

'Similarly, I think it would be better if your little adventure goes unremarked. I will make sure that the man says nothing of your not being here when he arrived.'

In spite of the smile there was a cold reminder that each of them had something to hide.

Having settled the girls comfortably, making sure that they were as warm as could be made possible, he made his farewell. Holding Margery's hand for perhaps a second or two longer than was customary, he raised it to his lips. She cast her eyes downwards in embarrassment. This was the first time a young man – or any man at all – had done such a thing. It was all the more surprising for she had long been aware of his antipathy towards her. This day was to have been simply the day when by virtue of leaving school behind, she crossed the threshold into womanhood. Now it had become a day more eventful than she could ever have dreamed of, one that would lead to greater changes than she would have believed possible.

That she would also have cause to remember this day on the day she died was a thought that did not then disturb the myriad of images which filled her head. As the carriage left the town and bumped its way over the uneven country road that would bring them to Sternfield, she sat close into her corner seat, hugging her secret thoughts to herself. Anne interpreted her closed eyes as a sign that Margery had still not fully recovered from shock and surprisingly, she had the sensitivity not to force conversation upon her.

In the scene being played out in Margery's head, a male figure, who wore the clothes of John Beddingfield but had the facial features of the fire-eater mixed with those of one of the models from the waxwork tableau, knelt before her and asked her to become his wife.

'But I could not think of such a thing!' Too late, Margery realised she had spoken out loud.

'What thing?' Anne looked at her quizzically. Deep in her own thoughts, she wondered if she had missed some earlier remark by her friend.

'It was nothing. I was dreaming, I think.' She felt the lameness of the excuse but it appeared that Anne accepted it. For several minutes both continued silent, then in a whisper Margery asked;

'Anne, do you ever think about . . .being married?'

'Lord, yes!' She laughed. 'I think about it a great deal.'

'You do?'

'Why don't tell me you don't? Surely you are not so goody goody that you've not let your thoughts wander to what it will be like on your wedding night. What will happen when the curtains are pulled round the big bed and your husband gets in beside you and . . .'

'Hush, Anne, hush!' She covered her ears to blot out the crude comments now, as she had always done at school when the other girls had talked of such things. Her father had impressed upon her from an early age that indulgence of the body in any way whatsoever was the work of the devil and she had been careful never to give in to temptation to satisfy any physical longings she might have. Of course she knew that the purpose of marriage was procreation but she had only the vaguest notion of how this was achieved. In so far as she had ever given the matter any thought, marriage meant a man and woman living in the same house, with the woman supervising the household and bringing up the children. Occasionally the married couple would sit and converse with each other and even more occasionally might attend a social function together. Such a limited view was almost inevitable for one whose experience was based solely on those households where she had made short visits. Certainly her own home could provide no example. Her mother had died before Margery, her only child, was a year old. Her father had never remarried, leaving the early nurture of his child to an elderly housekeeper.

Like most girls of her age she had read poetry and some fiction which told of romantic love but the gallant salute of the knight's lips to the maiden's hand bore, as far as she could understand it, very little relation to the getting of offspring.

Margery closed her eyes again and considered her future. The immediate future, that is the next few weeks, were taken care of. She was to stay with Anne. But after that? In reality there was no question. The matter had already been decided for her. Her father's letter in which he gave his reluctant permission for her to spend a holiday at Sternfield had made it very plain that now that her education was completed, she was to return to his house and take her place as a daughter's duty demanded. The aged housekeeper would be pensioned off and Margery could take on the running of their very simple household. More usefully, now that his eyesight was failing she would also act as his secretary, read to him, transcribe the notes for his 'extempore' sermons and possibly accompany him on his preaching missions around the countryside.

Unsure of so many things, of this one thing she was certain. She did not want to spend her life in the way her father had planned for her. But what alternative had she? She had no money except that which he gave her – and that sparingly – neither had she any relations who might offer her a home with them.

She envied Anne who had a happy home with doting parents and a brother who, although he teased her, obviously loved her. She had also, married step-sisters who often invited her to stay, thus widening her range of acquaintances. Lucky Anne. If only she could change places with her, if only she could stay at Sternfield forever. As the last wish flashed through her mind, she saw again the figure of John Beddingfield raising her hand to his lips. Then she knew where the answer to her future lay. She would marry John and Sternfield would be her home for evermore.

Two

MAY 1759

John Beddingfield surveyed himself in the glass in his mother's room. Turning slightly to the right, chin uplifted, he squared his shoulders then ran a hand down from his chest to his abdomen, well pleased with the firm flatness it encountered.

'Well, Mamma, will I do?' The question expected no answer.

'This shade of blue suits me, don't you think? I had doubts at first that it might be too dark, but now I see it on, it does very well . . . I might even start a new fashion,' he laughed.

'I should not have to remind you, John, that even this colour is hardly appropriate – within a month of your father's death. I don't know what people will say.'

'A fig for that! It matters not as much as that to me,' he flicked thumb against finger with a satisfying snap, 'what the people about here have to say . . . on any subject.'

'But you should care. These are now your people – most of them – dependent on you. And how you conduct your life affects them and their livelihood.'

The widowed mother tried hard to be severe with her beloved only son.

With outstretched arms, he took hold of her elbows and gently rocked her on the spot, laughing as he did so.

'Oh, little mother, really! It does not suit you to play either the grieving widow or the concerned chatelaine. You and I are too much alike for either of us to pretend to be what we're not.'

He kissed her lightly on the cheek before relinquishing his hold.

'As for my father's death, though regrettable, it was timely, for I doubt I would be receiving his blessing this day. He certainly did not look to his son and heir being married off so young . . .'

'Or as hastily,' his mother added with a frown.

'John, it does worry me. You are too young for all the responsibility you are undertaking. Barely come of age and already you have to deal with the management of a very substantial property. Fortunately, as far as this farm is concerned, you have Chandler Cobb to guide you and keep you in the ways of your father . . . Yes, I know,' she forestalled his interruption, 'that you find Cobb too strait-laced for your taste, but he's an honest man and does his work well. Your father valued him greatly which was why he made it one of the terms of his will that Cobb should remain bailiff for his working life.'

As the mother paced the floor of her room, the son sprawled, one leg over the arm of the chair, a nonchalant arm across the back. The expression on his handsome young face changed from amusement to the flush of anger at the mention of the bailiff's name.

Mrs Beddingfield had paused to stare out of the window. Below, as far as the wooded horizon, stretched the fields and pastures that had been her home for the past twenty-five years. That she was to leave it all next day brought no great sorrow. She had never considered herself anything but a townswoman, escaping, whenever she could during the past quarter of a century, to enjoy the society of London or Bath. She had found the lack of sympathetic neighbours in Suffolk a great trial. The trouble with being one of the daughters of a penniless member of a very minor branch of a noble family was that one had the taste for the good life without the income to satisfy it. Marriage to a wealthy farmer had enabled her to buy her way into London society but not into the county set. Welcome awaited her at many a good Town house dinner, ball or card game but when she was at home she was but a farmer's wife and as such found the doors of most of the big houses firmly closed against her.

It was this that had her determine that her step-daughters,

and later her own daughter, should marry into those families where access had been denied her. When this had proved fruitless, she had resolved that her precious son, heir to a sizable property, might well be looked upon with favour by one of those county families who had rather more daughters than they would find baronets for.

She let out a deep sigh as she turned from the casement for, yet again, she was to be thwarted.

'Why, oh why, did you have to become entangled with that girl? If your needs were so pressing, then why could you not have found some lusty village wench who would have been quite happy to serve you and would certainly have made no fuss about a bastard, provided you had settled for its keep.'

'We have been through all this before, Mamma. I love Margery and I would have married her even if . . .'

'Her father hadn't demanded it! Really! These country folk are so narrow in their outlook. I can't see why Rowe could not have sent her away somewhere to have the child. I could have given him several addresses of reputable houses where she might have been well attended and the child put out to adoption. It happens all the time, even to girls from the best families. And since he had taken the trouble to send her to school, he could always have told the curious that she had gone to another to improve her French or drawing or whatever little accomplishment she needed to develop. And, naturally, we would have borne most of the expenses. But no! I have had to sit in church for the past three Sundays and listen to my son's name being called out linked to that of a little chit of not yet seventeen who should have known better than to behave like a kitchen maid.'

She sank down on the chest at the foot of the bed that she had shared with her husband, the bed in which this errant son of hers had been conceived. Tomorrow he would bring his bride to this bed and the child which had anticipated the marriage service would in fullness of time be delivered there. As for her, once she had overseen the nuptial feast – and a shabby affair that would be compared with what she had dreamed for her son – she would leave the house and start a new life for herself.

'And as for love,' she snorted over the word, 'what you feel is good honest lust. You can dress it up all you like with poetic language, but the pair of you are no different to any other young animals who felt the urge to satisfy their basic instincts.'

'Mother!' Her plain speaking shocked him.

'You listen to me, John. No good will come of this hasty marriage. For a start, you hardly know each other . . . and you are both far too young.'

'Now, Mamma. That won't hold water. You were not much above seventeen yourself when you married my father.'

'True,' she conceded, 'but your father was a good twenty years my senior and had experience of life . . . how to manage people . . .'

At that, the son exploded with laughter.

'He might have been able to manage those who worked for him, but, confess it now, mother dear, he never, ever, managed you. If ever a wife had her own way, it was you.'

He took advantage of the smile of agreement that crossed her face.

'And, dearest Mamma,' his voice adopted the wheedling tones he had so often used as a boy to get his own way, 'you will admit, I believe, that if I were today marrying one of the Vernon or Dudley girls, you would have thrown off your black gown and been one of the first to dance at the wedding feast.'

'Talking of which, you, milord, had best take off that fine coat and breeches if they are to look anything in the morning.'

She rose from her seat, aware that she had failed. Both in her last attempt to save her son from the disaster she saw ahead of him, and in the way she had raised him. Too late, she realised that her indulgence of the boy accounted for the determination of the young man to continue to have his own way. Perhaps if she had not been so adamant last Christmas that his attention to Margery was likely to be misconstrued, then he might not have shown the interest that he had. He had ever been contrary – she had known when he was a child that if she wanted him to accept something then the quickest way to achieve it was to pretend to deny it to him. She should have remembered that four months ago but then she had believed that her son had left childhood behind.

Too late now for regretting what had passed. For the present, there was still much to be done before she could shake off her responsibility for this household.

'I must see how the preparations are faring in the kitchen.' She turned when she reached the door. 'If you should see Chandler Cobb in the yard, would you ask him to send up one of the men to carry down the rest of my boxes? They are to go to the carrier's tonight.'

John felt a twinge of guilt as he returned to his own room to change. He knew that his mother had always planned that in the event of her widowhood she would set up a household in London, either alone or with Anne if she were still unmarried, but he was aware that his marriage had precipitated matters.

For the life of him he could not see why she would not stay. Why things could not go on as before. Margery liked his mother and he was sure that they could have lived together quite happily. When he had discussed it earlier with his mother, she had talked loftily of the 'status of the mistress of the house' – as if Margery would care about that! He was sure that his future wife would be perfectly happy for things to remain as they had been when she stayed in the house as a guest. Since the days when she had first come home from school with Anne, she had fitted in just like another daughter. Then, even his father had remarked on her sweet nature and quiet, gentle ways, adding that he wished that some of her good qualities might rub off on his own rumbustious daughter. Sending Anne to be educated at the Young Ladies' Academy in Lowestoft had not achieved the results he had looked for. But then, his wife had reminded him, they hardly led a quietly religious life at home as was Margery's case.

Replacing his fine clothes with those more suitable for everyday, John realised that this would be his last night in this room. Tomorrow he – and Margery – would go to bed – together

– in the parlour chamber, the best bedroom. The awesomeness of the thought sent a shiver through his lower regions. For the first time he confronted the magnitude of the step he was taking.

Opening the drawer which held his shirts and cravats his eye fell on the little red leather case which tomorrow he would give to Margery. He took it out and opened it to reveal a pair of three-drop ebony earrings lying against a bed of white silk. Carefully he placed one of the delicate pieces in the palm of his hand, intrigued by the way light was reflected by the tiny facets. He was as pleased now with these ornaments as he had been the day he had bought them, that day when he had carried the unconscious Margery from the crowd to his father's carriage.

His mother might disparage the idea of romantic love, but John Beddingfield was convinced that he fell in love with Margery that day. He had felt then an emotion quite unlike anything he had ever experienced before. He had looked down at the delicate figure in his arms, lifeless and vulnerable and he had been filled with an overwhelming desire to protect her and keep her always close to him.

Afterwards, when she and Anne had driven off, he had entered the inn in need of strong liquor to clear his head of the notions that filled it. He could not for the life of him understand why he felt as he did. He was not some innocent young boy, he had had as much, maybe more, experience of women than most young men of his age and class. Like them, he was accustomed to satisfying his bodily needs either with those who sold their services or having a casual but enjoyable, passionate romp with any willing girl he might meet. Just occasionally, a particularly fine looking girl might capture his imagination for a week or so making him go panting after her. But usually his encounters were limited to once or at the most thrice. He had no wish to become stale, and there was always the promise that the next girl might prove even more exciting than the last.

He gave no thought to the women as anything but physical creatures; beautiful, warm bodies in which he could lose himself. Certainly the idea that one day he might marry one of these creatures had never entered his head. Marriage would come one day, of course, but that would be very different. Marriage was what one's parents had and was nothing whatsoever to do with what he did in inn bedchambers or haylofts.

That night, finding himself very poor company which drink did not improve, he had set out to wander through the market before finding the fellows with whom he was to spend the rest of the evening at cards. Finding nothing on the various stalls or in the booths to catch his fancy, he had turned from the market square into one of the narrow lanes which housed the shops of craftsmen. One of these he knew well. It belonged to one of those sons of Judah who had been forced for his religion's sake to flee his native Holland. A fine silversmith and watchmaker, he had also built a reputation in the few years he had been in residence of dealing sympathetically with young gentlemen in need of ready money in exchange for the pledge of a gold or silver watch or some piece of family jewellery.

At that particular moment, John was not in need of funds since he had been very successful the previous day in his bets at a cock-fight. Thus it was mere whim that led him to enter the narrow little shop-cum-workroom. The shopkeeper was in close conversation with a man who, John observed, looked as if he had fallen on very hard times. Despite the bitterness of the weather outside he was without either overcoat or travelling cloak, not even a waistcoat covered his dishevelled shirt. He looked as if he had walked many miles. But in these days when men often had to go far to seek employment, the sight of a homeless traveller was not remarkable. And it was apparent that this man must have come a great distance for the Jewish trader whose own English had been learned locally appeared to be having some difficulty in making his customer understand him.

In some desperation the shopkeeper turned to John for assistance. Could he impart to the other man that he only lent money against pledges, he was not in a position to buy outright. On the counter between them lay a small box containing several trinkets, but what at first caught John's attention was the heavy gold ring set with a fine cornelian.

'What an odd coincidence!' The other two looked at him questioningly.

'I was looking for a gift for my father . . .'

The unspoken questioning looks remained.

'My father . . . his name is Cornelius. You see, a cornelian for Cornelius?' His voice tailed off. The others looked at each other uncomprehending.

'How much do you want for this?' He held up the ring.

Before he could answer, the pawnbroker clutched John's sleeve. 'We do not buy. The ring, the other jewels . . . may be . . . thieved.'

'No!' The denial from the traveller rang defiantly. 'My own. I have to have . . .' he seemed to be fumbling for the word. Finally it came, 'monies.'

The watchmaker shrugged his shoulders in a gesture of futility but John, still holding the ring, looked at what else lay in the box. Beside a little silver thimble engraved with the most delicate pattern, there was a pair of jet black earrings, each one made up of three carefully cut and fashioned pieces increasing in size from that of a seed pearl through to a half inch pendant. The moment he saw these, John knew that he must have then for Margery.

'How much?' he asked again.

The traveller looked at him and for the first time John was aware that there was not only hunger in the man's eyes but fear too. Here was a man who was desperate, who would be prepared to take very little for his trinkets. John was ready to drive a hard bargain but then the thought of Margery wearing the jewels in her ears softened him. He took out his purse and holding several gold coins in his palm held it towards the man. For a moment the wayfarer hesitated, then looked John straight in the eye and took all but one of the coins, placing them swiftly into his own purse. Then he took the remaining coin and gave it to the watchmaker who had stood by watching with curiosity. With a flourish, he bowed to them both and pausing at the door to say, 'Bon soir,' he disappeared into the darkness outside.

'Well, I'll be damned! A Frenchie!'

John laughed while the watchmaker wondered, not for the first time, what gave the English such a peculiar sense of humour. John did not think for one moment that the security of his country would be at risk as a result of his buying trinkets from an enemy who was down on his luck. In fact he gained a perverted sense of amusement from the thought that he had been instrumental in helping the Frenchie evade those blundering self-opinionated troopers who had brushed him and his fellow civilians to one side earlier in the day.

'It is good. You have bought well,' the shopkeeper observed, passing John the box that had held the jewellery.

'You think so? I have no idea of the value of these things. I merely liked what I saw.'

'Then you have the good eye, sir,' the other replied. 'In my country we have some sayings for these things. This,' he held up the ring, 'is the lover, a man with fire in his heart. That one is for the young girl soon to be a wife.' he hooked the silver thimble on to his little finger. 'But these,' holding the jet drops up to catch the light, 'these are for the handsome widow.'

'What nonsense you speak!' John assumed a haughty manner. 'Let me have my purchases and I will be on my way. I think,' he added, 'that you have been well paid for whatever part you may have had in these dealings. I bid you good day.'

He was annoyed that the watchmaker should try to spoil his pleasure but he determined to forget at once the superstitious rubbish he had uttered.

And if he had been one who took notice of omens, then he would have said that the day had been the start of a run of good luck for him, for that night he had gambled for high stakes and won. His luck held over the next two nights' play so that by the time he returned to his home in Sternfield he had about him a good supply of cash as well as a bond on a fair sized property that a young heir-apparent had put up as a security.

But now he replaced the box in the drawer and left the room, descending the backstairs to the kitchens and then out into the yard. Crossing towards the outbuildings where a sick cow was housed, his mind was still full of thoughts connected with the past. He recalled how elated he had felt that afternoon when he had ridden up to the house. He was aching to tell his father of his acquisition for he knew that Cornelius would be pleased to hear of an old rival being within their power even if he would not be too pleased with John's manner of acquiring a hold on the property. Cornelius was a gambler too, though the sport he played was grasping at any and every deal that looked as if it would bring him additional money and power. He appeared to have a sixth sense which alerted him to the misfortunes of others, and there he would be, offering to buy up land cheaply as an alternative to some unfortunate soul being made bankrupt. Gradually he had added to his holdings, conscious that while few thought land a safe investment at that time, the day would come when he would hold the whip hand and be able to make a huge financial killing. It pleased him that his son had spirit but one day, he would have to settle down to run things in the way of his father. That time, he believed, was still a long way off, so he allowed the boy to have his head, sow his proverbial wild oats – just as long as the gambling at the tables did not become out of control.

'I was coming to find you, Mister.' Chandler Cobb's voice held that note of disapproval which had become habitual in his speech to John over the last few months. He had the ability to make the young man feel guilty regardless of whether or not he had done anything to cause such a reaction.

'We have lost the beast. And 'tis my fear that in spite of all the remedies we try, this will not be the first and last one. We haven't had the cattle plague hereabouts for seven years or more and shouldn't have done now, if we'd kept to known stock.'

Rage boiled up inside John. Cobb's impertinence was beyond endurance! Just because he had been with his father for more than twenty-five years, did not give him the right to criticise the way John was running things. The man had resented John taking the decision to buy new stock at market last month. In the past Chandler Cobb had accompanied Cornelius on major buying expeditions, but the last thing John wanted was the dour old bailiff breathing down his neck, watching his every move like some elderly wet-nurse! So, he had made a mistake. How was John to know that the cow was diseased? It had looked healthy enough to him and the seller was an old acquaintance.

The two men looked at each other; one with loathing, the other with irritation for unnecessary stupidity. John's resentment of the man grew daily, but at present he controlled himself sufficiently to say curtly,

'My mother would like you to send someone to bring down her boxes.'

He would have liked to order the man himself to do this menial task. He needed to be brought down to size, to be reminded that he was, after all, only an employee and, like it or not, that he was dependent now on John Beddingfield for a living.

It was Cobb who had spoilt John's homecoming that day before Christmas. As John had ridden into the yard, Chandler Cobb had emerged from the stables with his face as doom-laden as ever. While John dismounted, the bailiff had poured out the news. In the stables as John took care of his horse, he had to hear that prices of feed had risen sharply, there had been several cases of serious poaching, and two of the lads that they relied on for help during the busy time of the year had taken it into their heads to enlist on the last occasion that the recruiting party had passed their way. None of this made much impact on John. It seemed to him very like the gossip of the kitchen, but he was taken up sharply by the news which the man had savoured till last, prefacing it with the fact that his father was not at home.

'He went off about midday yesterday, when it became truly clear that the young madam had gone.'

John longed to shake the older man who, now that he had got John's attention, seemed bent on telling the tale in such a manner that it was difficult to follow.

'For God's sake man! Who has gone where?'

'There's never any need to invoke the Lord's name in vain.'

Cobb's piety almost drove John to violence but he resisted the temptation to hit him hard with his riding crop, slashing it instead against the stable door as he cried out, 'Will you tell me quickly what has happened here?'

Composing himself, Cobb related what he knew.

'Miss Anne and her friend came home three days ago . . .'

'I know that,' John cut in. Cobb ignored the interruption.

'Little Miss Margery was not well so she went to her bed straight away and stayed there the following day. The mistress was afeared she might be going down with the winter fever so she advised Miss Anne to keep from her for a day or so. Well, Miss Anne did that all right! That young woman came to me two days gone and said she wanted to go for a long ride. Said she had missed not riding these past weeks since the summer holidays and that she meant to get herself back into practice before you came home.'

He stopped to draw breath and to allow the implication to sink in that John was somehow involved in these events.

'Well? What happened next?'

'Her old mount was prepared for her and away she went . . .about nine o'clock, I suppose, saying that we were not to worry if she were late back.'

'And?'

'We took her at her word, of course. But then, when it became well into evening and she still not returned, I asked the master if we should go to look for her. Master and mistress talked it over and thought she might have decided to stay the night with one of the neighbours or at her sister's house. They hourly expected a messenger to come with news of where she was. There was no moon that night, so we would not have been able to follow her tracks, but in any case, no one thought any harm had come to her. Your parents are too trusting by half, Mister John, as they have now found to their cost.'

'Quit the sermonising, man, and get to the end of this tale,' John demanded, fearful now of its outcome.

Cobb looked resentful at the admonition but the desire to tell more overcame any affront he felt.

'A messenger did come at last, yesterday morning. The ostler from the King's Head at Wickham arrived bringing our horse with him – and the news that Miss Anne had taken the early coach to London.'

'By God! She's eloped, has she?' John had arrived at the same conclusion as everyone else when they had heard of Anne's sudden departure.

'As to that, I have not been made privy to any other information your father might have.' Cobb was at his most insufferable, John thought. 'All I can tell you, is that the household has been turned upside down and your father, who had a cold upon him, has gone charging off to search for her.

'This man really does consider himself my father's keeper,' John thought, but he said nothing and leaving Cobb to mutter his dire warnings to himself, he went in search of his mother.

He found her sitting with Margery in the little parlour off the kitchen. Both had a pile of sewing beside them but it was obvious that neither was in the mood to give much attention to darning stockings or repairing linen. John was struck by the very normality of the scene with its air of tranquillity. Even with so much pressing on his mind, he was conscious that this must be Margery's influence. He had expected to find his mother full of excited alarms, perhaps pacing the floor, certainly not sitting calmly with her needle.

Both women looked up anxiously at his entrance. He ran to his mother and embraced her while looking with slightly pounding heart at the girl who had smiled before dropping her eyes in modesty.

'Here's quite a to-do, mother, unless Chandler Cobb has made more of the event than it warrants?' He was deliberately light-hearted in his tone.

'I have no doubt he and all the servants have made the most of the story. At present all we know is that your sister rode to Wickham where she boarded the London coach. Why she has done so, without telling anyone of her intentions, is something we still have to discover.'

'Was she alone when she left?'

'That, naturally, was the first question your father asked the ostler. But he could not be certain. He said he had not seen anyone in particular with Anne – no man that is – for we have all come to the same conclusion, of course, that she has eloped. Yet Margery here, says that Anne never spoke of anyone who had captured her affections. There was no drawing or dancing master at school who paid her the sort of attention which might cause her to run off with him. Did she ever confide to you, John, that she was enamoured of someone? Someone of whom her father and I would disapprove? For that can be the only reason why she felt she had to take such a step.'

John considered the matter, trying to recall any conversation he might have had with her during the summer that had in any way touched on the subject of romance. He drew a blank. Anne had seemed to him then, as she had when he had met her three days earlier, still the boisterous companion of his youth. She might now be officially grown up, but to him she was the same immature girl who had made jokes about those who succumbed to love affairs and romantic dalliances.

Cornelius Beddingfield had returned home two days later – alone. Enquiries at the Coach offices along the route had verified that Anne had indeed travelled as an inside passenger to London. The landlady at the Belle Sauvage in Fleet Street remembered serving her with a meal on her arrival. She was certain that the young lady was on her own. No one had come to meet her and she had not given any indication that she was expecting anyone. The landlady, who had seen enough of such things to know all the signs, volunteered the opinion that Anne was not eloping. Or if she was, then she was the coolest runaway bride-to-be she had ever encountered. She had talked quite freely, giving the landlady the impression that she was a frequent traveller. Given the time of year, the hostess had assumed she was making a Christmas visit to friends or relations. She could not recall that the young lady had mentioned going on to another part of the country. On reflection she rather thought that London had been her final destination. Further inquiries around the inn and among cab drivers had proved fruitless.

Cornelius, an infrequent visitor to the city, did not know where to look. As he waited for the coach to bear him homeward, he was forced to admit that rather than rushing off as he had the previous day, he would have done better to have taken his wife with him. She knew London – had friends and contacts there to whom it was possible that Anne had gone. But why? That was the question they all asked themselves and each other, over and over but none of them could find a satisfactory answer.

Christmas Day passed almost unmarked apart from attendance at church in the morning. Cornelius felt duty bound to sit down to the customary Christmas dinner with his workers, but this year they were not encouraged to stay to drink too deeply before being sent off to carry plates of roast beef and plum pudding home to their wives and children.

Two days later Mrs Beddingfield set out for London to seek for news of her daughter. She went alone except for the maid Phoebe who usually accompanied her on her trips to the city. She explained to her husband that she would probably have more success on her own, but secretly she was concerned for Cornelius's health for he had not been able to shake off the heavy cold he had had for three weeks. Beddingfield men were known to have a weakness of the lungs and the last thing Cornelius needed now was to spend time in a city where the damp foggy air held captive the noxious effluent from the workshops of dyers, tanneries and soap manufacturers.

John had expected to go with his mother but she rejected his offer saying that she wished him to stay with his father and relieve him of as much of the farm business as he could.

'The old adage about the ill wind is certainly true here, John,' she had confided to him. 'I have long thought that you should do more of the management of the farm – that your father has let you play too long, but that was his way. Now you can quite naturally take over some of his burdens. While his chest still gives him trouble, you will make sure that he is out of doors as little as possible. You can make whatever calls are needed. It will be good for you to be occupied, rather than mooning about the house so much and turning poor Margery's head.'

His attempts at remonstrations were brushed aside.

'Oh, my boy! Do you think I am blind? I have seen the way the poor thing looks at you. And you, are a mite over-gallant! It is good to see that you have indeed acquired some gentlemanly manners – and I suppose it is good too, to have someone to practise them upon, but be wary – Margery is a sensitive little thing and, unless I am much mistaken, she could easily misunderstand your attentions. Oh, she is a dear, sweet creature and she has been a great comfort to us, otherwise I would have packed her off home to her father, but . . .' she paused and looked straight into the wide eyes of her son, 'Margery Rowe is not the sort of girl for you.'

For a moment, John was transported back to childhood with his mother telling him firmly he could not have some trifle or other that he craved. His annoyance now was every bit as strong as the anger and frustration he had felt as a child.

Had she been just that little bit wiser, Mrs Beddingfield would have insisted that Margery's visit be brought to an end, but in truth, the girl had established herself very firmly as a calming influence over the whole household. Mrs Beddingfield had become accustomed to using Margery as both confidante and deputy. The domestic staff too, had accepted her without question; she was prepared to work alongside them without fuss and when she had to pass on an order, she did it with such pleasantness that no one could fault her. Although Mrs Beddingfield, and everyone else for that matter, tended to refer to her as 'little Margery', her slightness of stature belied her inner strengths. It was on these that John's mother had come to rely and why she now felt she could leave her home at this time, secure in the knowledge that Margery would keep every thing running smoothly.

The girl was severely tested over the next month for it seemed that crisis followed upon crisis.

For ten days nothing of importance was heard from Mrs Beddingfield. Then came the news that she had finally learned of Anne's whereabouts. To her horror, she had discovered that the girl had attached herself to a theatrical company! This, she was told, had just left Town to perform a winter season in the provinces. Until Mrs Beddingfield had more specific details she would remain in London. Then, when the company's exact itinerary was known, she suggested her husband should join her to find and extricate their daughter from this entanglement.

Cornelius read the letter in his counting house-cum-office and then went in search of John to show him. He got as far as the middle of the yard when he collapsed with a choking fit. He must have lain in the mire for some time before the furious barking of the yard dog alerted the dairy maid.

Severe congestion of the lungs followed with the ever present fear of pneumonia. The surgeon was called but he could do little more than Margery had already set in motion – steam kettles, a rub of hyssop mixed with almond oil and tinctures to increase expectoration. John was amazed at her resourcefulness. How, he had whispered as he stood beside her at the foot of his father's bed, had she known what to do?

Margery had been a little taken aback by his surprise. She had accepted it as part of every girl's knowledge. She had been brought up to the idea of service to one's fellow creatures and ministrations to the sick were a major part of that. She had little expected ever to be grateful to her father's austere regime of upbringing, but here it was, increasing John Beddingfield's admiration of her.

For several nights the pair of them had sat and watched over Cornelius. They talked little but John became more and more attracted to her. He watched her every move, marvelling at the strength she seemed to find to deal with the invalid. He was impressed too, by the gentleness of her touch and the modest way that she coped with the patient's intimate bodily needs. Once, when Cornelius managed to sleep, Margery had allowed herself to doze for a while and John had had the most powerful desire to gather her up in his arms and hold her close to him. She looked, he thought, like a child, yet he was so aware of the woman. He had suppressed the urge but had been forced to leave the room.

Cornelius began to mend but was still not allowed far from his chair by the fire. Margery, when she was not attending to household duties, sat with him, sometimes reading aloud from the county newspaper. Occasionally she would write letters for him, particularly to Mrs Beddingfield who had been torn between pursuing her daughter and returning to look after her husband. In the evening, John would join them and Margery would sit quietly with her sewing while the men talked over farm business, drew up accounts or discussed market prices.

Margery was living in a dream world. In her imagination she was mistress of this household which had already accepted her as a deputy. It was altogether a more enjoyable place than that of her father to which she would soon have to return. In her dreams, she remained here for ever. The only problem was that to do that she would have to marry John, and although in her dream world she pictured him as her husband, the reality was that he was still very remote from her. She was conscious that he liked her, even admired her, but she was convinced that in his eyes she was nothing more than a friend – not just of his sister now, but of the whole family. Indispensable though she might make herself to the household, Margery believed she was incapable of making herself important to John.

So she was in a state of indecision. Part of her was happy and contented, the other full of misgivings for the future. In addition she was still tired from those nights when she had lacked sleep.

It was almost the end of January. The weather had been severe. Snow had not yet fallen but there had been several days of freezing fog and others when gales had lashed the countryside. It was still blowing hard on that day when John had returned home very late from market.

Margery had sat up for him until ten o'clock. Then she had

dismissed the servants to their beds, even the watchful Chandler Cobb had retired to his room at the back of the house having stated that if the young master had any sense he would, because of the inclement weather, stay overnight in the market town. Margery made sure that doors and shutters were secured and the fire well made up but safe, before going off to her bed. She had become accustomed to leaving a candle burning in her room in case Cornelius needed her during the night. And that night she was glad of the little comfort it gave. It was not a night when sleep would come easily however tired she might be. The wind kept up an unceasing high pitched whine which seemed to penetrate every recess of her mind, while against the casements the constant drumming of the rain set up a counter rhythm. A battle seemed to rage between the house and the elements and Margery lay in her bed listening to every skirmish.

Suddenly she was taut with fear. Amid all the noises outside there were new ones. Was it thunder, that frightful thumping? Did she imagine she could hear someone calling, calling her name? Holding her wrap closed with one hand, she took up the candle with the other and went quickly to the head of the stairs. Calmer now, she realised that someone was hammering on the door from the yard and that it must be John returned after all.

'Thank God!' he muttered as she finally unbarred the door and he staggered into the kitchen, slumping down on a stool.

'Let me help you.'

She eased off the sodden coat and threw it over the settle. Then she knelt before him and drew off his boots.

The man was soaked to the skin. 'Come,' said Margery, 'the fire in the little parlour should be burning still. Go through and get warm while I get your night clothes.'

Never for a moment did she stop to consider the impropriety of her entering John's room and bringing down his nightgown, cap and wrap. In her haste she forgot the slippers but remembered to bring towels from the linen store.

'There. You get dry and changed and I will make you a hot drink.'

She poked the fire into a blaze and threw on another log.

It took slightly longer than she had hoped to get the kitchen fire to heat the milk. While she waited she cut off some slices of bread and beef, convinced that he must be hungry.

'I have put some rum in your milk. That should help to warm you right through,' she said as she walked into the little parlour. But when she saw him, Margery the busy little housewife was quickly replaced by Margery the naive young woman. She was filled with embarrassment as she saw him standing before the fire in his night attire and then she realised that she too, was dressed in similar fashion.

She felt the flush to her cheeks, but the light in the room was insufficient for John to notice such details. He took the cup and plate from her.

'What would we do without you, little Margery?' His tone was reassuringly normal.

She backed towards the doorway to leave him.

'Don't go.' He pleaded. 'I know it is very late and you must be tired, but please stay and talk to me while I thaw out.'

She found herself being led to a seat by the fireside. John finished the food and drained the cup.

'Is there any more of that?' He referred to the drink.

'I can easily get more.' Margery leapt up, glad of something to do.

'You heat the milk – why don't you have some too? And I'll get the bottle.'

Margery allowed herself to be persuaded to have the liqour added to her milk. 'It will help you sleep,' he said.

They sat companionably by the fire, John telling her of the terrible conditions he had met with on the road home. Trees had been uprooted and huge branches blown down to block the path. The force of the wind was so great that for much of the journey he had walked, taking much, much longer than he had anticipated.

'But why did you not stay at the inn and come home in the morning?'

'I had thought to do that, but then when the late post came in and I read my mother's letter, I wanted to be home as soon as possible.'

'May I know what she says?' Margery asked diffidently.

'Of course you may. Who better than you? Our little friend and comforter.'

He leaned towards her and touched her hand. She did not draw it away. As his fingers tightened so hers responded. Somehow – and afterwards neither could quite tell how – they were both kneeling, facing each other, close, very close. Then they were in each other's arms, locked in an embrace which carried them both to the summit of consummation. On the hearth the fire roared as the wind in the chimney fanned the flames into life.

Three

JULY 1760

'Go in, Starkey, do. My wife will be pleased to see you. We don't see much in the way of company these days.'

John ushered his guest into the house.

'Margery, my love, are you there?'

The kitchen was empty and so, too, was the little parlour but the door from there to the flower garden stood ajar and gave a clue to Margery's whereabouts. That and the murmur of singing, a softly intoned air which seemed in keeping with the sultriness of the late afternoon. Margery was seated on the low swing that John had rigged up for her from the boughs of the old oak. Needlework in hand she gently rocked herself to take advantage of the little breeze she generated.

At the sound of his footfall, she looked up, her face alight with the pleasure of his approach. He crossed rapidly to her and as she rose he asked,

'Should you be out here in this heat, dearest? And are you sure that swing is safe?'

Starkey, who was a bachelor, took several moments to register the reason for John's concern. He found it a most odd situation to see this former companion, once as carefree as himself, interested only in having a good time regardless of the consequences, now so completely tied to a woman's apron strings.

John turned from her to make the introduction.

'Look, here is an old friend of mine, William Starkey now from Lowestoft way. Starkey, this is my wife, Margery.'

The other man could hardly resist a smile at the emphasis John had placed on the word 'wife'. Indeed, it really did seem that the fellow was besotted with the little woman.

Seated in the cool of the parlour, the men with a tankard of the Beddingfield brew beside them, the visitor took the opportunity to study his hostess. One did not need to be more than an adequate observer of human nature to know that here was a woman who exuded contentment with her lot. He would not have called her pretty, although he had to admit there was something in her looks which gave her a strange sort of beauty. He recalled that he'd heard – where, he couldn't say – that in pregnancy even the plainest woman could appear handsome. He was able to conduct his examination unhindered for John and Margery looked only at each other as John explained how he had come across Starkey at the local market.

'It was a very poor showing today. Another outbreak of the sheep ague. It's this weather, I believe. Too hot one day and too much rain the next. I can't see harvest starting for another month at least at this rate, can you, Will?'

John did not expect an answer or give time for one.

'Will used to live at Glemham but went off some time ago to take over his uncle's estate on the coast. That's right, isn't it?'

This time he did allow time for a reply.

'I believe I must have left the area the same week your father died, John. My uncle had had his first stroke and I went in haste, otherwise I would have been over to offer my condolences.'

'And if you'd stayed a month or so longer you could have come and wished us joy at our wedding.' John laughed good naturedly, brushing aside the reference to death.

Even now, Margery did not like to think of Cornelius's death. In those odd moments, usually in the early hours of the morning when hidden thoughts have a habit of pushing themselves to the front of the conscious mind, she was ridden with guilt that she had not heard Cornelius cry out for assistance. Had she and John not been so rapt in their lovemaking that she had been oblivious of all else, then she might have been able to save the old man.

Now she again refused to face the thought, asking instead, 'And what brought you back today, Mr Starkey?'

The visitor explained that he'd had some legal business to attend to. That having been completed, he had wandered into the market, met John and been persuaded home to dine with them. However, as they had reached the farm, so had his horse gone lame on him.

'So Starkey not only dines with us, dear, he will stay the night. I'll tell Betty to make up the guest chamber.'

'I'll go.' Margery put her hand on John's arm.

'My love, I have to move about, I can't sit still for ever.' She laughed gently and again Starkey was conscious of intruding on an intimate moment between them.

To ease his embarrassment he said rather too loudly,

'Gad, you really are well and truly settled, my lad. I never thought to see the day.'

'Aye. Nor I! Yet I tell you, Will, it was the best day's work I ever did when I married Margery. We suit each other so well that I have no mind to go looking for other diversions. Had you told me some eighteen months ago that I'd say such a thing, I'd have laughed you from here to Harwich.'

'And now you're to be a father! What took you so long, you old rogue?'

John's face darkened. 'I'd rather you didn't say anything to Margery on that subject. She miscarried our first child at seven months. Just at the stage she is now which is why I am perhaps a trifle over-concerned for her.'

Margery herself gave no indication that she was in anything except the finest health – positively blooming – as her maid Betty was wont to tell her at least once a day. Certainly this pregnancy had been much easier than the first; little sickness at the onset and at present neither heartburn nor the night cramps which last time had seized her legs in a vice-like grip filling her with a fear that she would remain set fast forever.

Apart from those days of sticky heat which could weary most folk, she felt full of energy and in very good spirits. This evening she felt exceptionally well, enjoying her role as hostess. She and John had entertained little beyond the occasional immediate members of the family and even that rarely. This was the first time she had sat down with one of John's men friends and she was justly proud that her housewifely skills had withstood the test of being able at short notice to serve up a dinner suitable for a guest.

They had just finished eating when there was a tap at the door and Chandler Cobb walked in.

'Beg pardon, Mistress, Master.' He looked at Starkey. 'I don't like to be the bearer of ill news, but I have to tell you, sir, that horse of yours has a great place on his leg that needs a good looking to. I've put on a bran poultice but I doubt he'll be fit to ride for nigh on a week.'

Starkey looked aghast but managed to thank the bailiff for what he had done.

John said: 'Well done, Cobb. Is the animal fit to be left for the night?'

The man assured him it was. Then he wished them good night and went off to his own quarters over the back of the house.

'That's a good, thorough fellow you've got there.'

John sighed. 'He's conscientious, sure enough, but he's so glum – and he's always right! If only he could make the occasional mistake like the rest of us, then I could like him better. But no – whatever it is, Chandler Cobb knows best.'

'He gives me the shudders! Look.' Margery held out her forearm for inspection.

'See. I've gone all goosey.'

Both men laughed, then Starkey inquired, 'Do you have a spare mount you could lend me to ride home upon tomorrow? '

Before John could answer, Margery sprang up from the table and ran round to perch on his knee. Winding her arm round his neck she cried, 'My love, are you very busy at present? Could you spare a day away? I have a great desire to look at the sea again so could we not all ride in the chaise to Mr Starkey's house and perhaps take a turn on the promenade at Lowestoft on the way back?'

'A capital idea, Mrs Beddingfield. Better still, why not make a holiday of it and allow me to return your hospitality by inviting you to spend the night at my home. And as for Lowestoft, there's no need for you to go there. If it's a view of the sea you want, I can take you to the very cliff's edge on my own property. Do say you'll come, John. I'd like your views on my fields and stock.'

Starkey had become quite excited at the prospect.

John looked first at the animation in Margery's face and then at that of his friend. He suddenly realised that like Chandler Cobb he was beginning to take life too seriously. Why should they not all be carefree again – at least for two days.

'Why not?' He shouted throwing all cautious thoughts aside. 'It's a wonderful idea. What a clever little wife I have. Why didn't I have enough brains to think of it?'

He kissed her long and hard and again poor Starkey felt *de trop*. He was not at all used to such displays of marital affection. He began to think that if he endured much more of this he might well be tempted to seek a wife of his own!

With injunctions not to drink too much, Margery left the men to talk while she went to the kitchen to check that Betty had cleared all away before she retired for the night. She told the servant of their plans for the coming day, mentioning the chores which were to be done during her absence.

From the big chest in her bedroom, Margery removed spare nightwear and a change of clothes ready for the journey, then lay down to sleep well pleased with the day and the prospects for the morrow.

They were on the road early next morning for it promised to be another very hot day. The highway was busy but most of the traffic, horsemen and gentlemen's carriages, was going in the opposite direction making its way to the races in Ipswich.

'We went last year but Margery didn't really enjoy it. She's not at her happiest in large crowds, are you my love?'

'Nor at losing great sums of money either!'

Margery laughed but Starkey had the impression that there was meaning behind this remark. The John he remembered had liked to risk a wager whether it be at cards, a cockfight or a race. Here was yet another example of what marriage had done to him. It would not surprise him to learn that old John had even gone so far as to get himself elected a churchwarden! True he hadn't mentioned it when they had been alone last night but even then, without the restraint of his wife's presence, there had been little sign of the Beddingfield he had known a few years earlier.

Conversation was desultory. Margery, in particular, was taken up with all that was to be seen along a road over which she had not travelled since that day she had left school. Starkey suddenly remembered a sight he had witnessed the previous day but too late to distract her attention as they reached the crossroads. In his concern he made matters worse.

'I wouldn't look there, Mrs Beddingfield.'

'Where?'

'There.' The man blushed scarlet as her gaze followed his finger and she saw the very spectacle he had wished to avoid. A body, swathed in chains swung from the gibbet. From the state of its decomposition it was clear that it had been there some time.

Margery turned very pale but was still able to ask if Starkey knew the history of the corpse.

'A very nasty business. He was a drummer in Lord Riches's regiment which came to camp here for the summer.' He hesitated, wondering how much detail he should give.

'It was the old story I'm afraid. Begging your pardon, Mrs Beddingfield. You know, too much to drink and then he picked up a young woman. He was found the next morning still in a drunken stupor lying beside her dead body.'

'How awful.'

Margery looked back towards the crossroads where the figure swung gently back and forth, the clanking of the chains cutting through the heat haze.

'As you say, an awful outcome to what ought to have been a simple night out.' John perhaps remembered his own similar escapades.

'No, I mean how awful for the soldier. His being so very drunk he would not remember what he had done. And just suppose he didn't kill the girl! Suppose somebody else did and realising that the man was dead drunk he put her body beside him to let him take the blame.'

'Oh come, now, Margery! That's hardly likely.'

'But how do you know if he was guilty or innocent?' She turned to Starkey.

'Mr Starkey, you obviously know the details of this case. Now, when it came to court, had anyone actually seen the pair together?'

'I think all that was known was that the accused was found with the body when the search party went looking for him because he had failed to return to quarters.'

'There you are. No proof of his guilt!'

'Oh, Margery. It is very kind of you to try to defend the villain, but he must have been guilty otherwise they would not have executed him.'

'As to that, I am still not happy that anyone should be convicted for a crime when there is no real evidence of guilt. I wonder how many innocent people have been put to death for crimes they did not commit?'

'Not many, I'll be bound. If you behave foolishly, then you must be prepared to take the consequences, whatever they may be.'

'That sounds very pious, husband dear. I wonder if you always thought like that in the past, eh?'

John laughed. 'All right. I confess that I have had my fair share of carousing nights, as has Will here, but the pair of us are as likely as you are, my dearest, to murder anybody.'

The conversation took on a lighter tone and the rest of the journey passed with Margery and John questioning Starkey about his property and his plans for the future.

Before they sat down to dinner Margery asked if they might walk a bit. She was stiff after such a long drive and felt the need to take some exercise but more important she was longing to go and stare at the sea and smell its strong tang.

Starkey led them across the high pastures towards the edge of the cliffs. Breathing in the bracing salty air, Margery ran ahead of the men to get the first sight of the ocean.

'Be careful!' John shouted.

'Don't be tempted too close to the edge,' Starkey warned 'They sometimes crumble without . . .'

Margery had turned to hear what he said and in doing so, missed her footing and fell. Mercifully, she was still some distance from the edge.

'Oh my God!' John sped towards her screaming her name.

'It's all right. I am quite unharmed!' Margery picked herself up. 'Just a wrench of the ankle, that's all.'

'Are you sure? There is no other place that hurts?' John dared not ask about the baby.

'No. But I will be good and ask for your arm as I go to look down at the water.'

They stood for some time watching the waves rolling in to crash against the base of the sandy cliffs. Margery seemed mesmerised by the regularity of the relentless force which gathered up the body of water into a foaming arch to throw it hard upon the beach before slowly sucking it back to the deep again.

Reluctantly she allowed herself to be taken back to the house where a meal awaited them. Margery was surprised to find herself with an unusual appetite.

'Your sea air makes a glutton of me,' she remarked as she helped herself to more of the cold fowl and vegetables. She also did justice to the dish of late strawberries covered with thick cream and did not refuse either a second glass of wine or later the French liqueur, the origins of which she felt it best not to inquire.

She was in lively form and joined in the conversation of the men. Although it was mainly about farming, John had so often discussed the workings of their own that she was well informed about new trends as well as the problems caused by foreign imports.

At length they all retired for the night, it having been agreed that after a late breakfast, John and Margery would set out for home.

Starkey's last thought before sleep overtook him was how pleasant the last two days had been and how glad he was to have renewed his acquaintance with John Beddingfield.

'I must make sure that I do not lose contact with them. We must see much more of each other.' He yawned and leaned over to extinguish his candle.

A little after midnight Margery woke suddenly from a deep sleep, conscious that something untoward had occurred.

The damp clamminess in which she lay was not, she quickly realised, that of a violent sweat produced by the heat of the night.

She turned and touched the naked chest of her gently snoring husband.

'John,' she whispered.

For a moment he stopped snoring and then turned on to his side.

'John, please wake up.' Her voice was louder and more insistent but still there was no response from him. Desperately, she grabbed his arm and shook it furiously.

'John! The baby's coming!'

A searing pain in her lower back caught her unawares. Without realising it she sank her fingernails deeply into the flesh of his arm.

Instantly he was awake.

'What's happening?' He sat up clutching the injured arm.

'It's the baby. My waters have broken! Oh, John – it will be just like last time.'

She began to sob hysterically.

'I'm so sorry. I should not have left home . . . I should have been more careful and not have fallen . . .   I should not . . .'

The list of self recrimination stopped as she was engulfed in another wave of racking pain.

John leapt from the bed and groped for his clothes. In the unfamiliar room he was unable to find the candle but streaks of the early dawn gave sufficient light for him to manage.

'What must I do?'

His sense of present helplessness was increased by the recollection of the last time they had faced this situation. Then, they had been in their own home with reassuringly knowledgeable womenfolk to hand.

'Rouse Starkey,' she panted. 'One of his serving women must be able to help.'

'Go – now!' The scream of fear and pain which rent the air as John flung open the door was sufficient to disturb the rest of the household.

Starkey's housekeeper took quiet but firm control of the situation. The men were banished to the ground floor while she and the maids did all that was necessary in the guest chamber.

John was totally despondent. Blaming himself for giving in to Margery's whim to go travelling at this stage, he convinced himself that he would be returning home childless and very possibly, he considered in his darkest moments, without a wife.

After what seemed an interminable age but was in fact under three hours, a maid slipped into the room where the two men sat staring blankly into space.

'It's all over, sir,' she announced tentatively.

John let out a hoarse groan and buried his face in his hands.

'Oh, no, sir! It's not like that.' The poor girl grew flustered at the misunderstanding.

'If you please, sir, the baby's here – safe and sound – and the young woman is as well as can be expected.'

The words tumbled out. The young girl had just witnessed her first birth, an event that had both horrified and excited her.

'Missis says you can come up now.'

Full of self-importance, she led the way. Starkey who had been unwittingly caught up in this domestic drama followed without thinking.

Within the room all was now calm and ordered. Fresh linen

had been placed on the bed and Margery lay against the white pillows, her small face looking so very young and vulnerable. Her pale cheeks contrasted with the red creased face of the tiny infant she held close to her.

An air of expectancy filled the room. Housekeeper and maid stood, almost to attention, at the far side of the bed. Proud of their role in the event which had taken place, they now seemed uncertain of what must be done next.

Starkey who had rushed up the stairs behind his friend held back by the door, unsure if he should follow any further. John stood at the bedside transfixed by the sight of his wife and child. There was no movement anywhere. No one spoke. It was almost as if no one breathed. The whole tableau could have served as a model for one of the old Dutch painters.

Then the baby opened its eyes and let out a whimper which turned into an insistent yell. Instantly all the adults were galvanised into action.

John fell on his knees beside Margery.

'Oh, my love – my little love.'

'Which of us do you mean?' Margery managed a laugh.

As if reassured by the gentle sound, the infant cries stopped and the baby fixed John with a long watery stare.

The man was overwhelmed. There was so much he wanted to ask, so much he wanted to say but just at that moment no words would come. He could only stretch out a long thin finger and timidly touch the child's cheek where a tiny teardrop still lay.

'So how do you like your daughter?'

John thought his heart would burst within his chest. He had a daughter. Margery had said when she first knew she was pregnant that this time they would have a perfect girl to make up for the child they had lost and then, when she was sure that she knew how to do it properly, they could have the all important son. He was not worried about sons, all he wanted was a healthy child.

'John, will you apologise to Mr.Starkey for all the bother I have caused him.'

'No bother at all, dear, dear lady.' Starkey said from his discreet distance. He too, was feeling sentimental and ashamed at admitting to such an emotion. He signalled to his housekeeper and maid to follow him from the room so that the new parents might have time to themselves. Somehow, Starkey felt that he was a different person from the one who had set out the previous morning from Sternfield with the Beddingfields. Yesterday he had been a young man. Today he felt he had truly gained mature adult status.

In the month that followed he was to learn even more about domesticity. Once she had been reassured by the old woman who acted as midwife and general nurse to the locality that her baby was perfectly formed in spite of her premature arrival, Margery wanted to go home. She felt perfectly fit within herself. The birth had been remarkably straight forward and she had suffered no post natal symptoms, therefore, she argued, there could be no earthly reason why she and the baby should not be tucked up in the chaise and carried home.

All the women involved in her case shook their heads and threw up their hands in collective horror. She must be confined to her bed for two weeks at least. Then she might be allowed to sit out within the room for a longer time each day, eventually she would be permitted to come downstairs. By this time she would have healed inside and the baby would be feeding strongly and putting on weight. That, she was told, was how it was with most women and she must obey the rules.

Poor John was torn between her pleas to return to Sternfield and the advice he was given on all sides. In addition there was the farm to consider. Much as he hated leaving Margery it was essential that he should go back and see that all was in order. For once he was grateful that Chandler Cobb was there. On the day of the birth, John had sent a messenger to Cobb telling him what had occurred. The return message that all would be taken care of was reassuring but there were some things that even Cobb could not see to, like the payment of bills, ordering stock or selling. These John must do for himself. So for the next four weeks John was back and forth between his own home and Starkey's. Towards the end of that time as Margery increased in health and strength, John began to look strained. A prolonged spell of fine dry weather had brought on the harvest and he and his men often worked late in the evening to get it in. At first John had tried doing a full day's work then riding the thirty or so miles to Starkey's. Often this meant that by the time he arrived all he was fit for was to fall asleep over his supper. Margery found this almost as irksome as not seeing him so a compromise was found that allowed John to divide his time more sensibly.

Even with all the demands of the baby, Margery found her time hanging heavily. Without even her sewing to do she spent many hours reading what books Starkey had in the house. This was a fairly limited collection, mainly books of a religious nature that his uncle had purchased. She also wrote long letters. To John's mother and sister in London she sent minute details of the baby's progress and ended each letter with the hope that they would come to Sternfield for baby's christening.

'As to the christening', her sister-in-law Anne had written, 'what exactly are we to call this wonder child? Is she to be known as baby for the rest of her life? '

'She's right, of course.' Margery said after she had shown the letter to John. 'We really must decide on a name for her.'

'I thought she would be Margery like you,' John replied. 'Or perhaps you would like to name her for your mother – or mine?'

Margery considered the suggestions.

'No. Certainly not Margery. I don't really like the name for myself so it would be unfair to give it to poor baby.'

She gazed at the infant lying in the cradle which had held several generations of Starkeys and had been hastily brought down from the attic for this temporary guest.

'No! What I would like is something unique to her. A name that no one else has.'

'That, my love, is going to be difficult. Every name that exists must have been used by someone.'

'Oh, you know what I mean. I don't what her to be an ordinary

Elizabeth or Sarah or Anne – and certainly not a Prudence or Patience.'

'What about Grace? Or Charlotte? Ruth, Lucy, Clarissa?'

John's mind went over several of the young ladies he had known in the past.

'She's such a pleasant baby, she deserves an interesting name.'

'That's it!' John shouted with glee. 'How about Pleasance? I've never known anyone to use it as a Christian name and it would please my own godmother no end. She and Mr Pleasance were always very generous to me as a child. Pleasance Beddingfield – it has a good ring to it. It is a name to remember. What do you think?'

'Oh, you clever man. Yes, I like it very much.'

She looked down at the baby, longing for her to wake so that she could tell her that from now on she was Pleasance.

When she next sat down to write letters, Margery told the family in London of the date fixed for the naming. She wrote also to Mr and Mrs Pleasance inviting them to the ceremony and after much thought she wrote again to her father. She had told him of the arrival of his granddaughter but she had had no acknowledgement of her letter. In fact she had not spoken to her father since her wedding day when he had grudgingly given her away. He had deplored her choice of husband and was appalled that his daughter had behaved no better than a common servant girl in giving way to the lusts of the flesh. He had cursed her for her sin and for the shame she had brought upon his name. Margery had tried hard not to let his bitterness spoil her happiness. In the early days of her marriage she had made several attempts to heal the breach, inviting her father to share meals with them but he remained constant in his vow that he would never cross the threshold of the Beddingfield farmhouse. Once, Margery had gone to call at her old home but an unfamiliar servant, deputising for the housekeeper who was sick, had left her standing at the door and then returned with the curt message that 'the master will not see you.'

Hurt and humiliated, Margery had vowed that she would

never think again of her father but this she had found impossible to carry out. From Chandler Cobb who attended chapel with her father she found out how he was, worrying when Cobb reported a sudden loss of weight in the older man.

The birth of her daughter had seemed a good time to heal the breach. And because she had been confined away from home, there would be no need for the father to feel he must visit and Margery could tell herself that this was the reason he had made no attempt to see her. But she could find no excuse for his not answering her letter. Nonetheless she would try again. Just a note, simply inviting him to be present when her daughter was baptised. In her heart she knew she was wasting her time and she knew too that the name she and John had chosen would not find favour with him, it being neither biblical nor a good plain English one.

By the end of the third week Margery was well enough to leave her room for a good part of the day. The sticky heat of July had changed to August's clear blue warmth which made one long to be out of doors soaking up the sunshine. Heedless of the dire warnings of the household women, Margery and her babe lay out on a rug, only seeking shade from the trees as noon approached. In the late afternoon she walked in the meadow near the house carrying the child, quietly singing. Then she would make her way to the end of the lane where she would sit on a fallen tree to wait for John to ride into view.

Great was her disappointment if he did not come. On those occasions Starkey tried very hard to make conversation which would amuse her. In those last days she joined him for his evening meal. To her, he was an extension of John and thus she had become quite fond of him. He was like a brother. Starkey, however, had begun to have more than filial feeling for her and was torn between acute jealousy of his friend, longing for Margery to go and let him return to his former ways and anguish at the thought of what life was going to be like when she was no longer there.

Such were the mixed emotions which took hold of him on the

day when farewell embraces and thanks to the various members of the household were made and John finally put Margery and the baby into the chaise and the little family set off for home.

Four

MICHAELMAS 1761 — 1

The ball of dough hit the table with a thump at the same moment as the child's head banged against the door.

The resulting wail caused the woman at the table to look up.

'Oh, for goodness sake child! Do stop it. I've just about had enough of you and your whining. And why can't you sit still? I haven't got the time to chase round after you. I've got my work to do.'

The child was picked up from the floor where she had been crawling, given a quick shake, then promptly put back on to the piece of matting which was there for her use.

'There's only one way to deal with you, my lady.'

From a drawer the woman produced a length of old sheeting, one of the strips torn off to make bandages, and proceeded to tie one end round the infant's middle, the other she secured to the leg of the sturdy old kitchen table.

'Let's see how far you can get now!'

The dough was given further pounding, angry fists beating the soft pliable mixture.

The child sat still and sobbed, quietly at first. Realising that this was having no effect, she stopped, took a deep breath and let out a howl.

'Shut up, Pleasance, do! Your mummy will be down in a minute. At least I hope she will because I can't stand much more of this. You must be a good girl. You've had your breakfast, now it's time for baby to have his.'

'You sound very flustered, Betty.'

The maid looked up crossly. Here was to be yet another interruption to her routine.

'And so I might be, Miss Anne. I ain't no nursemaid. I come here to do kitchen and dairy. Not children. I don't even like children. And this one, who I used to think was quite reasonable for a baby, has done nothing but whimper and whine since her little brother arrived.'

Anne, who was dressed for riding, put down her crop on the edge of the table and bent down to rescue the little girl.

'Come, my pretty,' she said softly, her tones contrasting to those of Betty. 'Have you a lovely smile and a kiss for aunt?'

The little tear-stained face looked into Anne's for a minute then the tiny arms encircled the woman's neck and the miniature lips puckered and were placed firmly against Anne's cheek.

Holding the child to her, Anne seated herself on the stool close to the fire.

'So, Betty. What is ado here that has left you as nursemaid? Where is Prue?'

'Gone'.

Betty drew her mouth into a thin line as if to imply that nothing would induce her to say another word on the subject.

Anne took her cue and remained as if indifferent, giving her whole attention to the child.

In silence, Betty divided the dough into pieces. When all had been shaped, the loaves were put to one side to rest while she started on the pastry making.

She continued without speaking until she began to roll out the pastry and then it was as if the taking of the rolling pin into her hands unleashed her thoughts and with them her tongue.

'Little hussy! Fancy carrying on like that!'

Anne was longing to ask for some explanatory details but was fearful that any interruption from her might make Betty clam up again. Far better to let her have her say and try to work it out afterwards. She could, of course, ask Margery, but somehow, she thought, she would be more likely to get the riper details, if there were any, from Betty while her friend would furnish only bare facts.

'And under our very noses too. Well, all I can say is she must have been pretty desperate for a man. Huh! Man! And him barely fourteen and looking as if he could well serve as one of master's scare-the-crows. A puny wretch and her a lumpen great wench.'

Anne felt she now had the gist of the matter and ventured to say,

'Prue always seemed very good with the child. I got the impression that she really loved babies.'

'Well, now she'll find out what it's like to have one of her own, won't she?' The maid was grim-faced again. 'And she'll find the inside of the Workhouse is a hard price to pay for a few nights frolicking.'

'Oh, poor girl. Has it come to that? Would her family not have her back?'

'Certainly not.' Betty was shocked that Anne should consider such an idea. 'They are respectable, God-fearing people!'

Anne suppressed a smile. It never ceased to amaze her that peasant folk should have so much higher moral standards than the rest of the population. Surely Betty, who had been with the Beddingfields for the last ten years, must have been well aware of John and Margery's hasty wedding. Or perhaps it was all right because there had been a wedding. And what about her own case? Did Betty stop to consider what Anne's life had been for the year that she had been away? Or had that been all hushed up for the sake of respectability?

'So everything's topsy-turvy at present, Miss Anne. Who would have thought Chandler Cobb would have to leave Beddingfields before his time. What with him going and Prue and that boy – useless though he was – I don't know what to think. Master has gone to Tunstall for the Fair, but it won't be the same in this kitchen with all new people, I can tell you.'

She cut out the lids for her pies, sighing as she did so.

'I sometimes think perhaps I ought to have looked out for a new place for myself too.'

'Well Betty, you know that if things do become too difficult for you, mother and I would be pleased to have you. The girl we brought with us from London is no match for you. Mother swears her pastry is responsible for her present bout of indigestion!'

'Thank you, Miss. That is a comfort. As it is knowing that you are not so far away. I have more than once walked of an evening over to your place to sit and talk with Phoebe. I like to hear her tales of London but, Miss Anne, I was very glad when Missis decided not to settle there but to come back down home.'

'And so was I!'

Both women started, neither had heard the light tread of Margery as she entered the kitchen.

'Anne. How lovely to see you and how well you look.'

'Which is more than I can say for you.' Anne's blunt comment was out before she had time to consider the effect it might have.

With her mother's arrival, Pleasance leaned away from Anne and put out her arms to Margery. She wriggled and then cried until Margery took her. Once in Margery's clasp, she put her thumb in her mouth, nuzzled her head into the little mother's shoulder and closed her eyes ready to sleep.

'Poor baby.' Murmured Margery against the little blonde curls.

'Yes, she is still only a baby, isn't she? It must be very hard for her to have to become 'big sister' at barely a year old. Especially when you – and John too – have made so much of her. I can understand that she must resent the time you give to the baby – I know I would have done.'

Margery said nothing. Her thoughts seemed elsewhere as she rocked gently on the spot, perhaps soothing herself as much as the child.

'Are you going to ask me to stay for a bit? I wouldn't mind a sit-down after my long ride.'

Her less than subtle hint penetrated Margery's thoughts.

'Of course, let's go into the parlour. The baby should sleep for sometime and maybe Pleasance will, too.'

'You look as if you could do with some rest yourself. You look awful.'

'Thank you. I have never been one to seek compliments on my looks as you know, and at present I have more on my mind than my appearance or how I look to an outsider.'

'Oh, Margery! Is that how you see me? An outsider? My dear, I am not criticising . . .'

'It sounded that way to me.' Margery's raised voice took on unusually harsh tones causing the child in her arms to stir and whimper in her sleep. Immediately she softened, rocking on the spot and gently hushing the disturbed one.

Neither woman spoke. Anne sat grim-faced staring blankly at the wall at the far end of the room, her sister-in-law and erstwhile close friend stood, hunched around her child as the tears silently flowed from eyes hollowed with lack of sleep.

Anne was overcome with remorse that the remark which she had made out of concern should have had such an effect.

'Here, let me.' She took Pleasance from her and tried to put the child on the sofa. But in her sleep the little girl clung to the woman.

'You see. She won't sleep unless she's held. We have no peace from her at night unless she shares our bed or that of Prue. And now the baby cries from the colic every evening so he too needs to be nursed.'

She sank down into one of the high backed chairs beside the fire. She seemed dwarfed by its size making Anne realise just how much weight the girl had lost since the birth of the new baby. The tears still came.

'Our old nurse used to say you'll feel better for a good cry.' Anne tried to sound cheerful.

'Then my cries must all have been bad ones! I seem to be tearful most of the time and it certainly has not made me any better.'

She attempted a weak smile. 'I'm glad you came and I'm sorry to be such a pitiful sight.'

'I only wish I'd come sooner. It was unfortunate that mother and I should have gone to visit my step-sister at Felixstowe so soon after your confinement. Had we been here we might have been able to help in some way. What can John have been thinking to let you get into this state.'

If Anne was expecting an answer to this enquiry she was

disappointed. Margery chose that moment to examine the state of her hands.

'My nails are roughened. I must make sure that I do not harm the children when I change them.'

Anne looked at the hands seeing not just broken fingernails but chapped red hands.

'Are you doing the children's washing too?' she demanded.

'How long is it you have been without Prue?'

Margery looked vague. 'I can't remember. Two – three weeks. It seems like an age. John did try to find someone but there was no one wanting work who was willing to live-in. We did have a washerwoman for a bit but she didn't get on with Betty. And then there was all that trouble with Chandler Cobb and John so angry and now . . .'

Her sobs were heartrending. Anne felt useless. Her instinct was to take Margery in her arms and comfort her but the child was already there and if she was put down she might wake and howl, demanding attention. But action was needed. Stepping briskly into the kitchen she demanded that Betty should stop whatever she was doing and hold the child. Then she returned to the other room, helped Margery from the chair and led her upstairs to her bedroom.

'There. Just you lie down. No! I will not let you resist. You are to lie there and forget about everything for a while. Sleep if you can. Betty and I will see to the children . . .Yes, yes, I know that you will have to suckle baby but you can do that – when the time comes – from here. This is a belated present to you. The gift of a day in bed. So make the most of it.'

She stifled all Margery's protests. 'Don't be selfish, my dear. How often do I get the chance to play 'mother'?

Margery lay back and closed her eyes. Anne watched and saw how tense she was but after a few moments she began to relax and her breathing became more regular. The watcher could hardly believe the change which had taken place in her friend. Even when she was very heavily pregnant she had kept herself well groomed. But now her hair which had escaped from her cap hung lank and unkempt, circling the face with its sickly pallor which emphasised the dark shadows beneath the now closed eyes. Anne could not help noticing that stains from the tears seemed to indicate that her face had not been washed recently. But the biggest shock of all was in her clothes. Far too big for her, the old gown was generally grubby, as well as stained where the baby had regurgitated milk, and her white apron and stockings were dingy from prolonged wear. Anne looked down at her own neat attire and then back at the girl on the bed. Girl! Not yet out of her teens, today she might be taken for an old woman. If this was what marriage and motherhood did to you, then it was not for her, or at least not unless she married a man who could make sure that she would never be left without a nursemaid for her child and domestics to make sure that the laundry was always spotless.

What was John thinking to let things come to such a pass? Had he, who she had always known was fickle, at last tired of his wife? It had come as a tremendous shock to her that he should have been attracted to Margery in the first place and when, after her bid for freedom, she had returned to Sternfield, she had been both surprised – and a little jealous – to see how much they cared for each other. They had been married nearly a year when Anne and her mother returned to live nearby in what had become dubbed locally as the dower house. Anne had widened her knowledge of life considerably in the months that she had spent with the touring theatrical company. She had learned a great deal about relationships between men and women as well as the harsh reality that she was neither a very good actress nor had she sufficient beauty to make up for the lack of talent. She had agreed to return to live with her mother. At least the widow Beddingfield had a zest for living and although their base might be in the country they would still continue to make long visits to Town. Both women enjoyed an independent income that enabled them to support their chosen life style. Nonetheless, Anne had felt the loss of both her brother's attention and her friend's devotion and admiration. And when she first saw them together as a married couple she had been filled with an envy of which she had not thought herself capable.

Over the months this had lessened, and with the birth of Pleasance she had been able to take on a more acceptable role for herself as welcome aunt.

And this was how she saw herself now, taking charge of Margery's household – even if it were only for the day. She had never regarded herself as in the least bit domesticated, her mother had not encouraged that, but she knew that a firm hand was what was required at this moment.

Noiselessly, Anne slid out of the room, passing through the adjoining one where the baby slept contentedly in its cradle beside the bed which should have housed the errant Prue.

Briskly she entered the kitchen where Betty was chafing at not being able to get on with her work.

'Is there nowhere we can put Pleasance where she can sleep comfortably and soundly, Betty?'

'If you ask me, that's half little madam's trouble. She had to give up her cradle for the baby and she didn't take kindly to being in the big bed even when that Prue was there with her.'

'Poor mite, you can hardly blame her, it's such a big bed in comparison to a cosy cot. I wonder . . .if, just for now . . .'

Anne disappeared into one of the big walk-in cupboards and returned with some sacks. Next she went to the linen press and retrieved a thick blanket.

'Let's try this.'

Deftly she made a nest of the sacks and blanket under the kitchen table.

'See if you can lay her down in there without her waking.'

Betty bent slowly and carefully and almost holding her breath deposited Pleasance in the hollow that had been made. Both women waited expectantly. The child turned slightly on her side but slept on.

'Well, I never did.' Betty marvelled.

'I'll tell you what. Unless it has been thrown out or given away then my little bed should be up in the attic. Do you mind keeping an eye here, while I go and see if I can find it?'

Relieved now of her burden, Betty would have agreed to anything.

Using the back stairs from the kitchen to ascend to the rooms in the roof space, Anne fondly recalled how, as children, she and John had loved to play up here among the accumulated discarded and rejected objects of family life. Here on very cold or wet days they had used their imaginations to weave exciting stories in which they were the chief participants. A broken chair became a throne or a chariot, an inverted table a Roman galley or a pirate ship on the Spanish Main. Anne's roles had varied but rarely was she called upon to act a female part. The other good thing about this area beyond the rooms inhabited by servants was that it offered dark, secret places in which to hide, perhaps from a parent's wrath but more likely from a brother's teasing.

Anne realised how much of her life was associated with the assortment to be found up here. However, she resisted the temptation to linger and revive memories. So she pushed and tugged various items, disturbing dust and sleepy spiders until she found what she was hunting for. Bigger than the traditional infant cradle, but still with the security of solid wooden sides, this small carved oaken cot had been hers until such time as she had been big enough to sleep happily in a proper bed. Then, for a very brief time it had stayed in her room to house a family of peg dolls. Quickly dispensing with such a silly pastime in favour of boyish activities, she had asked for it to be removed and had promptly forgotten its existence.

All sorts of memories flooded to the surface as she carried the little object down to the kitchen.

'There! What do you think little Miss will make of that?'

Betty was very taken with it, having never seen such a thing before. In her experience you progressed from cradle to a share in a communal family bed. This 'in-between' emphasised to her the wealth and position of the family she served.

But having admired, she was also eminently practical.

'It needs a good clean', she remarked reprovingly, as if she half expected that Anne might put the child in it just as it was. There was also the unspoken reprimand that she already had enough to do without being asked to undertake more.

However, Anne seemed to have the ability to read Betty's thoughts.

'Tell me where you keep the beeswax and rags and I'll have it gleaming in no time.'

Settling herself away from the table where Betty was still busy with food preparation, Anne began her polishing. Both women worked in silence for some time.

Returning from the larder where she had replaced unused flour and preserves, Betty said, half to herself, as she probably had a number of times in the last few days,

'I do hope Master will find good help at the Hiring.'

Anne, who had heard her, did not think she was expecting a reply. But Betty's thoughts had been running on the subject for some time.

'You must notice that things here are not what they were, Miss.'

Still Anne refused to be drawn. She knew Betty well enough to know that very soon she would explode and reveal all the intimacies of the household.

'What your mother must think! And I dread to think what the late master would say if he could see what has happened here'.

Now was her opportunity –

'And what exactly has happened, Betty?'

The fish was caught, the floodgates were open . . .out it all came.

Betty related a story of people under pressure. Again Margery had given birth just as the harvest was beginning so there had been all the extra work that had brought to the house, as well as supplying the needs of the additional harvesters. John, like other farmers, always negotiated a special rate for the gathering-in of his crop and took on casual labour to assist his regular men. Amongst the casuals was a young fellow who, it turned out, had absconded from the military the previous year just before his regiment was due to return to his native Northumberland. He had managed to support himself by casual labour since then but was looking out for a settled position. John had been impressed with him, finding him a hard worker but he had not enamoured himself to the other men, mainly because his good looks made him attractive to the local girls. And that had been the spark which had ignited the eventual conflagration.

The former soldier had cast his eye on Prue when she had taken food out to the harvesters. For two or three days a little flirtation had been carried on between them but then one evening Prue's lover, the young apprentice who lived-in, had caught them cuddling and a fight had broken out. It was one of those summer nights when the air hung heavy and electrical storms were rumbling in the distance.

Work came to a standstill as the men gathered to watch the two opponents. Casual remarks made half in fun opened old wounds and before long a general brawl was in full swing. Chandler Cobb who had been supervising operations in the stackyard arrived back in the field with the cart just in time to see the boy deliver a punch that sent the ex-soldier reeling to land with his leg impaled on the prong of an upturned fork. His screams of pain had halted the rest of the men.

'I was just walking up to the field to find out how long they would be working when it happened.' Betty continued.

'By the time I got there, they had pulled the fork out of his leg and were tearing up a shirt to make a bandage to staunch the blood. Chandler Cobb was white faced, but he remained calm as he gave orders as to what was to be done. Me, I felt sick seeing all that blood, and that stupid girl Prue went and fainted in the middle of it all.'

Anne hid a smile at this, somewhat relieved to have a break in the tension of the narrative.

'Then what happened?' she asked.

Betty thought for a moment, mentally reviewing the scene and trying to recreate the sequence of events.

'That's right. I had to see to the girl of course and a couple of older women who had come to walk home with their menfolk, they helped Chandler Cobb with the injured man. Then they had him lifted into the cart and Cobb and another man drove off to see if they could find the surgeon. Before he left he told all the men they should stop work for the night but that he wanted to see them all the next day. And he told the lad that he was to wait up for his return.

'Well, none of us felt like going to bed after that anyway, so we three were all in the kitchen when Chandler Cobb came back.

'I can see him now. He walked in very slow, his face, never very open at the best of times, was full of doom. I was sure that he was going to tell us the soldier was dead.

'We all stood and looked at him. I wanted to ask but was too scared of the answer. Then he said, ever so quietly, 'You women get to your beds.' Prue and I went up the back stair there, but Prue stopped halfway to listen and so I came back to join her.

'We heard Chandler Cobb call the boy to stand in front of him. Still very quietly, he asked him to explain what had happened. As the lad told his side of the story, it was if Chandler Cobb suddenly went mad. He must still have had the horse whip in his hand because he started lashing out with it and we could hear both the whiplash and the lad's cries.

'Prue was down the stairs and through the door before I could stop her. She shouted at Cobb to stop and tried to grab his arm. In his frenzy he hit her. Then the boy shouted out that it was a cowardly thing to do to hit a woman, especially one with child.

'This made us all stop and take notice but within seconds Chandler Cobb was ranting at Prue, calling her the sort of names you only ever hear from the Old Testament reading and he was whipping her as if he would have liked to kill her.

'I yelled to him to stop and both the boy and I tried to get hold of him but he seemed possessed of a demon strength that let him shake us off.

'Then the outer door opened and in walked the master. He bellowed at Chandler Cobb and when he took no notice he set about Cobb with his own riding crop.

'It was then that the young Mistress appeared from her bed

wanting to know what all the noise was about.'

'She looked so young and frightened as she stood there that I suppose it brought us all to our senses. Master told me to take mistress back to her room and sent Prue off to her bed. Master said I was to go straight off too, so I don't know what happened down here after that.'

Anne had listened with mounting horror as the story unfolded. 'This was only a week or so ago, you say?'

Betty nodded. 'Nearer three, I think. It's hard to remember because there was so much to do. Mistress was very upset that night and took a lot of settling and both the children became fretful. Next morning Prue was sent away and that upset Mistress and Pleasance who was very attached to her. The boy went that day too. I didn't see him go but I did see Chandler Cobb.

'He and Master were shut up for ages in that room off the stables and I heard both of them shouting. At one time I had need to go across the yard and I heard Master say, 'You have no right to take these matters in your own hands, I'm master here.' And then Chandler Cobb started quoting from the Scriptures about rooting out evil, and Master called Cobb a ranting old fool – and other names I can't repeat. Then he said he'd just about had his fill of him and he'd better pack his bag and go.

'Then Chandler Cobb reminded Master that under old master's will, he had a job here at Beddingfield's for life.

'Master swore at him and told him he'd best go and find a lawyer but as far as he was concerned Cobb was dismissed and he had twenty-four hours to clear out.

'I must say, Miss, I never thought Master would be so hard on Chandler Cobb. I mean, he's been here so long and the old master always said that he was the best any man could have.

'When he came into the kitchen later, he never said a word about his dismissal – and of course I couldn't let on what I'd overheard. He just went to his room, packed up his things and then he came to say goodbye. You know, Miss, he was always a man to keep himself to himself and even then, although I'd known him all those years, all he said was that I should continue to behave myself and look after the mistress.

'I can tell you now, I actually wept as he went through that door. He looked a broken man. All his life's work to end like that.'

'And since then, I suppose my brother has had to do Chandler Cobb's work as well as his own? And that's why poor Margery looks so ill. Oh, Betty. What a sorry state of affairs.'

Anne finished her polishing while she mentally digested all she had learned. There was just one point she had to clear up.

'What happened to the man who had caused the upset in the first place?'

'They say he lost his leg. Gangrene set in some days after so surgeon chopped it off.' Her tone was matter of fact but she changed it to chide Anne with, 'I am surprised, Miss, that you ain't more concerned with what has become of Chandler Cobb.'

'Ah, but you see, Betty, I had heard his version of this sorry business and I know what is to become of him. '

'You do? Oh, go on, Miss, do tell! I have so worried about him.'

'Employment has been found for him with my uncle in Norfolk. As you heard him say, he believed that my father had made provision for him to remain here and boldly took himself to see our family lawyer. I truly believe that the man has got above himself and I gather that his tone to the lawyer was almost threatening. My mother was consulted and though it was made plain to Cobb that his behaviour in usurping my brother's authority and in his assault upon him, left the family under no obligation to him, it was felt that in recognition for his previous service, he should not be dismissed out of hand. And as luck would have it, my uncle was looking for a new man. I think he will be very well suited there. It was not an ideal situation here for him having to take orders from a master whom he had known as a child and a somewhat wayward youth. So all is well on that score. I wish a happier outcome could be found for poor Prue.'

'You have put my mind somewhat at ease but I don't know as how he'll settle to Norfolk. He's a Suffolk man born and bred and they are very different up there. Why, when that chapman from Norwich called at the door I had to call Missis because I couldn't understand a word he said.'

Betty chose to ignore the reference to Prue. Remarking on how fine the child's bed now looked, she left the kitchen for a few moments to return with an armful of bedding for it.

'Look, Miss. I found this in the linen press.'

She held up a little patchwork quilt that exactly fitted the bed. 'That must have been mine.' She examined it closely. 'Oh dear, it has been somewhat chewed either by the moth or a mouse, but it will do for now. And I can spend my long lonely evenings making another!' She laughed heartily at this picture of herself. Then she set about other chores before the child asleep under the table should wake and demand her attention. But like Betty, she could not help sending up a silent prayer that John had learned enough from the recent experience to choose his new help wisely . . .

Five

MICHAELMAS 1761 — 2

The Green Man at Tunstall was filled to overflowing. The Hiring Dinner was long since past but still people were pushing through the doors to join the crush inside. It was rare, in these times, for so many to gather. There wasn't the money to spend on drink when many had neither a roof over their heads nor food in their mouths. Although rushed off her feet the landlady paused for a moment to consider the scene, savouring a sight she doubted she'd see again for some months, perhaps not until this time next year. Shouted orders for refills brought her out of her reverie – at this rate her cellar would run dry for she had not thought the demand would be so great.

'But then,' she told herself, 'it would be a different story if they were doing their own paying.'

She brought another jug round from the back and almost spilt its frothing contents down the front of the dress of the young woman who had just managed to squeeze herself through the crowd of men standing in the doorway.

'Hold hard there, my gal! You'd look a pretty sight with ale down that fine gown of yours. Now where are you off to in such a hurry?'

The girl jumped back from the landlady, treading on the foot of a man sprawled at one of the trestles still standing from the dinner. He made a grab for her, pinching her backside and letting out an obscenity followed by a throaty laugh.

'That'll be enough of that, thank you. You'll be pleased to leave the young woman alone or . . .'

'Or what, young master? Quite the proud little lord, ain't we?'

The two men faced each other, one lithe and in his prime, the other red faced, stout and approaching middle age. Those immediately around them fell silent waiting for the outcome of the confrontation, some even moved back to make room for the fight which must inevitably follow. The noise from the rest of the room seemed even louder, emphasising the tension and drowning out the attempt of the landlady to defuse the situation.

The girl put her hand on the arm of the young man.

'Richard, please, leave it. He's had a drop too much. He meant no harm, I'm sure.'

'Oh, so Missy's going to fight your battle for you, is she?' taunted the older man lunging at the other.

A gleeful shout went up from the onlookers. Now the festivities would really get started. A fight was a signal for a general free for all. Old scores could be settled, fresh accounts opened just for the sheer fun of it.

'That'll do, lads, that'll do.' A slow but commanding voice sounded from the doorway of the inner room where the farmers of the surrounding area had met together over bottles and pipes to discuss the vexed problems of agriculture.

'If you men value the jobs you've just got, then you'll either sit and drink with each other in companionship or you'll get off home to your beds and keep out of harm's way.'

He paused to let his words be absorbed by all, even those furthest away who had no idea what was happening.

'And you, Joseph Stagg, learn to keep your hands for what they're best suited, the skinning of dead beasts not the mauling of young women! Now, let that be an end of it. If there's any more trouble, then I'll clear the place and you'll all be the losers.'

'Except the masters – they'll be saved paying for the ale,' an intrepid wag called from a far corner bringing laughter to start them off on the next part of the evening and take away the chill of the threats made by the Chief Constable's deputy.

The young man involved in the original skirmish took the girl's arm and led her outside into the late September dusk. The brilliant sunset had left a thick band of deep crimson across the horizon where later the huge golden orb of the hunter's moon would light up the sky and provide illumination for the homeward travellers.

The pair found a seat on a tree stump that had been set for that purpose outside the inn.

The man slumped forward elbows on knees, staring unseeing into distant space before speaking.

'I hadn't expected to see you here, Liddy.' His tone was flat.

'I'm sorry if I've spoiled your evening, Richard, but I couldn't wait to tell you my news.'

She snuggled up to him, linking her arm through his. 'You'll never guess. No, I can't wait, I must tell you.' She took a deep breath and came closer so that she could see the look on his face as she said, 'We're not going to be parted after all. Master Beddingfield has hired me too! There, what do you think of that?'

The news evidently took the young man by complete surprise. He turned to stare at the girl. In her boundless excitement her arms went round his neck, forcing his head down towards her. Her mouth on his was full of an eager passion which could have been hard to resist. But here, outside the Green Man with people coming and going, was not the place to give in to whatever desires he might have. And what ever his body might tell him, the mind of Richard Ringe was far from happy to hear that Liddy Clebold was to accompany him to his new employment.

He pushed her off and muttered that she ought to be getting home.

'Will you walk back part of the way with me? Then we can talk about our new life.'

Her own happiness as she slipped her arm through his obscured his lack of enthusiasm. She immediately began chatting, not waiting for any reply, which was just as well for Richard was deep in thought.

He should have known that today's stroke of luck was too good to last. It was always the same. Just when things were going well for him, something would come along to change it all. Just as it had when hard upon his eighteenth birthday his mother had broken the news that the little farm that they had been running together since his father's death two years before and which he had dreamed of expanding was in fact to be taken from them. Their rent had risen steeply each year until they were barely able to scrape the money together to pay it. They would have continued to struggle but the squire, like many other landowners, had decided to merge several of his smaller tenancies. And with the price of corn being what it was, then he too would turn to sheep and would have no need of all the husbandmen he was making redundant.

So Richard had gone from son of a yeoman, his own man, to being hired help. He had dreaded then the ignominy of having to come to the Michaelmas Hiring but luck had smiled upon him in the guise of an old neighbour whose health had dictated the need for an extra pair of hands. His mother, who had the reputation of running one of the best dairies in the neighbourhood, was able to secure employment as head Dairymaid at a large and prosperous farm near Southwold. So, although it had been a sad day when they saw all their furniture sold and they left their home for the last time, at least they were able to console themselves that they had good prospects ahead of them.

For three years Richard had worked assiduously, gradually making himself indispensable to the farmer. He was an old bachelor who actually held the freehold of his land and as time passed, Richard began to have hopes that when the old man was too old to work – or if he should die – then he, Richard, would inherit and once more be a man with a secure future. Life was indeed sweet, especially when the attractive young Liddy with her raven black hair and dark flashing eyes had joined the household. Her aunt was housekeeper and like her employer getting older so she had begged to have her niece come to help her with the cooking and especially the sewing.

With Liddy had come a freshness to a house which was old and stale. Her pleasant manner brought good humour to both farmer and housekeeper who were charmed by her, as was

Richard. But he knew, what they did not, that under that smiling exterior there lurked an uncontrollable passion that could be consuming.

Then suddenly, their lives had been turned upside down. The long established bachelor had finally relinquished that state. He had made the acquaintance of a farmer's widow who did not intend to stay that way long; a lady with winning ways and three healthy young sons, all well trained in the ways of agriculture. As soon as the nuptials took place, all the existing members of the household were given notice as from Michaelmas.

To soften the shock, the housekeeper was given a cottage, rent free, at Saxmundham and a small pension, but Liddy and Richard were forced to seek alternative employment. Liddy and her aunt moved as soon as harvest was finished, the older woman hoping that the girl might find work close to her. But Liddy had other ideas. She refused to commit herself until she knew where Richard was going. She believed herself to be in love with him. Certainly he was the most handsome young man she'd ever met and he was quite unlike the usual rough working lads with whom she had grown up. He always – well nearly always – treated her like a lady. He had good manners, but then, she told herself often, he had been educated and had known proper young gentlemen and had once been his own master. And he would be again, as he had frequently told her. In their walks together on fine evenings or in their more intimate moments stolen after the old folks were in bed, Richard had confided his ambitions to her. And while Richard dreamed of one day owning the largest farm in Suffolk and perhaps becoming a magistrate, Liddy saw herself at his side as mistress of the farm and mother of the son who would inherit and the daughters who would marry into the leading county families. Both saw themselves as special people who would achieve fame, whose names would one day be on everyone's lips. Such were the dreams. Reality was very different, particularly now.

'You're very quiet.' Liddy had come to the end of her speculations.

'Aren't you pleased that I'm coming with you? Master Beddingfield said he thought it a very good idea when he found out that we'd both come from Carter's. He said we would know each other's ways and be company for each other.'

She gave him a knowing look.

Annoyed with his lack of response she tried another tack.

'He's a handsome man, isn't he? Would he be taller than you, do you think? And he's very muscular – you could see that from the fit of his jacket. I like men who have that almost straw coloured hair but he didn't have the creamy white skin that sometimes goes with it . . .'

'For heaven's sake, Liddy!' Richard turned on her. 'You're talking about a farmer, not some fancy drawing room beau! A man who spends his working life out of doors is hardly likely to have a lily white skin.'

'You don't have to snap my head off.' She looked up at him mischievously. 'Perhaps you're a bit jealous of him. After all he can't be much older than you and he's got all the things you want.'

'Jealous of John Beddingfield!' he scoffed. 'If only you knew the half of it.'

They had stopped, still some distance from her aunt's cottage. Liddy tried to smooth the tension between them. 'What should I know?'

But he was not to be cajoled. There were some things which were better left buried in the past.

'Come on, walk the rest of the way with me and I promise I won't quiz you if you don't want me too.'

They continued along the road in silence. Liddy's thoughts hovered between her fancies as to what might befall her and Richard in their new positions and the striking image of her new employer. They had talked not above a quarter of an hour yet she found that she could recall practically every detail of Beddingfield's clothing, his stature, even the sound of his voice but most of all she could see the full sensuous mouth which he had brought close to her face as he had put the coins in her hand which sealed their bargain that she would enter his service for the coming year.

Describing the composition of his household, she had been a bit taken aback at the mention of a wife – he looked too young to have taken on that responsibility. She would have thought he had enough to do with running the farm. She was even more surprised when he told her that her task would be mainly to look after the two children. She had assured him that she adored little children. She had, of course, had experience of nursery work, she being the eldest and her mother producing a baby a year and sometimes twins. She did not tell her future employer that the reason she had gone to live with her aunt was to escape from babies and small children.

In her imagination now she peopled the house. Betty, the other maid, was obviously old – thirty at least – and probably crabby because she hadn't found herself a man. She would have to watch her step with her. And the mistress, well, she was probably old as well. Liddy had seen enough of the world for herself and had listened to the stories of her aunt to know that it was often the case that a farmer's spinster daughter who had inherited the land would look around for some healthy young man to run it for her and that even more often these working partnerships developed into the permanency of marriage. It was nothing nowadays for a woman to marry a man half her age. The weekly Journal gave case after case of such happenings, especially where the woman had a large fortune. Why only last week she had read out to her aunt the report of a lady in Derbyshire who had taken as her third husband a young officer of twenty-five and she was seventy-one!

As Aunt had said, when you have money you can take care of yourself and buy all the pills and potions to hide the ravages of time. Good dressmakers and wigmakers could achieve miracles!

'But you can't disguise an old body in bed.' Liddy had not dared to say this aloud to her aunt. The pair of them might speak in innuendo but there were some things that a supposedly innocent girl of seventeen did not say to her maiden aunt.

As they walked on both locked in their individual reveries, Richard was reliving his encounter with John Beddingfield earlier that day.

It had been fortunate for everyone that the day had dawned fine and remained so. No one minded standing about on the wide strip of land that fronted the Tunstall Green Man where, by custom, all those in search of work and those who sought labourers would gather. The unemployed arrived first, jostling for the best spots to stand to attract notice. It was decreed by the chief Constable of the Hundred that the Hiring Sessions be conducted according to strict rules. Hence all those of one trade stood together. Specialists like shepherds were much in demand at present, while there was always a steady call for horsemen and gamekeepers, woodsmen and those who could turn their hands to several skills.

Richard had been unsure where he should stand or how he should advertise his expertise. For that he certainly had. All that he had learned in the three years helping his mother run their own mixed farm had been greatly extended in the following three spent at Carter's. There he had been in charge of the labourers, had planned and ordered the day-to-day routine, and had often taken Carter's place at markets around the county. For so young a man Richard had shouldered much responsibility – and he had carried it well.

One of his greatest assets was an ability to learn fast and absorb new knowledge. There had been times when he was a boy and had longed to be out in the fields that he had resented the time spent away at Mr Scrivener's school in Framlingham. He could see no sense in learning Latin or Greek. But he had relished the instruction in mathematics and astronomy for he could see the relevance of these to his daily life. Old Carter had been mightily impressed by Richard's quickness with accounting, both in his head and on paper and was thus quite happy to leave him to do business deals at market.

It had been back during a transaction over the sale of some barley that he had first encountered farmer Beddingfield. Richard was negotiating with a buyer for his crop when suddenly this arrogant young man had pushed him aside, greeting the potential buyer by name and dragging him off for a drink with him. Later in the day he heard that Beddingfield had sold his own barley to the man – at a higher price than Richard was asking. The episode had rankled and lingered. Had he been his own master, he would not have received such treatment.

Beddingfield, of course, had long since forgotten the encounter, if indeed, it had even registered in his consciousness. On that occasion he had simply done what he always did, went straight for what he wanted.

And what he needed now was someone to act as his right hand man, a foreman to replace Chandler Cobb, someone who was both a good worker and malleable.

Richard had stood alone. Each foreman or bailiff kept aloof not only from the main work force but also from the possible competition. There was no interchange of conversation or banter as with the shepherds or cowherds. Each face of the eight or nine men present bore a look that varied from embarrassment to despair or resentment that they should be here at all. As prospective employers spoke to one, the rest would feign indifference while straining to hear what position was on offer.

Richard had kept his gaze forward, trying to will the ideal employer to come his way so he was unaware that he was under detailed scrutiny from his right.

'I say,' a voice had drawled,'don't I know you?'

Richard felt the light touch of a riding crop fall on his shoulder.

'Yes, I'm sure of it. Can't for the life of me remember your name, but I'll swear you were at old Scrivener's at Framlingham.'

Richard started and looked into the face of the man he'd seen two years before at the Corn market but this time, he too remembered where he'd seen him before.

'Well, I'm blessed! Fancy finding an old school fellow here! I thought all the fellows there had places of their own to come into. How come you've fallen on hard times?'

He had seemed genuinely interested in the story Richard

outlined, commiserating with him over his double misfortune. They talked as equals, as they had been seven or eight years previously. As Richard talked of his life at Carter's, a farm Beddingfield said he had heard good reports of, there was something nagging at the back of Richard's mind. Something that had happened at school but what it was just would not come.

'You seem to be just what I'm looking for, Ringe. See, I've remembered your name after all! I've remembered too that you were something of a wizard where the figuring is concerned – could do that dashed algebraic stuff of old blind Noah Whatsit.'

'Girling.' Richard supplied the name.

'So, is it agreed? Will you come to me?'

He named a wage that seemed reasonable adding that he thought Richard would find his accommodation at the farm more than adequate.

'The old man did a lot to make the place more livable in when Ma decided that my sisters were all to be ladies and get themselves fine husbands, so more money was spent on parlours and bed chambers than on barns and cattle sheds. Now I'm trying to do what's needed in that direction.'

Richard hesitated. The offer was tempting and no others had yet come his way. Suppose he turned it down and at the close of the Hiring he was still unemployed. What would he do then?

He had asked himself this question over and over and the answer he came up with each time was that the best he could do was try his luck as a teacher of mathematics at a school like the one he and Beddingfield had attended. At worst, he could enlist in the army.

'I'll take it.' He stretched out his hand to shake that of his new master. He swallowed his pride as he accepted the traditional coins that sealed the bargain.

Beddingfield was delighted. He put his arm round Richard's shoulders and led him into the Green Man to celebrate their contract.

'Well done, Ringe. You won't regret this, believe me. I foresee a long, fruitful relationship ahead of us. You have made the right decision, my lad.'

As they downed their ale, Richard desperately wanted to believe him.

But already things were going against him. He had enjoyed his dalliance with Liddy but he was not prepared to shackle himself to her in marriage. The one redeeming feature he had seen in their having to leave Carter's farm was that he could bring the affair to an end without any recriminations.

He had wanted to carve out a new life for himself with people who knew nothing of his past. He wanted to enter the house as Richard Ringe, bailiff, master's right hand man. But now he would have Liddy, flaunting their intimacy and no doubt ready to pass on titbits about their previous life to the other servants. He wished he could be rid of her, yet her talk of how attractive she found Beddingfield annoyed him intensely.

Deep down he had the feeling that it would have been better for all concerned if he had gone to join the army.

Six

AUTUMN 1761

'I don't know what it is gal, but however hard I try the butter just won't come.'

Betty stopped churning and straightened her back. Liddy continued her task of skimming off the cream from that day's milk. It made a change from looking after the children and gave her a chance to gossip with Betty while they worked.

To the surprise of both, they had discovered that each quite liked the other. Betty was not as crabby as Liddy had expected and Liddy was more sensible than poor Prue had ever been. Betty did have certain reservations; the new girl sometimes gave herself airs and tried to imply that she was not really born to be a servant, but this cut no ice with Betty. She knew a real lady when she saw one and that did not include Liddy Clebold. Nevertheless, it had been a relief that the new girl was clean-spoken and well mannered. Without a doubt she had been well trained and could turn her hand to most things that needed doing.

'There's a storm brewing nearby. That's why your butter won't come. My aunt says milk is always the first to know about storms.'

Liddy bent over the cream pan and sniffed.

'I shouldn't be a bit surprised if this lot don't curdle before morning.'

'Go on with you! That's as fresh as you could hope to get.'

Betty added more salt to her churn and started again when suddenly the whole house shook. The force of the tremor flung open the door to the dairy filling the room with unseen swirling air.

Betty ran to close the door but it was impossible to block out the awful noise. A hundred forges, with all the smiths working flat out, could hardly rival the clamour which filled the air.

The two women clung to each other in terror. Neither had ever heard such a storm as this.

'The mistress and the babies!' Liddy gasped. 'Do you think they are out in this?'

Betty glanced fearfully through the louvres trying to judge what the time might be. Normally she could have estimated by the amount of light left in the late afternoon but today all that could be seen was a sky that resembled a huge angry bruise.

'Let's pray she's still over at Old Missis's. Mayhap they will have seen this coming and persuaded her to stay.'

Betty couldn't help feeling that this was a vain hope. She was almost sure that Margery would have started for home a while back. But there again, if she had, it was just possible that she and the children had taken shelter in one of the cottages. That is if she had gone round by the lane rather than across the fields.

This would have to happen today, the first time that Margery had felt she could cope with both children on her own again. Betty had glimpsed some of her mistress's old spirit returning as she had talked that morning of taking the little ones to visit their grandmother and aunt. St Luke had been generous with his late summer that year and the air was still fine and warm. Margery had seemed so excited at the prospect of spending time walking through the meadows with the children. Pleasance had just begun to walk and the baby could be comfortably carried.

When John heard her plan he had suggested she should take young Will Nunn, the yard boy with her. The ten year old lad had also been taken on at Michaelmas as had John Masterton. But where Beddingfield could find plenty of work for the older boy at this time of the year, he sometimes found himself inventing jobs just to keep the younger one occupied. However, the boy had proved himself very amenable and had fitted well into the household, often lending a hand before it was asked of him. He could not do enough for Margery and she had laughed and said that if she had been a rich lady she would have made him her page boy. His eyes had widened when she had explained what his duties would have been. He was a bright lad, eager to learn and Margery had promised that when the winter evenings came she would teach him to read and write. He was, perhaps, one of the few children who actually listened to the Bible readings in church and from these and the powerful sermons of the minister he had formed his view of the world.

So Will went with her. He took turns to carry the baby when it got too heavy for Margery and held Pleasance's hand to give her confidence and encourage her onwards. He was good with children. He had had to be, being the eldest of the family and a brother or sister coming almost every year. Now that the sister nearest him in age was able to do more it had become time for him to leave home to make more room for those coming up. Master Beddingfield would now feed and clothe him but when he was older like the fourteen year old Masterton, he would be able to save most of his wages to take home when he was given some time off.

He didn't really miss being at home. He enjoyed the luxury of sharing a room and bed only with Masterton rather than his four younger brothers. And of course, there was far more to eat at Beddingfields! After only three weeks he could barely fasten the jacket he had arrived in, so it was a good job that master provided good sturdy slop-suits for them to work in.

But what he enjoyed most of all was being able to talk to someone who would both listen to and answer his questions. As they had walked out during the morning, Margery had tried to explain to him about mountains. Not easy for a lad who had lived his ten years among the flat lands of eastern England. Will had been very taken with the Old Testament passage from the first book of Kings which he had recited to her with care: " Go forth, and stand upon the mount before the Lord. And behold, the Lord passed by, and a great and strong wind rent the mountains, and broke in pieces the rocks before the Lord, but the Lord was not in the wind; and after the wind an earthquake;

but the Lord was not in the earthquake; and after the earthquake a fire, but the Lord was not in the fire; and after the fire a still small voice."

Margery found herself wishing she had paid more heed to her father's religious teachings as she tried to wrestle with some of the boy's questions. It also struck her that it was a pity that Chandler Cobb was no longer the overseer. He would have relished taking young Will in hand. As it was she did the best she could. And she admitted later to her mother-in-law and Anne that it did her good to think of things other than babies and the household's affairs.

Time had sped past. The grandmother had enjoyed the novelty of the children, doting on them but fully conscious that she would not wish to have them about her all the time. Anne had been pleased to see how much better Margery looked now that she had regular help. And the young mother was also beginning to show interest in what was happening beyond the confines of her own home.

She had listened with pleasure as Anne wickedly described some of those who had been present at the first of the winter concerts held earlier that week at Saxmundham. When Margery and John were first married they too, had attended the concerts.

'And is there to be the Ball as usual in December?'

'But of course, my dear.' Mrs Beddingfield senior had replied. 'If I remember aright, the date is the ninth. An early concert to be followed by the dancing. Shall we make up a party? Will young John be able to be left for that length of time by then?'

The technicalities of suckling infants were unknown to the older Mrs Beddingfield. She had engaged the services of a wet nurse for her children, preferring neither to being tied to a routine which would interfere with her social life nor having to endure a regime which would not allow her to regain her figure as quickly as possible. In her opinion, confided only to Anne, it was the constant nursing of her two children that had been responsible for Margery's weak state of health.

Margery said she thought that she could manage for one

evening and just for a moment her pale face was flushed with anticipation.

'Oh John will enjoy that so much. We haven't been out together for so long and he is so good. He could, I'm sure do as other men do and stay over after market to drink or play cards but he always comes home. Almost straightaway.'

Anne averted her eyes at this statement. She, like her mother, had heard rumours that John was not always as punctual as his wife seemed to think him, but it was not for them to disturb Margery just when she seemed happy.

Instead she turned the conversation to relate the amazing adventure which had befallen some ladies whom they had met at the concert.

'Can you imagine,' Anne cried, 'waking up in one's room to find a robber at one's bedside!'

'But how did he get in?' Margery thought of the bolts and locks on the doors at home. 'Did no one hear him enter the house?'

'But that was what was so remarkable, my dear. The robber used a ladder and came in by the upper window. The lady said she surprised herself that she remained so calm. She did not scream out, mainly because she was anxious that he might have a pistol, and use it. So she just sat up in her bed while he went through her jewel box. She even told him where she kept her purse! But then, and this is the odd bit, he took up her watch and at that she did cry out, saying that the little locket on it held the picture of her lover who had died in the war. At that the robber stopped and looked at the picture. Then, according to the lady, he fell down on his knees, begged her forgiveness and leaving emptyhanded he went out of the window through which he had entered! Now what do you make of that?'

'Did the lady have any explanation for it?' Margery asked.

'Her only thought was that perhaps her robber was an ex-soldier, as so many of the footpads and highwaymen seem to be and that he had served under her late sweetheart.'

Margery considered this. 'Certainly, it shows that even the most hardened of criminals can have a heart that can be touched. No one is wholly bad.' She sighed. 'What a lovely story. I must remember to tell John when I get home.'

'Don't expect him to be so sanguine in his reaction,' said his mother. 'He'll probably tell you that he'll keep a loaded pistol beside the bed just in case this Sir Galahad of robbers should try entry to your house. Mind you,' she laughed, 'it will be worth telling the tale just to make sure that rick ladders are not left lying about for the convenience of those who wish to enter premises unlawfully.'

It was time for them to go. Will was called from the kitchen where he had been helping while he waited. Unfortunately both children were now tired and a little irritable, Pleasance demanding that her mother should carry her and not the baby. Because of this, Margery decided that it would be quicker to cross the fields rather than go round by the lane.

They were within sight of the farmhouse but still some distance from it when, without warning, the storm struck, a titanic explosion, shattering the peace of the late afternoon. They stood transfixed, not just by the suddenness and enormity of the sound but by the sight and smell which accompanied it. Ahead of them, coming as it were from behind the house, was a huge ball of fire wreathed in billowing smoke. Flames appeared to be leaping upward within the ball, then swirling round and down to lick their base. As they watched, the fiery monster whirled up and down across the sky streaking the darkening heavens. Four times they saw it rise and fall, each time coming a bit closer to the meadow in which they stood. And all the time the same dismal and constant roar – nothing like the usual crash and crack of thunder – and with it the choking, hideous, nauseous smell of sulphur.

Will stood close to her clutching baby John.

'The Devil's come, Missis. It's the end of the world!'

With that he laid the child at Margery's feet and flung himself prostrate on the ground.

'Pray, Missis, pray! Say the Our Father and perhaps we'll be saved.'

'Don't be silly, Will. It's not the devil, nor the angel of death . . .'

Margery had to shout to make herself heard above the clamour to which was now added the cries of both children. Pleasance clung howling while Margery attempted to pick up the frightened baby. Leaning forward she was almost blown off her feet as a wind whipped across the meadow carrying with it leaves ripped from trees and turnip plants torn out of the earth in adjoining fields.

Then the rain came. Like a blessing to wash away the loathsome noise and obnoxious smell. A gentle rain at first, but a thoroughly wetting one.

'Get up, Will. At once!' Margery commanded.

The boy seemed unable to hear her so she struggled on without him, getting wetter and wetter.

Head down, concentrating only on making sure that she did not fall with the children she was unaware of the pounding footsteps behind her until a gasping voice called out:

'Here, Missis, let me take the little ones from you.'

Margery turned and looked up into a face which showed deep concern for her plight. It was the face of Richard Ringe.

Such was her relief at seeing him that she allowed each child to be taken from her and to her surprise neither demurred at finding themselves in his strong arms. Margery had no breath for speech. She attempted a weak smile of gratitude but before she followed his lead, she looked back for Will. Unmoved from the spot where he had fallen, the boy still lay stretched out on the ground. Seized with the most dreadful fear that he had been killed by a bolt of lightning, Margery ran back to see. Thoughts of what a burned body might look like interwove with those of how she would break the news of his death to his parents.

Anticipation gave way to anger when she found that far from being dead, he was lying there sobbing like a baby for his mother. She grabbed the back of his sodden smockfrock and dragged him to his feet. Snatching hold of his hand she pulled him after her. No words were exchanged. Every bit of effort was needed to help them pick their way over the soggy ground as visibility became more and more difficult with nightfall and the thickening rain. Margery felt thoroughly chilled as the rain penetrated to her skin. Her garments clung heavily further slowing her movements.

Then just when it seemed that she must drop in sheer exhaustion there were lights and voices. Richard had given the babies into Liddy's charge and he and Masterton came out with lanterns to look for Margery and the boy.

In the kitchen Betty had built up the fire and had water on the boil for a mustard footbath for Margery and a hot drink for them all. Liddy had already put the children into dry clothes for the night and Margery quickly followed to do likewise.

Now that the danger had passed, there was almost an air of celebration in the farm kitchen as they gathered round the table for supper. Margery said they should not wait for John who had ridden off that morning to do business and dine with a neighbouring farmer and was not expected back until the late evening. So with the little ones sleeping soundly, everyone in the house relaxed. The combination of shared experience with the warmth of the kitchen and the measure of rum which Betty had added to their heated milk because she was sure 'the master would have ordered it if he'd been here' produced a sense of drawing them together which had not been there before. Perhaps for the first time in the few weeks that most of them had been at the farm, they were able to talk freely.

The storm with all its attendant peculiarities and horrors was the starting point, each contributing a different aspect, each offering an explanation for what they had seen. John Masterton who had been with Richard on the far side of the turnip fields swore that he had seen the huge ball of fire actually touch the earth causing it to shake before bouncing back into the sky. Only young Will remained silent, seemingly intent on the contents of his bowl. Then Masterton made a laughing comment to the effect that God must have been striking down sinners and that He was on the look out for Will. The boy looked up, his face pale with anguish. It seemed likely he would shame himself again with tears but both Margery and Richard had caught sight of the stricken face and in attempting to save the boy's feelings both spoke at the same time.

'I beg your pardon, Mistress.'

'No. You say on. It was nothing but a trifle I had to say.'

'Bless me, if I had over-much to say beyond isn't it strange that after all the upset in the weather, it should have turned into such a quiet night.'

Everyone listened intently. It was true, there was nothing to be heard outside, no beating of rain against the window shutters, no tap of branch stirred by a breeze.

Ringe had successfully diverted attention from the boy but had also broken in upon the comfortable mood of the company. That would not now be regained. So he remembered his role as overseer and said,

'Now, young Will, you should be in your bed. And John, it's time we did a last look round outside to make sure all is safe and secure.'

Margery was surprised that Richard should have been aware of the boy's sensitivity and was grateful that he had saved Will from possible teasing.

She looked more carefully at the man as he rose from the table. He had, she realised, quietly become part of the household almost without her noticing. True, she had been more interested in Liddy since the girl was to work closely with her, and Will had quickly endeared himself to her, but Richard and John Masterton were more part of her husband's domain than hers, though of course, they all lived under the same roof. Most days they all ate together as they had done this evening. Conversation then tended to be about farm business with John giving orders for work to be done and Richard perhaps making a suggestion or comment. Usually, Margery was too concerned with one or other of the children to give much attention to the new bailiff. She had only noted that he was young, had a pleasant manner and, what was most important, seemed to suit John. In fact, she had noticed that her husband was so satisfied with the man that he left him more and more to do.

Freed from the dour Chandler Cobb breathing dire warnings as to the state of agriculture in general and his farm in particular, John felt he could enjoy more social contact with his neighbours and cronies. He would slip away to attend a bare-knuckle fight, enjoying the thrill of the gamble on the outcome of the match as much as the bout itself. For the first time since he'd inherited the farm, he felt he was truly the master.

'Goodnight, Mistress Beddingfield.' Richard took up the lantern and he and the lad went out.

'Ringe seems a very pleasant fellow,' Margery remarked to the maids as they carried dishes through to the larder and left the kitchen tidy before going up to bed.

As the senior, Betty felt it incumbent upon her to comment. He was, she told her mistress, a fine young man who was most thoughtful for others. He didn't expect to be waited upon hand and foot just because he was a man. In fact, she had had some trouble in the beginning to make him accept the services that were offered, like making his bed and doing his laundry. Now, that cheeky young monkey, Johnny, he expected too much and she'd had to tell him plain exactly where he stood!

'And what about you, Liddy? Do you like him?'

'Oh, Liddy knew him afore , Missis.' Betty volunteered. 'They were together at their last place.'

'Then you will know him well.' Margery's remark brought a smirk to Betty's face and Liddy wished she'd held her tongue and not been so ready to confide in her fellow. She wasn't sure how the mistress felt about close relationships between hirelings.

But Margery failed to see either Betty's smirk or Liddy's discomfort. Her thoughts were only of how good it was that the man had come to her assistance earlier and to Will's just now. Sympathy and kindness were not characteristics she had met with often in her limited experience of menfolk.

'Which of you will sit up for the master?'

Betty regarded this as very much her prerogative but tonight she was tired so she was more than willing to let Liddy do the duty.

Liddy prepared the candlesticks for Richard and Masterton as well as for John. For him too, there was a place laid with a plate of cold meat and a jug ready to be filled with beer should he require it.

The two servingmen returned from their yard duties and the younger one went to his bed immediately. Richard was about to follow when Liddy pulled at his sleeve and whispered that she wanted a word with him.

He hovered by the door. 'Well?'

Liddy edged towards him, her movements sensuous. She stood in front of him and smiled, the long, slow smile that a few months earlier would have stirred Richard with longing.

'What's the rush, Dickon?'

He flinched at the use of the familiar name she had adopted for him. He tried to turn from her but she caught hold of his waist and pulled him to her.

'I'm to wait up, so shouldn't you bear me company? I'm sure Master, and Mistress too, would think it most kind of you to stay with me, especially after a day like this has been.' Her face was very close to his. He could feel her warm breath teasing against his cheek. Part of him desperately wanted to take her there and then, regardless of where they were and who might come in. But there was the other part, the one that said he would be foolish to give way to mere animal lust, the one that told him he must play cool otherwise he would lose again. Already he was building a role for himself in which there was no place for this girl. Yet he might need her help at some time in the future, so better not to repel her too much.

He kissed her long and hard but steeled himself against full arousal. Keeping his own passion under control he was able to prevent her from going any further than he wished.

Drawing away, he explained that they both had to consider the future. 'If it was discovered that we were lovers, then without doubt we'd both be sent packing. And jobs are hard enough to come by at the best of times, let alone this time of year.'

He led her back to the stool by the fire where she had been

sitting earlier. Standing before her he reminded her of the tale Betty had told of the hapless Prue and her boy lover.

'Let's bide our time, Liddy. One day, I promise you, we will be able to tell the world, but for now, let it be our secret – and only ours,' he added as a caution.

He looked at her closely to see the effect of his arguments. He was rewarded with a look of tenderness if not understanding.

'The mistress was asking about you while you were outside.'

'Yes?' He tried to appear unconcerned. 'What did she say?'

'Not much, just that you seemed pleasant enough and what did Betty and I think about you?'

'What did you say?' He could not keep the tremor out of his voice.

'Ah, that would be telling, wouldn't it?'

She tried to keep her tone light and bantering, knowing now that he would be angry if he discovered that she had revealed the knowledge of more than their casual acquaintance.

The barking of the yard dog and the sound of hooves put an end to any further discussion between them. Richard quickly went to his own quarters before the master of the house came in.

Her body aching from Richard's rejection, Liddy greeted John Beddingfield with more enthusiasm than he was used to among the serving women. She chatted brightly as she heated his milk which she laced with the accustomed medicinal dose of spirits. As she helped him off with his riding boots she dramatically related the events of the afternoon, laying particular emphasis on the part played by Richard. Flushed with thoughts of the man who had been able to resist her, Liddy's hand lingered longer than it should against John's leg as she eased the second boot off. Instantly, he was aware of her as a woman. Had he been given more time he might have been tempted to steal a kiss or fondle the eager young breasts which peeped above her dress, but before either had opportunity for an action that might be regretted, the door was flung open. Clad only in a nightgown stood the distraught Margery, the baby in her arms.

'Thank God, you've returned,' she gasped. 'The babe is far from well. Listen to how he breathes!'

There was no need for them to be silent. The wheezing and bubbling which came from the infant's lungs filled every corner of the room. Margery's own breathing was falling into the same rhythm of short sharp bursts.

John was by her side, peering into the tiny pinched face of his son. There was no colour anywhere, not even in the little cheeks. In its place a pearl-white tinged with a hint of blue around the miniature mouth which only that morning the father had remarked as full and rosy as the child had suckled.

He took the child from her. There was a flicker of movement in its eyelids as if acknowledging the change of handler but the effort to breathe was as much as the frail body could stand.

Liddy stood looking at the parents, conscious she ought to do something but unsure as to what. Margery looked bewildered as if now that John was there he would shoulder the responsibility. But what was he to do? What could he do? Then he recalled how Margery had nursed his father. She had been so competent then so why did she now seem so hapless? He resisted the urge to shake her, hard – to make her do something constructive to help his son.

He spoke brusquely. 'You, girl, make up the fire at once and put pans of water to heat.'

Liddy did as she was bid. To Margery his tone was a little less commanding but nonetheless urgent.

'Margery!' He rarely used her name, she was mostly 'my love' but some inner sense told him he had to deal firmly with her, make her become practical.

'You remember when my father had the congestion of the lungs you kept him easy by filling the room with steam. We shall do the same for the babe.'

Margery fought to bring herself out of this nightmare of unreality in which she was caught.

'Can you also recall what remedies you added to the steaming water? Or do you have any medication to hand that will help the little one breathe?'

Margery sprang into action then. Taking up a candle she went into the storeroom off the back kitchen where she kept her homemade remedies. Shivering as she stood barefoot on the cold stone floor she held the candle up to the shelf where the medicinal jars stood. She had let things slide here, so there was little order upon the shelves. Frantically she had to sort through the infusion of white lilies for severe cuts, tinctures of valerian for nervous upsets and the emetic tartar John used for a vomit when he had a stomach upset. At last, behind the oils of juniper, caraway and rosemary ready to be mixed with other herbs for specific use, she found the balsam mixture of aniseed, camphire and liquorice which was recommended for breathing problems. She just hoped that the potency had not gone from it. Tomorrow, she told herself, she would take stock of the shelves and make new infusions. Tomorrow . . . No time to think of tomorrow. What was she doing standing there thinking about domestic affairs when her child was fighting for its very breath. What sort of mother was she? How could she be so heartless?

Full of self-recrimination she returned to the kitchen where she found that John had brought down the baby's cradle and had placed it close to the fire. Liddy had rigged up a sort of tent of damp sheets around it, the heat from the fire increasing the steaminess within it.

Margery busied herself. She poured the friar's balsam into a basin of boiling water. Placed within the makeshift tent, strong aromatic vapours soon filled the air. The baby still wheezed noisily but no longer fought for each breath.

John realised that it would be no good to suggest that Margery return to her bed. No word passed between them on the subject yet it seemed understood that they would both watch. Margery, who was much more in command of herself now that she had something practical to do, told Liddy that she must go to her bed. When Liddy begged to stay and take her share of the watch, Margery reminded her that she was needed upstairs in case

Pleasance woke. How frightened the little girl would be if she called and there was no one to answer her.

Left alone John and Margery sat in silence, each occupied with fearful thoughts. At last Margery could stand it no longer. Staring straight ahead, her hands twisting in her lap she began to blame herself, first for taking the child out that day and then for not leaving her mother-in-law's house early enough to avoid the storm. Had the baby not been soaked through from the rain, he would not now be lying there suffering. It was all her fault. For the first time that night, she wept. She sat, straight backed in her chair, never taking her eyes from the cocooned cradle. Her tears flowed silently. She dared not sob aloud in case she missed some change in the child's condition. She desperately wanted to hold him close to her and make him well again. Reason told her this must not be. But reason did not explain why her husband did not comfort her. Why he did not come and put his arms round her and hold her as she wanted to do with the baby. Surely he must realise how she felt?

But John remained immobile, impassive, in the chair beside hers. Either one of them need barely move an elbow to have touched the other yet the distance between them at that time was insurmountable. Although he said nothing, in his innermost thoughts, John blamed Margery. She could not, of course, be held responsible for the storm but she could have taken more precautions with his only son. If only she had . . . he found himself saying over and over again.

They were isolated in their individual pain. Each needed comfort but neither was able to give it. Each would have done anything within their power to save the life of their child. But they were powerless.

So they sat marooned in their thoughts as the long hours dragged out their course. In the darkest part of the night, a little flame suddenly flared up from a green log and quickly fizzled out. Then all was silent. The baby had taken his final breath.

Seven

WINTER 1762

They had never known weather like it. Day after day of rain had followed the mysterious fireballs. Fields where the sodden soil could take no more were turned overnight into lakes as swollen streams edged relentlessly over their banks. Root crops waiting to be lifted rotted in the ground, while cattle and sheep waded disconsolately searching for sustenance before falling prey to disease. Everyone knew that food shortages were sure to come and with them even higher prices.

There were those who believed that it was yet another omen, a further sign of divine anger with a people who were constantly at war. How else, they asked, to explain, for example, that dreadful explosion which, according to all the English newspapers, had occurred just before Christmas in the Dutch town of Maestricht. Surely it was divine retribution that such a large store of gunpowder intended to bring devastation in battle should blow itself up. Of course it was a pity that eighteen innocent lives had been lost and three hundred homes either damaged or destroyed. But that was the price that had to be paid for going against heavenly law. Once peace was restored on earth, then Nature, it was believed, would regain her balance.

But the chance of peace seemed even more remote. Reports had it that even now Spain was preparing to take up arms against England. But then, said local gossip, it's an ill wind that does no one any good, relating that there was work in plenty to be had for craftsmen down at Ipswich. Double tides were being worked in the shipyards in preparation for the forthcoming conflict.

Then, without warning, the wind came. As the new year began, violent storms with gale force winds swept down from Scandinavia causing immense damage all along the coast. In the North Sea ships were overturned and sunk. Those which sought shelter inshore were hammered against rocks or driven fast upon banks of treacherous sand. Inland, windmills bore the brunt of the onslaught. Many were blown over, their sails pounded to matchwood, while adjacent cottages were lifted bodily to be blown across fields or even toppled over cliffs into the sea.

When the winds died down and the tides receded to their normal strength, many beaches from the Wash to the Thames were littered with unfamiliar objects, the strangest being beached and stranded whales. Until now, only those who had sailed in the whaling ships to Greenland had seen such creatures. Great was the curiosity of the public; at Gravesend there was one reckoned to be at least sixty feet in length. In Suffolk people were more than content to pay their pence to see the one, a mere third of that size, displayed at John Tillet's Nova Scotia Shipyard near the Bourne Bridge at Ipswich.

In the now calm seas off the East Anglian coast, His Majesty's ship Namur had surveyed the damage done to other members of the Fleet and was now lying at anchor on this Saturday afternoon awaiting orders. Seated at his desk in his cramped cabin, Sir George Pocock frowned as he carefully noted down the number of ships lost and damaged in the recent storms. More worrying for him was the severe shortage of manpower. Regrettably, there had been no possibility of saving any of those on board the two ships which had gone down and heavy losses overboard had been sustained on those vessels which, although they had survived, had been most dreadfully buffeted by the wind.

It was imperative that numbers were made up – and as soon as possible. Much as he hated recourse to such unpopular action he would have to agree to the solution suggested by his second in command.

Purposefully, he took a sheet of paper from his writing box, cut himself a new pen and began his letter to the Commander in Chief, the earl of Albemarle.

'My Lord,
The Commodore has a mind to make a sweep of seamen ashore in the night. I have no objection . . .'
He had, but what other means had they at their disposal? So he continued writing.
' . . .to his procuring as many men as can be picked up. I must have your Lordship's consent to the officers going about the town. I should choose this impress be made without creating any confusion in the town.
I am, my dear Lord,
Yours most truly,'

He signed his name with a flourish when he had read over what he had written and then realised that in his haste to be done with the affair, he had forgotten the most important part. So, entrusted to a postscript was the request for speedy permission as the following night was considered to be the most convenient time.

The letter was sealed, his servant called and given instructions for its immediate dispatch. Within minutes a boat was lowered and the request was on its way to the Commander in Chief.

In their own quarters aboard the Namur, Capt.Lloyd, some of his junior officers and young midshipmen were looking forward to relieving the boredom of being at anchor, anticipating the excitement of a night ashore as members of what on land had become known derogatorily as the Press-gang.

Lloyd and the others who were old hands at this method of recruitment regaled the novices with tales of their most recent exploits when they had conducted a sweep of the taverns and brothels around the docks of the City. The ease with which they completed their task there was in stark contrast to the problems encountered down on the marshes of Essex where the men had to be chased through ditches and channels to remote cottages and farmhouses. Like most of those who lived close to the sea, the Essex marsh-men were skilled not just as inshore fishermen. Economics of the time had encouraged them to diversify; ferrying illegal imports had brought both an increase in income and an aptitude for avoiding apprehension by the Excisemen.

Plans were now laid for the forthcoming sweep of the coastal areas of Suffolk. One party would concentrate on the harbour and its environs, another would take horses and venture inland to the town of Saxmundham and a third group, also mounted, would scour the villages and outlying farms in between. Lloyd was by this time an expert in such matters as commandeering suitable horses. His astute understanding of human nature meant that he knew when he could use an appeal to national pride rather than having to offer Government compensation.

Some of those listening questioned the reasoning behind making a raid on a Sunday evening. Surely a Friday or Saturday would be more fruitful since the inns and alehouses would be full of likely candidates just ripe for the picking. Capt.Lloyd agreed that in some areas this would be true but, quite apart from the fact that they could not wait for those days to come round again, he had had it on very good authority that in that part of Suffolk, the alehouses did better trade on Sunday nights than they did on Saturdays.

'Remember,' Capt. Lloyd told the men, 'when we go out, we are in the main, looking for those who have had sea experience. At this time of year there will be fishermen who are idle – they make us a good catch.'

He paused to wait for the dutiful laughter to come.

'Then there are those who have served time in merchant ships, made some money and come ashore to spend it. Look out for those who have gambled away what they had and are wondering where next to find funds. These are the fellows you're sure to find in the backrooms of inns and taverns, wherever there is a game in progress. A drink or two will suffice to get them to join up with us.'

A light-hearted squabble broke out as to upon whom would

fall the duty of standing treat in the local alehouses. Lloyd raised his hand for silence.

'You'll all get your chance, lads. Now. The local magistrates are constrained to let us have any malefactors that are suitable. No sense in locking up in the Bridewell a strong able-bodied fellow when he could serve his country on the high seas. So that should bring us in a reasonable haul.'

'But, what crimes, for Heavens sake, can anyone commit in such a dull area like this?'

The young officer who asked had been ashore and visited the quiet town of Aldeborough. He had found the slow pace of life there incomprehensible and worse was to follow when he hired a horse to help in his search for diversion and amusement. His ride had taken him through endless tracts of heath land and forest before he reached Saxmundham. But even there, in midwinter, there was little to tempt a man who did not know where to look for either games of chance or parties where ladies gathered to dispense their favours.

'Poaching, my lad! That's about the most heinous crime you can commit in the country – worse than stealing another man's wife, that is. And I can tell you now that most of those handed over to us by the magistrates will be those who have been caught helping themselves to a bird or two from the estates of those very same magistrates or their landowning friends.'

'Poor wretches,' murmured another young fellow. 'Can you blame them for trying to fill the bellies of children who are starving because the price of bread alone has risen to such an extent that the father can barely afford a crust to feed them. In similar circumstances I'd be tempted to help myself to birds or hares I happened upon, especially when I saw the over-stuffed gentry shooting or coursing just for mere pleasure.'

'That's enough of such talk, young sir,' barked Lloyd. 'You watch your tongue! You could well find yourself at the end of the yard arm for such radical speech.' His expression as well as his tone quelled any further comment.

'Remember, it is not our place to question. We are here to

uphold His Majesty's government and as such we do our duty... Now, where was I?'

Pausing briefly to let his words take root, he went on.

'Be on the look out for foreigners. Those who have entered the country illegally, Frenchies and the like, can be offered an amnesty if they sign up voluntarily. And a good deal they get too. A year or two in service for us and they can find themselves offered British nationality and the chance to be resettled in one of the colonies in the New World.'

'It's not likely we'll find many of those round these Godforsaken parts, Captain.'

'You think not?' Lloyd's tone was scathing. 'Then you may be in for a surprise. This coast is much favoured by those fleeing from the continent. Not just those who disagree with their own governments but young gentlemen who have been forced into exile to escape creditors, overstrict parents or even,' his face twisted in a sardonic grin,' anxious ladies with pistol bearing papas.'

He accompanied this last statement with a crude mime of both daughter and father. Amid the laughter that greeted this one or two looked uneasy.

'Finally, I have to remind you that no gentleman must be taken by force, neither can you remove any labourer actively engaged in field work.'

'But,' an earnest midshipman looked towards his captain.

'Yes, I know what you're going to say. At this time of the year there will be little work going on in the fields – and in any case, we shall be doing our little foray during the hours of darkness... Now... I wonder just why that should be?'

In the late afternoon of the following day, the little groups assembled on deck. Lloyd's cursory inspection revealed no other weapons than the permitted cutlasses and cudgels. Final orders were given, the boats lowered and a rising tide carried the hunters swiftly and silently towards their quarry.

On shore horses were ready, waiting for those who were to penetrate further inland. Capt. Lloyd took his work seriously, dismissing as unprofessional and slipshod those of his fellow officers who relied on haphazard and random sweeps to provide them with their quotas. It was his custom to make frequent trips ashore, sometimes leaving his shipboard base in dock somewhere while he rode into the hinterland to explore likely territory. Around the coast the major ports and their immediate environs had been pretty thoroughly worked over and it was now apparent that new sources would have to be sought.

It was while the Namur was lying in Yarmouth Roads that Lloyd had given any thought to the central area of Suffolk. Needing to make the journey by road to London, he had stopped to take refreshment at an inn in Saxmundham. Here, with his easy manner and open-handedness in buying drinks, he had ascertained that John Leatherdale, the licensee, was a former seafarer. Half his leg being blown off at the same time as Admiral Boscawen had received his wounds at the battle off Finisterre, Leatherdale had taken his pension and returned to his native town. Here he married his boyhood sweetheart who just happened to have become the widow of the innkeeper.

Leatherdale was the gregarious type who enjoyed nothing more than entertaining his customers with stories of his life at sea. The hardships, dangers and often sheer misery he had known grew less as the years passed and young men starting out in life heard only of the adventure, camaraderie and fortunes to be made from Prize money.

Lloyd had noted with some satisfaction that here was a centre where most of his work had been done for him. In addition to the easy prey eager for excitement in their lives, Leatherdale's also proved to be the gathering place for other former seafarers, not all of whom were no longer able bodied.

Encouraging those around him to talk, Lloyd had learned who among the locals had served recently in merchantmen. Like Leatherdale, they were often eager to boast of their exploits and if they themselves were reticent, then there were proud fathers keen to relate the prowess and daring of sons. Men who had travelled the high seas carrying cargoes from the African coast to the Americas and back – and survived in full health – were, from

Lloyd's point of view, the best to be had. Men already trained to life aboard ship were not wasteful of the time and money needed to apply the rigorous discipline necessary for the green landsman.

Lloyd's sharp brain had caught hold of names and locations, information to be carefully written down when he was alone and stored away until he was ready to use it. As he was now.

But even Lloyd, whose experience of inns and taverns could be said to surpass that of most men, was surprised at the noise which issued on that February night from the Angel. Seldom had even the roughest, toughest dockside establishment reached this level. Long before Lloyd and his small band reached the inn, the sounds of raucous laughter and voices raised, not in anger but simply to make themselves heard, were carried down the deserted main street.

'Seems you have some celebration afoot tonight,' Lloyd remarked to the elderly ostler who shuffled out to take their horses.

'Ay,' he sighed, 'when a man enters upon his inheritance on the Sabbath he'll have spent it all by Tuesday.'

Lloyd and the others gave this pronouncement the deep consideration the ostler seemed to expect. Then Lloyd, sensing that he was supposed to respond in some way, inquired,

'Of what exactly do you not approve, my friend? The fact that it is Sunday or that a young man should entertain his friends so soon after a bereavement?'

'Reavement! I said nothing about that.' The old man snapped. 'No one aint dead! When I spoke of inheritance, I was meaning that young James Scarlett had come out of his apprentice time and is to be master along with his father. And I bode fearful, having lived long enough to see many a man make a good living from a business which his sons have got through by their careless ways. Corny Beddingfield for one wouldn't lie straight in his grave if he could see how much of his money was going in cards and ale and his son is a boon companion of young Scarlett.'

'Surely,' said a young midshipman, 'you'll forgive Scarlett for painting the town red just one night.'

The joke had been carefully thought out but neither Lloyd

nor the ostler gave it a second's thought.

'I hope you gentlemen were not planning on a quiet night's sleep.'

'No. We're not staying. Just some refreshment before we're on our way again.'

'Oh, you'll find there's plenty of that. An extra special brew and plenty of good roast beef too, seeing how it's Scarlett.'

With no explanation for this final remark, the ostler left them and they stepped inside the crowded room. One look was all Lloyd needed to realise that they could not have come at a better time.

The place was filled with young men whose ages ranged from fourteen upwards to the late twenties. It was also instantly apparent that the party had been going for some time.

The majority had reached that stage where judgement is suspended, where every man is a close friend in whom to confide and all is well with the world. Another measure or two of the strong brew and the mood would swing wildly, old wounds would re-open, scores needing to be settled. At that stage present grievances would out – the nagging wife and irritable children, repressive parents, dissatisfaction with employment or the lack of it.

That would be the moment when Lloyd and his crew members would be able to throw back their travelling cloaks and reveal their uniforms, and with silken tongue beguile likely fellows to join them. Other suitable candidates they would earmark to follow homeward. These they would need to take by force so it was essential that their prey had drunk too deeply to make more than a token resistance. The closed carriage waiting at the edge of the town would later make the rounds to pick up all the new 'recruits' and by the time they had slept off the effects of the night's carousal they would be incarcerated either in the requisitioned fishermen's store on the beach or in the hold of the Namur. Neither location was likely to offer much comfort.

Once on board, the impressment officers relied on the results of a hangover and the acute nausea occasioned by being confined in the dark, dank and airless space below decks to keep their night's catch reasonably docile. Only the most foolhardy – or stupid – would attempt an escape. But all that was still to come. The host of the evening, the young man whose face tonight matched his name, lurched towards them in welcome. Lloyd responded, wishing him joy in his new status and gladly accepting the brimming tankard Scarlett pressed upon him. While drinking his health, Lloyd's eyes flashed messages to the rest of his party that this was one to be left unmolested.

Appraising those nearest to him he gave just the faintest nod in the direction of one and raised an eyebrow toward another as a sign of suitability. However, his lip curled as he watched the enactment of a little scene further across the room. A man in his late twenties, a gentleman by his clothes, moved towards his youngest midshipman. The youth, flushed with the excitement of his first such excursion ashore, responded to the greeting of the older man who put an arm round the young shoulders and drew him towards a table in the far corner. Lloyd tried to move closer but before he could reach him, a burly youth of perhaps sixteen or seventeen leapt out from the shadow and pushed the midshipman to one side, yelling an obscenity which pierced the din, bringing momentary silence.

Lloyd moved quickly, fearful that the midshipman should mar their enterprise by drawing his sword in self defence. He pushed through the crowd, grabbed his young officer by the arm, smiling as he said to the other two, 'He's with me.' They exchanged glances of understanding, while Lloyd indicated by gesture to his men that these two and any other of their tribe should be avoided at all costs. He also made a mental note to watch the midshipman closely in future lest he developed tastes in that direction.

By the time the festivities were coming to an end Lloyd had earmarked a number to be followed as they left the premises. One in particular, he felt, bore all the hall-marks of being unlikely to put up much of a fight. He had watched as the young man had come from an inner room. From his look and the odd snatch of overheard conversation, he had surmised that the young fellow had lost heavily at cards. Although obviously well known to all the company present, the man had chosen to sit apart, staring morosely into his drink. As a cat watches a mousehole, so Lloyd waited as his target seemed set to drink himself into oblivion.

Lloyd often filled his periods of waiting with pondering on the folly of human nature. What led an individual to desire to deaden intelligence; what could be so dreadful that there was an urgent need to escape from facing the consequences? In the dim light his victim's face appeared grey and haggard, ravaged with excessive care. Yet his body was that of an agile young man. Lloyd put him around the early twenties. Had he, the captain wondered, just lost everything in that fatal card game? An inveterate gambler, perhaps, now too scared to return home and confess that he had beggared his family?

Gradually the crowd began to thin out as those conscious of waiting wives and the start of a working week looming ahead left for their homes. Lloyd's men followed to shadow those they hoped to entrap. Lloyd himself remained, determined his prize should be the failed gambler. He moved towards the table where the other sat, thinking to engage him in conversation and win his confidence. Then he would offer to help him on his way.

But in this he was forestalled. James Scarlett, still just in command of himself, got to the table first and Lloyd heard him suggest that his friend should stay the night with him.

For a moment it looked as if Lloyd was going to be the loser but the drunken man struggled to his feet and declared,

'I'm going home! Going to my own bed – and by God – this night my wife shall be in my bed too!'

To the horror of those standing close by, he began to cry. Scarlett, plainly embarrassed, tried to make him sit down again and finish his drink. But the man would have none of it. He roughly elbowed Scarlett aside and reeled towards the outer door.

Scarlett, who had been winded by the blow, managed to say, 'He's not fit to walk alone to Sternfield. Someone should go with him.'

Lloyd seized the opportunity. 'Allow me. I haven't drunk as much as the rest of you. I'll see that the young man is taken care of.'

Scarlett seized his hand in maudlin gratitude. 'God bless you, sir. You will, one day, be rewarded for this night's work.'

'I will, indeed,' laughed Lloyd. 'And sooner than you know,' he added softly as he went out into the dark night.

Soon now, very soon, the cat would have his mouse.

Eight

WINTER 1762, SUNDAY

An air of unaccustomed tranquillity pervaded the kitchen at Beddingfield's farm that Sunday night. Margery sat alone with young Will Nunn. Over the last few weeks she had become used to spending her evenings with only the servants for company, her husband spending more and more time away from home.

In the beginning she had been hurt by his absence but now, she admitted to herself, she would rather he were out than remain to sit with her in the little parlour either re-reading every word of the weekly newspaper until he must have known it by heart or staring into the fire as if seeking there the answers to his unasked questions.

It had been like that ever since the night he had returned from the burial of baby John. Aching with her own great grief she had sought comfort from him in their bed. The harshness with which he had rejected her and the bitter words he had spoken to reinforce that rejection, even now made her cheeks burn with shame.

That night, and for several following, each had lain on either edge of the huge feather bed isolated in their individual unhappiness. As John slept, his breathing heavy from the excessive amount of drink he consumed between the end of his working day and bedtime, so Margery lay rigid with torment. In those direst hours between two and three in the morning she relived the agony of the child she had miscarrried and the nightmare of little John's death. Was it all her fault? Was she being punished for her wickedness in going against her father's upbringing? Would she never be allowed to raise the son for which her husband so yearned? How long would John go on hating her? How long must she endure this loveless bed?

Relief had come unexpectedly. One night as yet again she lay wakeful, she was aware that Pleasance's cries had gone on longer than usual. Creeping into the adjoining room she found Liddy sound asleep, oblivious to her charge. Margery gathered up her daughter and held her close, realising that in her own misery she had neglected the child. Pleasance had been fretful of late and it had been too easy to order Liddy to 'look to the child!'

Margery realised too that John now rarely cast an eye on the little girl. She still ran to him when he came into the kitchen but he no longer bent to scoop her up and toss her upwards as he used to do. Once he had revelled in her giggles of delight as he caught her, now he pushed her away when she attempted to climb on his knee as he sat down to dinner.

Gently rocking the child, Margery felt a sense of calm. She still had one child. It was up to her to make sure that Pleasance knew that she was loved by one parent at least. The night was cold and the pair shivered in the chilly room. It seemed then sensible to creep into the bed beside the sleeping Liddy for the rest of the night. After that a precedent was set. Margery explaining her action to the maid by saying that as Liddy had the care of the child by day along with her other chores, then Margery should be on hand at night.

But that still left the days to be got through. John gave his orders for what was to be done but wasted little speech on anything else. Sometimes he went away for several days at a time telling Richard, in Margery's hearing, that he had business to attend to in other parishes. To Margery he said little beyond what was absolutely necessary.

Richard was left to cope with the daily running of the farm. He could do the work easily enough, but feared to make decisions which might not be agreeable to his master. On more than one occasion the changeable nature of John's temper brought him to the point where he would dearly have loved to tell the farmer what he could do with his job but he bit his tongue and bided his time. It angered him too, to see the way his master treated Margery. It had taken great restraint on Richard's part not to say something when, one evening as the household sat round the table after work, John had been cruelly belittling of his wife in front of them all. Richard had seen the look of anguish in Margery's eyes as she bore the affront.

He was also concerned that accounts remained unsettled, John leaving him to deal with merchants who were reluctant to supply goods when payment was slow. It was Richard who now attended the weekly markets and it was there he heard rumours that his master was negotiating to sell off pieces of land in other villages. It made no sense. Land prices were at their lowest. This was just the time, the older farmers gossiped, when Master Beddingfield's father would have been buying – not selling. What, they asked Richard, could have brought young Master John to take such drastic action?

As he rode back, Richard had thought long and hard about this. Their own farm was productive enough, so why the sudden need for cash? Then it came to him. The thing that had nagged at him about their mutual schooldays. He remembered there had been a scandal. A group of older boys had been caught at an illegal bare-knuckle boxing match. Far worse than the mere sneaking out of school to attend the fight was the discovery that the boys had all bet heavily on the match – and lost. One of the youths, the son of a local attorney had actually borrowed money from his father's office to finance his ventures; another had stolen some of his mother's jewellery to pledge against his bet. Although Richard and the other pupils had never heard the full story, they had learned enough from rumour to know that this was not the first time that the group had indulged in such activity. There was talk of attendance at cock-fights and card games outside school while information was soon offered up that some of the youths had attempted to extort money from younger boys in simple games of chance.

Richard was able to recall the vivid picture of the malefactors lined up before the rest of the boys to receive their public flogging.

And yes, of course, John Beddingfield had been among them! It was the defiant curl of his lip as he had straightened up which had registered so deeply in Richard's mind.

Then everything fell into place. Richard's anger began to grow into a gnawing hatred of the farmer. How could Beddingfield who had everything – land , money, wife and child – be so careless of them all? Could the man not see that he stood in danger of losing it all? And what future was there for Richard? Was he to find for a third time that his hopes of a settled future were to be dashed? And this time as a result of the mere turn of a card or throw of the dice?

One evening after he had returned from Aldeburgh where a supplier had been particularly difficult about giving credit, he had attempted to talk to Beddingfield about the farm's financial state. Coldly, John had told him to remember his place. Angry with himself as much as his employer, he had sought refuge in the stables where he attended to the horses. When, later, he took up his coat again, he saw the packet he had purchased that afternoon from the Aldeburgh apothecary. Poison to deal with the rats which plagued the farm. The packet was in his hand as he crossed the yard.

In the kitchen, Betty was alone, heating milk for Beddingfield's nightly drink.

'He's got the old devil on his back again tonight,' she observed as Richard came in.

When Richard said nothing, she continued with the train of thought uppermost in her mind.

'He do make life a misery, these days. There don't seem to be anything a body can do right.' She sighed deeply. 'If only there was something we could do to make us all happy again.'

Richard fingered the little packet in his hand and then looked at the cup she was preparing.

'Put a bit of this in his milk, Betty, then all our worries would be over.'

'What have you got there?'

'Poison. For the rats. Go on, girl. Drop some of that in! He'll never taste it, not with all that rum. Do us all a good turn and get rid of the worst rat of all, the one who's gnawing at all our lives.'

Betty paused but a moment as she poured the spirits into the waiting milk.

'Get away with you, Richard Ringe. For a minute there I thought you were serious. As if I'd risk my place here, never mind my immortal soul, just to think of a such a thing. And you shouldn't say such things, even in jest. You know what the Good Book says about evil thoughts.'

Richard didn't, but neither did he wait to have the text quoted in full. He went out to the outhouse to lock up the lethal package.

The long winter days dragged on until that Sunday when by tradition servants had the day free to visit their families if they lived close enough.

Betty had gone to see her mother who lived on the edge of Saxmundham. She was to be accompanied there and back by Masterton whose family lived further along the same road.

Liddy was to visit her aunt in the town itself and Margery ordered that Richard should walk in with her and be there to ensure her safe return. This arrangement suited one but not the other. Liddy was overjoyed to have the opportunity to be alone with Richard and had already decided that her visit to her aunt would be a short one. Richard, with no filial duty to perform, had hoped to remain at the farm where there might be the chance of an uninterrupted conversation with Margery. He told himself that his interest in his mistress was only a desire to make her less sad. She seemed to appreciate his company on the rare occasions they had been alone, seemed to understand the sympathy he had for her plight.

In her quiet, subdued way, Margery was a complete contrast to the vivacious Liddy who took nothing seriously, was too ready to laugh at the least thing and flaunted herself at any man who as much as looked at her. Richard had seen the way she looked at Beddingfield, always pushing herself forward to perform little services for him; her hand touching his leg as she pulled off his riding boots or placing her body very close to his as she helped him off with his coat. Betty might be taken in by her, but Richard suspected the motive which made Liddy offer to be the one to wait up on those nights when John Beddingfield returned late.

Richard might no longer desire Liddy for himself, but he resented her giving her favours elsewhere, particularly to their employer. The prospect, therefore, of their being forced to spend time in each other's company that Sunday was a bleak one for Richard.

Only Will Nunn had been unable to go home. Several days earlier he had developed a severe sore throat. Ever fearful that the symptoms might develop into something worse, Margery had dosed him with her fig remedy. Will, whose job it had been in the autumn to gather the fruit from the gnarled old tree at the back of the farm, had watched with interest as Margery had prepared the concoction for him. Eight shrivelled fruit were simmered slowly in the large pan over the fire. When not much more than half a pint of the thick brown liquid remained it was left to cool. The boy was given a little night and morning to gargle with until his throat was clear of infection. When he got up on Saturday he assured Margery he was now fully recovered. However, he then found there was a final part to this cure. He was required that day to eat the figs to purge his system of any lingering ill effects. And so it was that on Sunday, Will had not dared to undertake the journey to his home.

Not that he minded. Apart from the upheaval in his stomach region, he was quite content to stay with Mistress Margery and young Pleasance. They had had a quiet, restful day, Will more than happy to sit and listen as Margery told Pleasance stories of fairies and magic carpets; handsome princes and beautiful maidens with long golden curls just like those the little girl had. The child may not have understood much of it, but she enjoyed her mother's undivided attention and sat on her lap snuggled close to Margery's thin body.

After the child had been put to bed, Margery had taken up her knitting, but for the most part her hands were idle as she concentrated on answering the boy's questions about the stories she had told. The intelligence of the lad amazed her as had the speed with which he grasped the ability to read. It was as if the knowledge of how to put letters together to make words was already planted in his brain just waiting to be released. To herself Margery compared it with a garden plot of freshly turned earth. One minute there is nothing but flat brown soil but following the next fall of rain the whole is covered with quick growing seedlings.

In keeping her promise to teach him, she had given her own mind a chance to escape from other cares. Will could now read to himself but he enjoyed it more when Margery listened to him and he could ask for explanations. She rose now from her chair and took down the Prayerbook from the shelf which held her few books.

'Come, Will, you shall read me the collect for the day before you go to your bed.'

He found the place. Slowly and carefully he read, "Grant, we beseech thee, Almighty God, that we, who for our evil deeds do worthily deserve to be punished, by the comfort of thy grace may mercifully be relieved; through our Lord and Saviour Jesus Christ. Amen."

'Amen, indeed,' echoed Margery. She shivered as she considered the verses. When, she asked herself, would she receive the relief from her punishment?

'Take your candle and be off with you. Goodnight.'

Will had got no further than the door to the staircase that led to his room above the kitchen when footsteps were heard approaching. The boy waited. He could hear Betty's voice raised in excitement. Something must have happened and he would rather hear it fresh from her than wait until Masterton came to bed and told him.

Margery rose to unbar the door and Betty almost fell into the kitchen in her haste to impart her news.

'Oh, Mistress, you'll never believe what a time I've had. Whoever would have thought such things could happen in Saxmundham? And on a Sunday too!'

Betty struggled with the strings of her cloak and bonnet while Masterton moved to the fire to warm himself. Betty didn't look in need of such comfort, her round face was flushed with excitement and the exertion of almost running back to the farm.

Margery waited patiently. She knew that when Betty had a story to relate she liked to take her time in its narration. So she sat back in her chair and waited.

At last Betty had removed her outdoor garments and was ready to begin.

'Well, you know, I had a funny feeling that something untoward was going to happen today. First, I heard three raps on my bedhead in the night, then this morning when I came down the cat sneezed and then the third thing was to discover it was to be full moon tonight – a Sunday!'

'Now Betty, you know, as we all do, that that is all mere superstition.'

'You may think what you like, Mistress, but I tell you, queer things have happened today.'

'Are you going to tell or not?' Masterton interrupted. "Cos if you don't, I will!'

Betty rounded on him. 'How can you, you stupid boy? You weren't there most of the time.'

'Well, if you don't get a move on, then I'll tell my bit and go to bed – before the full moon come and get me!'

Margery smiled at Masterton. She appreciated how he felt.

'So, Betty,' she prompted. 'What did happen?'

Betty plonked herself in the chair opposite Margery and continued her tale.

'You probably don't know, Mistress, but my mother lives alongside old Goody Culham. A fearsome old creature she is, with black flashing eyes that seem to bore right through you – and to my mind, when I was a child, I thought she was a witch. And come to think of it, she could be at that.' Betty fell silent as she pictured the woman who was unknown to the rest of them.

'Go on, for goodness sake,' urged Masterton.

Betty ignored him and looked at Margery.

'What you also probably won't know is that Goody Culham is Chandler Cobb's mother, she having married Culham after she had Chandler and his brother. I could tell you a lot about that . . .'

'Please Betty, let us have that another day. What is the significance of Goody Culham or Chandler Cobb, for that matter?'

'Well, don't you see? Chandler Cobb came to visit his mother! His new employers, who are very good folk by all accounts and think highly of him, allowed him two or three days to come and visit the old lady. She not having been in the best of health of late.'

'And?' Margery prompted.

'When he heard I'd come, Chandler stepped in to mother's to see me. We were having a rare old talking over of the old times when we heard a banging on the wall from his mother's tenement. Thinking she must have been taken queer, we all ran next door just in time to catch two men coming out at the kitchen door. "What's all this?" says Chandler and made the men go back into the house where old Goody Culham was sitting shaking like a jelly and crying fit to bust.'

'Good heavens,' cried Margery. 'Was she much hurt? What did the ruffians want of her?'

'Ah! They wasn't ruffians at all, Mistress. Them was supposed to be gentlemen. Officers they said they was, looking for young men to join up with them in the navy.'

'Pressmen – that's what they were,' Masterton interposed.

Betty silenced him with a look.

'Chandler Cobb made them sit down and explain their business and they said they had the King's authority to enter any house they liked to search for anyone who might be hiding. "That may be," said Goody, " but I don't suppose His Majesty told you to help yourself to my old man's brass tobacco box from the shelf – and that with my next quarter's rent money in it." She had recovered her spirits by then. So Chandler, cool as you like, made the men turn out their pockets and sure enough, there was old Culham's baccy box. Well, then there was a right old set-to with Chandler threatening to go off and report them to the magistrate.

One of the men, a quite good looking young fellow of perhaps seventeen years, drew his sword then and said if Chandler wasn't so old, he'd a good mind to take him. But the other laughed nastily and said they weren't that hard up and that if Chandler wanted to complain he'd find his chief at the Angel in Saxmundham. Then they pushed their way out saying they'd still got a night's work ahead of them.'

'We sat a while and talked things over and then I remembered that young Masterton here was supposed to be on his way to meet me and I was afeared that the Pressmen might get him – though why I bothered I don't know.' She glowered at the boy. 'So Chandler Cobb said he'd walk along the road to try and warn him.'

Betty sat back to gather her breath as well as her thoughts, so Masterton took up the story. A stolid youth, he lacked the maid's sense of drama and told his story plainly though he too, had had an adventure. He explained that his mother lived at the far end of a row of tenements which had been carved out of one single substantial house. He had just been preparing to make his farewell when a child from the other end of the row had come with the news that the Press-gang were searching the houses and had taken up a neighbour's son. Mrs Masterton had acted quickly. Taking up her candle she had bundled her son up into the space in the roof giving him whispered instructions on what to do next. Then she returned to her kitchen to await her visitors. As soon as the lad heard the men's voices below him, he carefully felt his way along the rafters which supported the roof of the whole row until he reached the far end. There he had waited. When all was quiet, he had let himself down into the bedroom beneath and so made his escape.

'I was wholly scare, I don't mind telling you. And cold too, for I hadn't had time to put on my coat. I kept as close as I could to the hedge but it was dark and dreary.' He looked at Betty. 'Your full moon didn't shine much tonight.'

Before she could say anything, he went on.

'Then I could just make out a figure coming towards me and

so I dived into the hedge and fell into the ditch bottom. I lay there aquaking, when a voice called out, "Masterton, I've come for you!" I thought that the Pressmen had found me out but it was only Master Cobb. He told me he was going to go to Saxmundham and that I should hurry as Betty was waiting for me.'

Margery, having listened to their accounts, showed immediate concern for their health. She sent Nunn for towels and ordered the other boy to take off his wet clothes. She also insisted they should take rum in their milk to warm them inside. Then she dispatched both boys to bed and bid Betty to do likewise. The older woman demurred, saying she would wait up with her mistress until the others came.

Both of them were so full of the events of the evening that neither noticed the air of restraint between Liddy and Richard when they returned.

Liddy came in first. Richard followed a minute or two later. Neither said anything beyond the usual evening greeting and both busied themselves preparing their chamber candles. Betty however could not resist a new audience and launched into a re-telling of the events of the night to which they listened with scant attention.

Each was preoccupied with the argument they had had on the way home. Richard had made it plain to the girl that he could not entertain thoughts of a permanent relationship while the future was so doubtful. Liddy had scoffed at the idea that Beddingfield might be heading for bankruptcy bringing with it a loss of employment for them both.

'What a foolish notion. As if the master would ruin himself like that,' she had said.

'It's not foolishness, just plain commonsense. I have seen the signs. He will come to a bad end, you wait and see.'

'Well, at least he'll have had some fun on the way. Master's more of a man than you'll ever be, Richard Ringe.'

Stung by the implication of this, Richard had grabbed Liddy's arms and pinioned them to her side. Holding her so, he asked the question which had been nagging at him for weeks. 'Has Beddingfield been your lover?'

Liddy shook herself free of him, laughing as she did so, 'Wouldn't you like to know!'

She had run off ahead of him, turning back to yell, 'And what if he has? If you don't want me, why shouldn't I let him have what his wife can't – or won't – give? She's a weak pathetic creature. With a bit of luck she won't last long – and then, who knows, Richard Ringe – I may become the mistress at Beddingfield's farm. How would you like that?'

Richard had caught up with her then and she was able to say in normal tones, 'Then you could make your great goose eyes at me instead of Mistress Margery and play the loyal servant for me, fetching and carrying at my every whim.'

He was not a violent man but his hand swung up to deliver a stinging blow to Liddy's cheek.

She recoiled momentarily, then laughed. 'Oh, I do like a man with some spirit! A pity you've waited so long to show it.' She had then turned and walked ahead of him for the rest of the way to the farm.

Now all Richard wanted was to take himself to his room to sort out his muddled thoughts but there was no immediate escape.

'Richard,' Margery's gentle voice broke into his thoughts, 'did your master say aught of the time he might be expected?'

'No, mistress, but I dare say it will be later than usual, if the noise coming from Master Scarlett's celebration was anything to judge by.'

He saw the pain in her face and again inwardly cursed Beddingfield.

'Then we will go to bed. Come, Liddy.' She dismissed the maid's offer to wait up. 'Betty, see to the fire and leave the master's drink ready before you go up.'

She turned back again to the man. 'Richard, will you wait to see the master's safe return?'

Nine

SUNDAY/MONDAY

Chandler Cobb was weary. It had been a long day. So had been the previous one on which he had set out from Norfolk, making his way on foot when he hadn't managed to beg a ride from a passing cart.

He now began to doubt the wisdom of his impulse to report the malpractice of the young officers. The magistrate certainly would not entertain a visit so late in the evening, so perhaps he should go straight to the Angel and make his complaint there.

As he neared the town, one of his feet began to throb unbearably. He could feel something sticking up inside his boot. It would have to be removed. Not as supple or as adept as he had been in his younger days, he needed to sit down in order to take off the boot. In the dim light shed by the moon through the thin cloud covering, he looked around for a suitable spot to park himself. Just ahead he caught the outline of the wall to the churchyard. That would have to serve. Limping towards the gate, he turned into the graveyard and felt his way to a large, flat-topped tomb of some past wealthy merchant who, reluctant to the last to leave this earth had insisted on being buried as close to the town as possible.

Cobb hoisted himself up on the tomb and pulled at his boot. He heard a piece of stone hit against the grave as the boot came off. Then came the struggle to replace his hot, swollen foot back inside its casing. The effort took its toll and he leaned back against the cold stone, fighting off the desire to lie down and sleep. He would give himself just a few minutes respite.

He must have dozed. For how long he had no way of knowing but he was brought to sudden consciousness by the sound of distant voices. Authoritative voices, calling on someone to stop. With the swift, silent skill of a man who in his time has had to deal with poachers, Cobb moved to a position beside the entrance to the churchyard. From the other side of the wall he could hear the stumbling unsteady gait of a man who has drunk too deeply. He realised that if he remained where he was, he was likely to witness the Press-gang make a successful snatch.

A law-abiding, God-fearing man, with a strict sense of duty to his sovereign and his country, Cobb had recognised the need for such measures to be taken for the defence of the realm. But that had been before he had had personal experience of the methods that were employed. He remembered the look of terror on his old mother's face and reflected momentarily on what might have become of her if he hadn't been close at hand to protect her. Why should these paid government louts be allowed to get away with such behaviour? If he could not complain through the proper channels, then he would seek his redress elsewhere. He would spoil their chances of a captive.

One quick movement and his hand was over the mouth of the drunken man. With his other arm round the man's waist he dragged him into the graveyard and threw him roughly behind one of the huge ancient yew trees.

'Lie there and be silent, if you value your life.' His hoarse whisper surprised Cobb himself by its strangeness.

Then he walked slowly back to the gateway reaching it just as the Press-gang drew level.

Capt. Lloyd raised his lantern to peer at him. 'What are you doing here, old man?'

Cobb, who had never knowingly told a lie, looked him straight in the eye, 'Answering an urgent call of nature, sir.'

'Have you seen a young man pass by here? A very drunk young man. He can't have gone far along this road.'

Cobb considered his answer carefully. 'I have seen no one pass by this spot.'

Lloyd failed to notice the slight emphasis on the word 'pass' being too busy giving the order to scout ahead. The young midshipman quickly returned to report that there was no sign of anyone on the road and nothing either in the way of habitation.

'We've no time to scour the hedgerows. Let's hope he's fallen into a well-filled ditch and drowned himself.' He turned to Cobb, 'and you, old man, get yourself off to your home or you might find yourself taken up for a thief.'

The posse turned back towards the town and Cobb returned to the spot where he had left the man. He was lying, flat on his back, sound asleep.

'Now what am I going to do with you? If I leave you here to sleep it off, by morning you'll be as dead as the rest of them in here. Come on up with you. I'd best take you back with me to mother's.'

In raising the inert figure he was able to see for the first time the man's face. What he saw startled him so much that he let go his hold and the other fell back heavily to the ground.

'Young Master Beddingfield!'

Chandler Cobb straightened up and stared down at the body. The irony of the situation was not lost on him. He had just saved the man who had quite ruthlessly ejected him from his home and employment. A year ago he would quite happily have wished to see his erstwhile master suffer torments far worse than being taken off to serve at sea. At that time he had longed to get his revenge on John Beddingfield, now the man's life was at his disposal. He could be vicious and go into town and report to the Officer-in-Charge that he had found the man for whom they were searching or he could callously walk away and leave Beddingfield to take his chance against the night.

Cobb allowed himself the luxury of considering the options. He made his decision. He bent forward and picked up the unconscious man, slinging him across his shoulder as he would a sack of corn. Then he stepped out into the road, his feet no longer hurting and began the walk to his mother's house.

Half a mile on, the burden weighed heavily. He stopped to

rest at a field gate beside a steaming dung heap. It was no good, he could carry the load no further. Resisting the temptation to throw his former master on top of the heap, he gently rolled the body on its side close to the base making sure that Beddingfield's face was away from the noxious pile. At least it would keep him warm.

When he reached his mother's home, he rested for an hour or so, for it would soon be time for him to set out on his return to Norfolk. With still an hour or so before daybreak he wrote a careful note giving details of where Beddingfield might be found, then made his way to the farm which had once been his home.

His approach to the house passed unheeded except by the old dog who acknowledged their former acquaintance with no more than an uplifting of his head. Pushing the folded paper through the gap below the kitchen door Chandler Cobb's night's work was done. He could set his way northward with a clear conscience.

A log shifted on the hearth bringing Richard into wakefulness. It had been some time before he had dozed and then fragmented dreams had tormented him. He sat up, wondering what had disturbed him. The fire was low and beside him the candle flame was flickering in a well of liquid tallow. It was obvious that his master had no intention of returning before morning so he might as well go to his bed for what remained of the night. He placed more wood upon the dying fire and prepared his own bed candle. As he took it up he caught sight of the paper lying by the door. Puzzled, he picked it up and took it across to the table. Setting down his light, he unfolded the note and read:

"Master was going home very drunk, hotly pursued by Press Men. I threw them off but he passed out. Couldn't carry him so far. Have left him beside dung heap at Further Fen. Best fetch him quick or he won't be. Have gone back."

Richard turned the note over. There was no indication for whom the note was intended, neither was there a signature. He read and re-read, trying to take in the full implications of the contents. He tried to recreate the scene in his imagination but was unable to find a face for the chief actor in this drama. Two sentences stood out. At "best fetch him quick or he won't be", Richard allowed himself a smile of appreciation at the unknown writer's sense of humour. How tempting to fling the paper into the fire and leave Beddingfield to rot along with the dung. As far as Richard was concerned it would be a fitting end for him. But what of "Have gone back"? He could only assume that the man, whoever he was, had returned to wait with Beddingfield until help arrived from the farm.

This put Richard in a quandary. Should he go now or wait until daylight? The messenger might well think that his note would not be found until morning, in which case Richard could linger as long as he liked before going – and who could tell if it might not then be too late? On the other hand, whoever had pushed the note under the door must have had some knowledge of the household, enough to know that a servant was probably sitting up against the return of the master. There was also the possibility that if Richard delayed too long, the mystery man might get help from other quarters.

He screwed up the paper and threw it on the fire. As the little ball hit the centre of the flames he made up his mind. Noiselessly, he let himself out of the house, crossed the yard to the stables, saddled one of the horses and led it out into the lane before he mounted.

The blue-black morning sky was streaked fiery red as the sun rose to sharpen the outlines of frost covered hedges and fields. Richard reached the gateway of the field known as Further Fen. He dismounted. There was no sign of life anywhere. He called softly but there was no reply. Slowly he edged towards the stinking, steaming heap. There lay John Beddingfield, on his back, rigid, and his mouth agape.

In the stillness of the wintry dawn Richard could hear only the beat of his heart drumming in his ears. Waves of nausea rose within him as he tried to focus on the scene before him. He had wished this man dead – and now he was. And he was here, standing by the body. Fear consumed him. Suppose someone else should pass this way and find them both? How would he prove he was not responsible? What must he do? Fear gave way to panic. He must get away! But where could he go? Not back to the farm. How would he explain where he had been? Easiest just to get on the horse and ride away – anywhere – as fast as possible. He tried to move but his legs seemed unconnected to his body. Then the thought flashed into his mind that if he rode off he would be classed as a horse thief, certainly hanged if he were caught.

The enormity of it all made his head reel and he lurched forward almost falling on the body. He stretched out his arms to save himself and a hand landed on Beddingfield's face. Immediately, his full senses returned as his cold palm was warmed by the breath of the 'corpse'. Almost hysterical with relief, Richard picked up his master, carrying him as carefully as he would some precious object and gently placed him across the back of the horse. Getting up behind him, he turned the horse towards the farm.

The household was up and in confusion. Betty, first to come down, had found the door unsecured. When the two boys reported that Richard was neither in his room – his bed never slept in – nor was he to be seen outside, Margery was informed. Liddy was sent into the parlour bedchamber adjoining the room she now shared with Margery to wake the master and tell him. She returned swiftly with the news that his bed was also just as it had been the night before.

As the early morning work of the kitchen got underway, Masterton came in from the stables.

'It get worse, Mistress. We've had a horse stolen in the night.'

'There, what did I tell you, yesterday? Didn't I say things weren't right here? I heard that tapping at my bedhead again last night and now Master and Richard be gone – taken away by the Pressmen, if not done away with by thieves in the night.'

'Hold your tongue, Betty and be about your work', Margery rounded on her sharply.

Behind her back, Betty made a face at Liddy. Wisely, Liddy said nothing. Recalling the previous night's conversation with

Richard, she was of the opinion that he had decided to cut loose, taking the horse as a way of revenge. More fool him, she thought.

They worked on in unnatural silence. Then the door was flung open and Will ran in shouting that Richard had just ridden in. The three women did not even pause to put on shawls but went straight to the yard.

'I've got the Master,' Richard called. 'He's in a bad way – not least for having spent part of the night on a dung heap. I should stand back a bit,' he cautioned as Margery ran forward. 'He'll need a bath before he goes to his bed. I'll take him out the back.'

'Quick girl – don't stand there,' Margery's voice rose impatiently. 'Get water to the tub as quick as you can and Liddy, put the warming pan to the master's bed.'

The maids scattered to their tasks. Margery longed to go to John but Richard and Masterton were already carrying him into the wash house, so she had to content herself with looking out a clean nightshirt to hang by the fire to warm and then preparing a cordial to revive her husband.

As the men stripped him of the rank smelling clothes, John began to stir. Still befuddled he struggled against them as they lowered him into the tub but then he relaxed as the warm water brought ease to his aching body. He lay like a child as Richard gently washed him from head to foot. Masterton stood slightly apart, self-conscious, holding the diaper sheet ready to dry his master. Outside the door, Betty hovered, waiting to pass clean garments to them.

So far no words had been exchanged between them. Richard's thoughts raced. How much could John recall of the previous night? What explanations would he, Richard, have to give as to how he had come to find him? Should he mention the mysterious letter?

Still without speaking, John allowed himself to be led into the kitchen where he paused for a minute to look around him as if he were unsure of his surroundings. Like figures in a tableau the rest of them stood motionless, waiting, for something momentous to happen.

Margery broke the tension, moving towards him with outstretched arms.

'My love, I was so worried for you.'

A look of blank incomprehension passed over his face. He turned away from her and before anyone could reach him he lost consciousness and fell to the floor.

From beneath the table where she had been hiding, Pleasance let out a wail. Margery was torn between comforting the child and assisting her husband but matters were taken out of her hands. Libby caught up the child and took her to one side while Richard gathered up John.

'I'll get him to his bed. Sleep is what he needs.'

'Should I go for the physician, Mistress?' Betty asked. White faced and close to tears, Margery agreed to this and then changed her mind, begging that Will should go instead, leaving Betty free to help watch over John.

Margery followed Richard up to the bedchamber feeling sad and useless. Even now, when he was perhaps close to death, John had rejected her. She smoothed the sheet on the bed before Richard laid her husband upon it, fussed with pillows – anything that would show her love and concern – and it was all unheeded. Except by Richard. He was only too aware of her wretchedness and longed to comfort her. As he stood very close to her at the bedside, he had to fight down the intense desire to put his arms around her, to protect her, to tell her he cared for her even if her husband didn't. If only it had been to him that she had whispered those words, 'My love, I was so worried for you.' The urge to touch her became even greater as Margery's stifled tears broke free.

He could not bear it. He left her abruptly, muttering as he reached the doorway that he had to see to his work. Margery did not even notice his going. She knelt by her husband's bed and wept; all the pent-up anguish of the last few months flooded out of her. She still had her face buried in the quilt when there was a movement beneath it. John had turned over on to his side. Just a hint of colour tinged his cheeks and his breathing was the regular breath of sleep.

Again Margery bowed her head, this time to offer a prayer of thanksgiving. Rising, she became aware of the cold in the room and practicality overtook her. She ran down to the kitchen.

From the strained silence which greeted her entrance it was obvious that she had interrupted Betty and Liddy in their speculation of events. Not for the first time she regretted the intimacy that living in such a household could impose, but she ignored this for the time being, there were more important things to be done.

'Betty, we shall need a fire in the parlour bedchamber. Leave what you are doing and see to it.'

'But, Mistress, Nunn's not here to carry the firings for me.'

'Then you must do it yourself. You are quite strong enough, surely?

Betty looked surly. Liddy smirked at her fellow but Margery catching her, said sharply, 'You, my girl, can leave Pleasance with me and go out the back and see to Master's clothes. Wash what can be saved but if his outer garments are beyond cleansing, then dispose of them.'

Liddy opened her mouth to argue but Margery's look and tone made her realise that it would be best to obey. Margery got a perverse satisfaction from giving the two women distasteful tasks, particularly Liddy. Until now, Margery had refused to acknowledge to herself that the maid was at times over-familiar with the master. Well, let her now have the pleasure of touching his clothing. She half hoped that sorting through the soiled garments would make the girl sick.

In the afternoon the physician arrived to examine John who had by then awakened with a blinding headache. The doctor found swellings on the back of the patient's head and some congestion of the lungs. There were too, still signs of an excessive intake of alcohol.

'How did you come to such a pass?'

'I can't remember.' John's head throbbed.

'Nothing at all? Not going to drink Scarlett's health?' The doctor was a party to all the gossip in town.

'Yes, I do recall something of that.' His eyes narrowed as he strained to bring a mental picture to mind. 'I must have been very drunk.'

'You were, by all the accounts I've heard this morning in Saxmundham. And, it would seem, lucky to be here at all. Some have said that the Press-gang went after you. Though had they taken you they would have been duty bound to let you go.'

John closed his eyes for a time, then turned to the doctor.

'I can't see in mind's eye at all, but I can hear things.' He became quite excited. 'I can hear footsteps behind me and voices, voices shouting and then . . . a cracking in my head. Nothing more.'

'I can see what happened.' The doctor spoke with assurance.

'The Pressmen must have caught you. Probably you struggled and in their efforts to restrain you they cudgelled you about the head. Then they must have realised from your habit that you were a gentleman and rather than face the possibility of a severe reprimand should you bring charges, they left you lying out to fend as best you could. Think yourself fortunate that your man found you when he did. More dead than alive it would seem. You are a lucky man to have such a good and loyal servant willing to place his own life at risk to save yours.'

'How so?'

'Think man, if the Press-gang had been still on the road when he set out to look for you, then he might have been taken – and there would have been no escape for him.'

'So I owe my life to him?'

'I fully believe so. Had you been left lying out any longer, I would now, most likely, be examining your corpse for the coroner.' The doctor rubbed his hands and laughed heartily at this prospect.

'Now, Mistress Beddingfield', he turned to where Margery stood at the foot of the bed, 'be sure he takes the purge. Keep him in bed for the week, dosing him with the lung mixture and he'll soon be on the mend.'

On his way downstairs the elderly physician dropped the bright manner he had adopted with his patient. While not wishing to alarm the young wife, he tried to impress upon her that John would need careful nursing to avoid a worsening of his lung condition.

'It's a family weakness. You remember his father. And I,' he stressed, 'remember his father before him. They were both prone to breathing problems. A sudden attack of either choking or the inability to exhale naturally can, in extreme cases, be fatal.' He became aware of Margery's pale face. 'Not that there is any fear of that. Your husband is a healthy young man.' He patted her arm reassuringly. 'But it is always best to take sensible precautions.' He turned as he reached the door to add, 'And keep him from the drink and anything that might excite him.'

It was a subdued group which later gathered round the table for supper. The stress and tension of the day had affected all of them. None of them was entirely at ease. Each felt the day had been exceptionally long. Will, having spent much time running errands on top of his normal work, nearly fell asleep over his food so Margery ordered him to bed immediately, bidding Liddy and Betty to follow as soon as they had completed their night's tasks. Gently she declined Betty's offer to sit up with the invalid, saying that she would do that duty herself.

When only Richard remained, she spoke to him directly for the first time.

'Richard, I don't know how to thank you for the service you have done this day.'

He looked at her, felt a pang of conscience and mumbled that he had done nothing.

'No, you must let me speak. I can only think that it was some divine direction which led you to go to search for your master. And I have already offered up my thanks for that but now, I must thank you, not only for saving his life but also, by all accounts, placing yourself in very grave danger.'

He dared not look into her face. She took his averted gaze as evidence of modesty.

'You are a very brave man. I hope that later I shall be able to reward you properly.'

She came closer and placed a hand on his arm. He trembled at the contact. She felt the tremor and interpreted it as a sign of his fatigue.

Her hand dropped to her side, concerned for him.

'You need rest! I should have given some thought to you sooner but I have been so rapt with my husband's well-being. We will talk of this some other time. Go now to your bed and sleep sweetly.'

She took up her candle and by its light he saw her gentle smile as she said softly, 'Goodnight, Richard – our very own hero.'

Margery took up her station by her husband's bed where she would watch throughout the night for any change in his condition. She was elated that now he needed her. She was filled with the thought that when he was recovered their life together could be as happy as it once was.

At the other side of the house, Richard lay for some time listening to the sound of the regular breathing which came through the thin partition dividing his room from that of the two boys. Physically exhausted, yet his mind refused to rest. So much had been crammed into the past twenty four hours. His brain tried to unscramble the various events, some of which were more insistent than others, refusing to disappear however hard he tried to shake them off. Worse than the mental pictures were the mixed emotions which took hold of him, feelings of which he had not thought himself capable. Self loathing overcame him as he yet again heard Margery's voice calling him a hero.

Ten

JUNE 1762

"This hempseed with my virgin hand I sow,
Who shall my true love be the crop shall mow,
I straight looked back and if my eyes speak truth
With his keen scythe behind me came the youth."

Betty sang as she churned, taking her time from the slap of the paddle. She looked across to where Liddy was skimming cream off the morning's milking.

'You'd be hard pressed to sing that, wouldn't you, gal?' Still pure at four and twenty, she had grave misgivings about Liddy's carryings on. For herself, she still lived in hope of finding her 'own true love'. Time was, she knew, passing her by. The youths she had known had long since found wives elsewhere and she had now to face the fact that if she were ever to attain the married state it would be, like as not, to a widower looking for someone to take on his motherless children and keep his house rather than the longed-for swain consumed with passion for her. Nevertheless, she would observe yet again the rites of Midsummer's Eve. This year, perhaps?

'You and your old superstitions!' Liddy emptied the first thick cream into a bowl beside her. 'I'm surprised you still hang on to all that rot.'

'You can scoff, my girl, but if you want to know if your lover – whoever that be,' she glanced quickly at Liddy's face to see if she could detect any little sign from it. Receiving a blank stare back, she continued, 'if you want to know if he is faithful to you or loves another, then you'll go out later and get yourself some Midsummer Men.'

'Who on earth are they when they're at home? I'm surprised at you, Betty Riches, egging on a poor young maid like me to go after not just one man but a whole load of them.' She was enjoying this but gave the other woman no time to reply. 'Are these Midsummer Men of yours like the dancers that come with the Mummers? 'Cos if they are, I've quite a fancy for them. I like a man who's light on his feet and not ashamed to lift his leg.'

'That's enough of that! I won't have loose talk in my dairy.'

'Why? You afraid it'll turn the milk sour? If anything will do that it's your face at this moment. Go on, you know I'm only ateasing you. Let's hear about these men of yours.'

'They t'aint men, you daft besom. They're plants. Some folk call them 'Live-longs' but whatever they be, on St John's day you pick some stems and tonight put them about your bed. Then when you wake, you look to see which way they be bending. If they all go to the right hand you know that your lover be true to you . . .'

'I know – if they go to the left then he's supposed to be false!'

'You've got it, gal.'

'That's a load of squit. You can make it go which way you want depending on where you stand to look.' Liddy was triumphant. Let Betty answer that!

'Not so, Miss Hoity-toity! You look from your bed before you rise. 'Course, if you don't know your left from your right, that's your look out.'

Refusing to let Betty score, Liddy changed her tack and asked in a tone which oozed a pretended innocence of Betty's own state. 'So you will be doing that, will you?'

'No, not this year. Tonight, I shall go through the door backwards into the garden and pluck a rose. Then I'll wrap it up and put it in my box till Christmas day. If when I take it out is as fresh as when I picked it, then I'll wear it and then . . . he who is to be my husband will come and claim it.'

'Now I've heard it all! You just make sure you don't trip over and break your neck with your walking backwards – or fall into the bushes and get rose thorns stuck in your backside.'

Liddy's laughter echoed through the dairy. 'You're better than a dose of physic any day. I wonder master didn't order a draught or two of your old superstitions when he was so ill, it would have done him a deal of good. Though come to think of it laughing so much might have made him cough even more.'

Betty's mouth opened and closed again. It wasn't worth the effort to convince Liddy of the power of the old ways. In any case she needed to concentrate, she had reached a crucial stage in the churning.

Pleased with her success over her fellow, Liddy took up the pan of skimmed milk to carry out to feed the young calves. If she timed it right, there was just a chance she might encounter Richard on his way back from Parham. Since that awful time when the master was ill, Richard had slowly become more attentive to her. They were still not as close as they had been but she had not given up hope. Although she scoffed at Betty's superstitions, had she known where to find a wise-woman, she would gladly have spent out on a love potion to use on Richard.

But perhaps she could work her own midsummer magic on him, especially as they would be almost alone in the house that night. A rare opportunity to be seized. She had started making plans in her head the previous day when fate seemed to be offering her a helping hand.

First the master had left by the early coach to attend to some legal business in Town. He expected to be away for the best part of a week. Then, in the late afternoon, a message had arrived for Margery from her father's housekeeper. Mr Rowe was running a high fever and the old woman thought Margery should come to see him, before it was too late.

Liddy had watched closely as her mistress wavered with indecision.

'You ought to go, Missis. If your father's real bad, you'd never forgive yourself for not going.'

She had read her mistress well.

'I know. That's what makes it so hard. But with the master away, if I go too, that means extra work for you and Betty. And I dare not take Pleasance with me, not to a house where there's fever and there's no telling how long I might have to stay.'

'We'll manage. We can do your work and look to the little one, don't you fear. Unless, of course . . .'

'Yes?'

'I was wondering, Missis, if perhaps Pleasance could go to stay a day or two with her grandma and aunt. They are at home just now, I know. And they do so like to see her. And,' pushing home the advantage, ' it would be a rare treat for Pleasance to have a little holiday.'

'Oh Liddy! Bless you! What a comfort you are.' Margery gave the girl a hug.

'I'll write immediately to my mother-in-law to ask what she thinks and you can step over with the letter and bring back her answer.

Liddy agreed, but not too quickly. She did not want her mistress to be aware of her keenness to have both her and the child away from the house. Nonetheless, she could not refrain from saying; 'You stay as long as you think needful, Missis. Betty and me will manage to keep all going here just as if you were here to give an eye to us.'

She had almost run to deliver the letter but when she had the answer she desired, she had returned more slowly, taking pleasure in devising her plan for spending time with Richard.

The household was astir very early the next day so that Richard, who was to drive Margery, would not have to lose too much time from his daily work. Pleasance, thrilled with the prospect of a visit 'all by mineself' as she told them over and over, got in the way of everyone until the maids were heartily glad to plonk her down in the gig beside Margery ready for the journey.

After a short delay as the child was settled in at the house of the older Mrs Beddingfield, who also insisted on adding another basket of provisions for the invalid to the one which Margery had already prepared, Richard was able to whip up the horse for the journey to Parham.

For much of the time, Margery was silent, anticipating what she might find when she reached her father's house. In her mind it was always just that – her father's house – she could not think of it as her old home. Home was a place of love and affection, neither of which had been in evidence during her childhood. Her father's increased coldness towards her since her marriage, his refusal to accept her invitations to visit, even his callousness in the words he had written in the two brief letters she had received from him in the last three years, none of these equalled the rejection she had felt as a child.

That was why her husband's off-hand behaviour to Pleasance earlier in the year had been so bitter for her. But things were very different now. She reflected, as she had so often done of late, at the strange twists and turns of events which shaped her life. At one time she had longed to be released from the deep, unremitting misery of those weeks following the loss of her baby son. Death had seemed the only way out. And then, suddenly, she had been faced with just that possibility.

Contrary to the doctor's optimistic view that John would be up and about in days, his condition had deteriorated, rapidly. Day after day he had lain, deathly white, rarely conscious. Margery hardly left his side. For four nights she sat, sleepless, watching every flickering movement he made, until finally, Betty insisted that she would watch while Margery lay down on the truckle bed in the corner of the room. She knew it was sensible, as Betty pointed out, what good could she be to the master if she was exhausted? When the maid made the further blunt remark that it would be very hard for Pleasance if both her parents died, Margery gave in.

Then John's lungs began to fail and the doctor ordered him to be taken from the bed and propped up in a high backed armchair by the fire where kettles constantly steaming against blocks of camphor slowly brought relief to his racked frame.

The experience Margery had gained nursing John's father stood her in good stead. She now had a practical way to show her husband how much she cared for him as she attended to his every need. John, too ill to remonstrate, both allowed and accepted her ministrations. When routine nursing tasks were completed, she would sit opposite him quietly, knitting or sewing, watching him but not intruding upon his own silence.

As he grew stronger, she offered to read to him and later, she started to talk of household affairs, reassuring him that the work of the farm was running smoothly. But she was careful not to tire him with needless chatter. For a long time he had found speech such an effort that he gave up the attempt. Only his eyes could give any acknowledgement of his feelings.

March went out like the proverbial gentle lamb and heralded in an exceptionally warm April. The doctor pronounced John's lungs clear of all inflammation; all that was needed now was to build up his strength and he would very shortly be able to leave the sickroom.

One day, early in the month, Margery had come up with some soup, bringing with her some primroses she had just picked. Her cheeks were flushed from the fresh air, her eyes bright. She set down the soup and held out the flowers. 'Aren't they beautiful?'

He did not take his eyes from her face. 'And so are you.'

She stood, hardly daring to breathe. Had she heard him correctly? The little nosegay trembled in her clasp. John's thin hand, the colour of cream that has stood too long, stretched out to take the flowers but grasped her wrist instead, pulling her to him. She fell into his lap, the primroses scattering to the floor.

Jumbled words came from his lips as he stroked first her hair and then her face as if trying to reassure himself of her reality. But words were not necessary neither then nor that night when Margery took her rightful place beside him in their bed, holding him in her arms, comforting as she would a child. As he lay sleeping, she gave thanks to – someone, something – for their second chance.

Happiness radiated from her after that day which, in her mind she called the day of the primroses, especially when John declared himself fully recovered and came downstairs. Amongst themselves the servants remarked on his much improved temper; wondering how long it would be before he was his old self again. Best of all for Margery was his rediscovered love for Pleasance. During the rest of April while he recuperated, he spent much time out of doors, playing with the child. Margery's heart would race as she watched them go off walking, hand in hand, the child's small delighted face turned upwards to her father, listening to his every word, while he discovered the joy to be had from her company. When she stooped to pick flowers he told her their names and then his laughter could be heard as she struggled to pronounce the strange new words. After the bleak winter which had so blighted them, it appeared that the blossoming of the spring regenerated new life in the little family.

They were approaching Parham. Richard, who had been absorbed in his own thoughts, turned his head slightly towards Margery to tell her that they would reach her father's house very soon. Before he spoke, he was surprised to see her gazing straight ahead, unseeing, yet smiling – that relaxed, contented smile which had lit her face so often these last few weeks. The pathetic look of anguish which haunted his dreams had been replaced by the reality of a vivacious countenance which when turned upon him stabbed at his heart as viciously as if she had used an actual blade.

The reconciliation of John and Margery had tormented him. He had tried to tell himself that his longing for Margery was wrong, that he had no hope of ever having her. He had deliberately sought out Liddy again in an effort to sever his attachment to Margery, but it was useless. There was only one course open to him now. He had already made his decision. Before Michaelmas came, he would give John notice that did not wish to be re-employed for the coming year. He would take his chance elsewhere – anywhere, the new world maybe. In North America he stood a chance of getting his own land, making a fortune. He filled his thoughts with images of himself, flourishing, becoming a respected and leading member of his new community, but always the mental pictures reverted to him returning to Sternfield a wealthy man, buying out John Beddingfield and taking his wife from him. Just how the last was to be achieved his imagination had not yet conjured up.

'We're almost there, Mistress.'

Margery emerged from her preoccupation and looked about her. As the gig turned into lane where her father lived her face changed – again that look of anguish.

Richard could hardly bear it as Margery's hand touched his as he helped her down. He carried the baskets to the door and then quickly returned to his place in the gig.

'I'll send word when I'm ready to return. I know that I can safely leave everything at home in your capable hands, Richard.'

'I hope you find your father improved, Mistress.' Fearing to say more, he deliberately kept his tone subservient.

'I pray so.' She smiled her farewell, then turned as the door was opened by her father's housekeeper

He had to go further along the lane before he could turn the gig, so he missed seeing Margery straighten her back and take a deep breath before she left the warmth of the sunlit day to enter the dark, cheerless house. She clenched her hands tightly round the handles of the baskets as if they were lines to the life she was temporarily abandoning. She bit her lip as she crossed the threshold, willing herself not to falter. She must be strong – not allow herself to become again the browbeaten girl who had once lived here and she made her first stand when the housekeeper cried: 'Thank goodness you're come, Miss Margery.'

'Mistress Beddingfield!' Margery corrected her.

'Beg your pardon, Ma'am.' The old woman gave a pathetic attempt at a curtsy. 'It's been so long and I do get forgetful what with all there is to do . . .' her voice tailed off into a whine. She gave Margery a worried look. 'Shall you be wanting to go into the parlour, 'cos I haven't cleaned there of late and there's no fire . . .'

"There's no need for a fire on a day like this, Mrs Jollye. And in any case, I will come into the kitchen and unpack the things I have brought.'

Margery had no desire to sit in the dismal parlour, redolent as it was of those days in the past when she had been forced to sit with her father listening to him preparing his supposedly extempore sermons or reading aloud from a religious treatise which exposed the evils of the world in general and of young women in particular. There had never been, as far as she could remember, any joyous moments in that room. Nor anywhere else in the house for that matter.

The kitchen was worse than she remembered. Her father had always kept a tight hold on domestic expenditure and it appeared that nothing had been replaced. All the cooking utensils were old, almost worn out. As she looked at the dingy room, desperately in need of a good clean, Margery had a fleeting thought of how it might have been had her mother not died or if her father had remarried. As it was, Mrs Jollye had battled on for years with a niggardly employer who offered her a roof over her head and a pittance in return for the service she gave. Margery suddenly felt intense sympathy for the woman. It must have been dispiriting for her to have to make the best of the little she had to work with. And now, although she must be well into her seventies, she was having to cope with nursing on top of everything else. For the first time it struck Margery that the poor woman must be worried sick as to her own future should her employer die. No doubt she had already seen herself entering the Poor House.

Softening towards the woman, Margery insisted that she sit down while the delicacies she had brought were unpacked. The housekeeper exclaimed with delight as pots and jars were placed upon the old table which was sadly in need of a good scrub. Urging Mrs Jollye to remain where she was, Margery took the fresh dairy produce, meat and eggs through to the keeping room. Only the briefest glance was necessary to reveal that the shelves were bare save for the odd long forgotten jar of preserves. No doubt, Margery told herself, she would find a similar story if she inspected the cupboards. She did not blame the old woman. Her employer's illness had left her without money to replace her reserves. It looked as if there had not been proper food in the house for sometime.

A pot of broth simmered on the fire, unappetising in both smell and appearance. Margery wondered how long it had been there. The first thing she must do was get rid of that and put on in its place one of the fowls she had brought from home. Her mother-in-law had provided meat, some of which would be ideal for beef tea.

Margery realised that in busying herself she was delaying the question which had to be asked. At length she forced herself.

'How is . . . your patient?' The word 'father' stuck in her throat. The sad old woman sighed heavily.

'Not good, m'dear. I do what I can to keep him comfortable but he do so rant and rave. Wouldn't let me get the doctor to him – says he's one of the Devil's men. Though a sweeter gentleman I've never met. And he don't eat. Yesterday he threw his cup of broth all over me – and the bed too. That make a deal of washing . . .'

On and on flowed the complaints. The old woman's ramblings giving a clear picture of what life had been like in recent days. Her weariness and inability to cope were pitiful. Margery let her talk without interruption, sensing that this was what she most needed, an opportunity to unburden her pent-up frustrations.

When she finally broke down, Margery put a comforting arm round her, saying softly, 'I'm here now to help. For as long as you need me.'

The woman lifted her head, her face streaked where tears had cleared channels through the accumulated grime. Margery overcame her momentary revulsion of the smell emanating from the ancient one's clothes and body as she held her, then gently she kissed a pitted leathery cheek.

'Bless you, Miss, Ma'am, Missis . . .'

'Margery will suffice, Mrs Jollye.'

Before any more could follow, Margery moved away, once more assuming a competent air.

'Shall you go up now and see him?'

'Not yet. We will attend first to matters here.'

She borrowed an apron, rolled up her sleeves and began on the practical tasks to be undertaken. An examination of the cupboards revealed what essentials were lacking. She made a list and then suggested it would do Mrs Jollye good to get some fresh air, so would she oblige Margery by stepping out to the shop to get them. The old woman hesitated. Realising the cause for her reluctance, Margery congratulated herself that she had thought to bring money with her. Taking out her purse, she placed it in one of the empty baskets with the shopping list and was rewarded with seeing the look of relief that passed over the other's face.

'I'll not be long, my dear. He should be all right but if he do call, then you'll go, won't you?'

'Take your time. Enjoy the sunshine – that's what you need. I will do whatever is necessary here – have no fear.'

Brave words. Margery was quite happy to throw herself into a hasty clean of the kitchen and the preparation of some nutritious food but what would she do if her father did call? Fortunately she was not required to answer that particular question.

Mrs Jollye returned, refreshed from her outing and was further elated by all that Margery had achieved in her absence. She was astute enough to understand Margery's reluctance to follow her to the sickroom, so she carried out her duties there, leaving the young woman to do what was needed downstairs. She reported that Mr Rowe had taken a little of the chicken broth and seemed a bit calmer in his mind.

By the evening, however, the fever again took its toll and he was restless, shouting out the names of those long gone mixed in with disparate quotations from the Old Testament. The sound of the wild raving echoed through the little house, reminding Margery of her childhood.

'It can go on like this all night. I'd better go up now.' Mrs

Jollye started towards the door, then stopped. 'Oh my lor, I've not made up a bed for you, Miss. Would you mind a lying on mine? The sheets be clean,' she reassured quickly. 'I've not been in them at all.'

'Then you must tonight. You must have proper rest or you'll be no good for anyone.' Margery found herself echoing Betty's words on a similar occasion.

'I will sit with . . .my father. No arguments, please, dear Mrs Jollye. I am well used to night nursing.'

It was a strange sensation entering her father's room. She could not remember ever having been in it, even as a tiny child. It was as bleak as the rest of the house. Sparsely furnished it contained nothing beyond the bed with its faded tattered hangings, the old chest for his few clothes, a chair and beside the bed a small table on which lay his Bible.

Bracing herself, she walked towards the bed. She was totally unprepared for what lay there. Her father had never been robust but now he had shrunk to nothing more than a skeletal figure swathed in a sheet. His hairless head had been reduced to a mere skull from which protruded staring eyeballs in their sunken sockets. A sagging lower jaw revealed gums almost devoid of teeth.

Margery suppressed the thought that this hideous frame had once throbbed with sufficient vigour to give her life. Could he ever have known the human passion necessary for procreation? It was almost beyond contemplation, yet as she sat beside the bed she allowed her thoughts to consider that he might once have loved her mother, that it was her death that had embittered him, causing him to find solace for his grief in his religious work.

Throughout the long night, he slept fitfully, with periodic bouts of wild raving. After each of these, Margery bathed his face with the aromatic vinegar she had brought with her. Occasionally she raised the withered body and held a drink to moisten the parched, cracked lips. In the morning early, as he slept, she crept from the room, eager to escape from the atmosphere of decay which hung there.

The next two days followed a similar pattern but on the third, the old man rallied sufficiently for Mrs Jollye to make a fatal error. Mr Rowe, having taken a good few mouthfuls of beef tea, commented grudgingly on its quality. Pleased, the old woman could not resist telling him the truth.

'Miss Margery made it for you. She's been so good. Done all she can to help.'

He appeared not to have heard, so she raised her voice slightly.

'Your daughter, Margery is here. Shall I send her up to you?'

Before she had a chance to move, the cup was thrown, missing her by a fraction before it hit the floor. The man rose up as though possessed and in attempting to get out of the bed, he too, fell beside the broken shards.

'Out!' he yelled, 'Get out!'

Mrs Jollye ran from the room calling for help.

Margery came and between them they lifted the thrashing body back to the bed.

'Father, please . . .'

In a voice which seemed too big for such a minute frame came the words, 'I am not your father. I have no daughter. You have no place here. Go woman – whoever you are, and leave me in peace.'

When Margery did not move, he screamed again that she was to leave his house. He lay staring at her – unseeing – his preacher's voice declaring, "Their daughters shall burn in the fire, burn and not be quenched." He paused as if waiting for a response from his unseen congregation then his cadaverous face twisted with a hideous leer and his voice changed to a thin high pitched wail as he screeched, "Heap on the logs, kindle the fire, boil well the flesh and let the bones be burned up."

The sight and sounds were so frightening that both women retreated hastily to the kitchen where for a time they stood unspeaking. The silence was finally broken by Mrs Jollye lamenting the fact that she had been so stupid as to mention Margery's presence.

'Perhaps it is for the best. I have done what I can here, and it is time I returned home. I will go and see if I can send word to be fetched early tomorrow.'

For the last time she watched by the sick-bed for part of the night but now she felt not the least flicker of compassion for the man who lay there. Mechanically she did what needed to be done. She had done her best to obey the commandment but surely parents should play their part too?

Waiting for Richard to come for her the next morning, she tried to comfort Mrs Jollye. First she gave her money, then she told her that she would make sure that Richard called at least weekly with supplies of fresh food and she begged that the woman would eat properly to keep up her own strength. Finally came the assurance that if on his death it was found that Mr Rowe had made no provision for Mrs Jollye, then Margery would undertake her maintenance.

There followed that painful time that comes just before a leave-taking when neither party knows quite how to fill up the long spaces of things thought but not spoken, when thirty short precious minutes seem to drag themselves into an hour. At last the sound of the approaching gig had Margery almost running out of the house and into the lane. Mrs Jollye followed slowly, her face contorted with a mixture of grief at losing the support on which she had so quickly come to depend and fear of what was yet in store for her.

Margery hated leaving the old woman like this so she endeavoured to cut short the farewell. Amid her sobs, Mrs Jollye choked out; 'Bless you Miss. If there really be an old Devil, then it's him in there.'

Margery's face was expressionless as she turned from her.

'Walk on, Richard. Let us go home.'

Eleven

JULY 1762

John had been very, very angry. He had returned from London the day after Margery to find her looking unusually pale and withdrawn. Thinking that her depressed state was in some way linked with his absence, which had been longer than expected, he had done all he could to make amends. When neither soft words nor the presents he had brought from Town lifted her sombre mood, he demanded to know the cause.

Hearing the harshness that had crept again into his voice, Margery had reluctantly given a full account of her stay at Parham.

'How dare he!' His fist hit the table. 'How dare he treat you like that! The miserable, canting old hypocrite. I tell you, Margery, you are to have no more to do with him. Do you hear? You can forget your promise to the housekeeper. There is to be no further contact with that house. I utterly forbid it!'

And that, as far as John was concerned, was the end of the matter. He had exerted his authority and expected his wife to obey him without question. Life could now return to normal. And that included his going out again in the evenings to visit old friends. His brief excursion to London had rekindled the pleasure to be had from a hand of cards and a bottle or two with congenial companions. He told himself that he was not being driven to the tables as a way of forgetting his troubles as he had at the time following the death of his son. No, a man had to have some relaxation after a day's work and if this was the way he chose to spend his leisure and a trifle of the money he had made on the land deal he had transacted in London, then who could deny him that?

Satisfied that all was now well between him and his wife, John had gone that evening to renew old acquaintances in Saxmundham. Margery was alone in the kitchen when Richard came in. She had gone over and over what action she should take to deal with the problem that was uppermost in her thoughts. Richard seeing how absorbed she was, simply wished her good night and prepared to go up to his room.

Instead of returning his greeting she asked, 'Richard, can I count on you as my friend?'

He looked startled but said firmly, 'You shouldn't need to ask that, Mistress. You surely know that I would walk through fire for you . . . I will do anything you want me to.'

She hesitated, wrestling with her conscience. 'Even if it means doing something of which the master would disapprove?'

He stifled a desire to laugh and say that would be the very best of reasons for doing it.

'Will you sit a moment while I tell you what's on my mind?'

Intrigued and excited he did as she asked.

Margery bent over the small garment she had been sewing. As the needle went slowly in and out forming a perfect line she endeavoured to make straight her thoughts so that the words were evenly matched. In the heavy silence that accompanied her noiseless movements the ponderous swing of the old clock's pendulum echoed loudly. Richard found himself waiting for the next beat, counting each dull thud as it came. At last he could stand no more suspense and shifted in his chair causing a floorboard to creak loudly.

Margery put the sewing aside, folded her hands in her lap and looked at him.

'My husband has forbidden me to have anything more to do with my father.'

He said nothing; unable to gauge what response she wanted.

'You know, only too well, how upset I was when I left Parham . . . and I have no desire to go there again but . . .'

'Yes?'

'I made Mrs Jollye a promise that I would send food and money – for her as much as my father. I said you would call to deliver these . . . and find out how things went there.'

'If you have made a promise, Mistress, then you must abide by it.'

'Even though my husband has ordered me not to?'

Richard thought quickly. 'As to that, I haven't been given any such order. There is no reason why I should not go – of my own accord –'

'Oh, I hoped you would say that. Yet I ought not to expect you to put your own position here in jeopardy. Should my husband find out he will be very angry – with both of us, but you could lose your job.'

Richard refrained from saying that he no longer cared about that.

'We shall have to be circumspect. No one else must know of this. I will make sure I have things ready for you on the days when you are going in that direction.'

Relieved that Richard had so readily agreed to assist in her scheming, Margery stood up too quickly, spun round and staggered, almost falling in his lap. He put out his arm to save her. Embarrassed by the contact, they both laughed a little too heartily.

'Excuse me!' Coming from the back kitchen, Liddy had witnessed the scene. 'I only wanted to know how the time went.'

Margery, having regained her feet, glanced at the clock.

'Is the brewing finished?'

Liddy looked from her to Richard. He was aware that her scowl indicated that she had read more into the episode than it merited. He no longer cared. Let her think what she liked.

Oblivious of any tension, Margery was concerned only with the task upon which the maid had been engaged.

'I will come though with you and see how things are. This brew is important. It is the one we will need for the harvesters.'

She indicated that Liddy should go ahead of her. She paused

at the door leading to the back kitchen where the brewing took place.

'I'll say good night, Richard.' Then with just the slightest emphasis, 'I believe you go to market tomorrow? I may have some commissions I'd like you to undertake for me.'

He understood her meaning.

While professing disbelief in such old fashioned notions, Liddy had not been able to get it out of her head that the silly old plants that she had picked at Betty's instigation had mostly leaned to the left on the morning of the longest day. At the time she had airily dismissed the event, telling herself that the heat of her room was responsible for the wilting. Nonetheless, she had counted up those which sagged to the right and had been forced to admit they were greatly outnumbered by those which leaned the opposite way. Thus when on that night she had come upon Richard in such a compromising position with the mistress, she had been forced to reconsider matters.

As the calendar year entered its second half, the gentle warmth of midsummer gave way to days of searing heat and nights of oppressive sultriness. As she lay unable to sleep in the airless room, Liddy resolved to watch closely for further developments in the relationship between mistress and manservant.

Unwittingly, they added more fuel to the fire of her suspicions. How she wished she had been able to read for she would have had no compunction in undoing the letter Margery asked her to carry to Richard's room early one morning before he was even up. She had contemplated not delivering it but she feared the consequences to herself if she did not. Instead she had to content herself with flinging it at Richard as he lay in his bed, saying with heavy emphasis, 'Here's a love letter from your mistress. I hope it makes you happy.'

She had been furious when he had looked at the inscription on the front and laughed before putting it to one side.

'Go on, don't mind me. You read her pretty words to you. I don't care.'

Had Liddy been familiar with the alphabet, she would have

known the letter was intended for Mrs Jollye. Richard was divided between revealing the truth and taunting the girl. He told himself that the only reason for his silence was his loyalty to Margery but in truth he was enjoying the intimate bond forged by their secret. It gave him power.

Noon was the hour for dinner at the farm. The menfolk came back from the fields to eat and rest for a couple of hours before resuming work that would go on far into the evening. In those first few days of July, Liddy noticed that on the days when Master Beddingfield was absent, Richard would hang back after the boys had been sent off to start on the rest of the day's tasks. Betty would be busy in the back kitchen with the pots and if Liddy tried to linger, Margery would dismiss her sharply to take Pleasance outside. Hovering close to the door to the yard, she tried to hear what was said but they spoke in low voices, their words a mere murmur to her ears. To make matters worse, on one of these occasions they had tried to make her a party to their deceit when Margery had called to her as she was leaving, 'Let me know if you see the master coming.'

Brooding on this secretive behaviour, she kept her thoughts to herself even when Betty remarked, 'I don't know what you think, girl, but I'm sure there's something queer going on.'

'Why's that?' Liddy feigned disinterest, knowing full well that once started Betty would chatter on.

'The mistress is hiding something from us.' She did not wait for Liddy to ask, she was only too eager to relate her story. 'I got the shock of my life this morning when I was changing the bed-linen. I went into Richard's room to strip his bed off and there was the Missis standing beside his box. The lid was up and I was just in time to see her put some coins in. She looked mighty flustered when she saw me and said something about having to hide money from the master.' She sighed heavily. 'You know what I think? I reckon he's back to his old tricks of drinking and gaming and the poor mistress is trying to keep him short. Oh dear, just when I thought things were better. It's a good thing Richard's a steady fellow that Missis can trust. I suppose she thinks the master would never dream she'd hide money away from him.' She considered the matter .'Though I'd have looked after it for her, if she'd asked.'

Liddy shrugged her shoulders in answer. She did not trust herself to make any comment but inwardly she marvelled at the older woman's naivete, her inability to guess at the true situation. For herself this latest happening merely reinforced her certainty that Margery was doing all she could to win Richard's affection. Fancy being so desperate that she had to pay him!

That same day Richard returned early from the market and a visit to Parham. When he made sure that they were alone, he reported to Margery that Mrs Jollye was now certain that it could not be long before the old man died.

'And about time too! I'm sorry, Mistress, to say it of any living soul, but he's wearing that poor old woman out. I wonder how long she can keep going with all she has to bear. I sat with her awhile and three times I heard him shout for her and she barely able to get up and down the stairs to him. The last time she said he seemed to know there was someone else in the house and had sent her down to get her besom to sweep the evil out. I know this must grieve you, Mistress but the sooner he dies, the better for . . .'

He broke off as Liddy came in with an armful of newly pressed laundry to be put away.

The maid's sharp ears had caught the last words and now her keen eye took in the pair standing grim-faced at a distance from each other.

As if in a trance, Margery glanced at her, then said, 'Take Pleasance's things up. And I'll come too, there is something I must do.'

While Liddy sorted the child's clothes, she was surprised when Margery knelt before the old chest housed under the window. She had never seen it opened before, though her curiosity had once led her to raise the heavy lid slightly in an effort to see what it contained. She had been disappointed to find nothing but clothes. She now watched intently as Margery took out first a black shawl and then a dress of fine black cloth.

Margery stood up and shook the dress from its folds, holding it against her as if trying to guess if it would still fit her.

Liddy felt she should say something but all that came out was 'Black do suit you, Missis.'

Absorbed in her thoughts, Margery seemed to have forgotten Liddy's presence in the room.

'As to that, I care not. But I believe I shall have need of these before very long. I wonder . . .' She went through to the other bed chamber and came back with her jet earrings.

'Here, Liddy, help me put these in.'

For a brief moment, the girl's admiration overcame her resentment of her mistress.

'They are beautiful,' she breathed. 'I'd kill for a pair of earrings like that.'

'What nonsense you do talk, girl. Though I agree they are very fine. Your master gave them to me as a love token.'

The girl was too rapt to notice then the reference to the master.

'And don't they just go with that dress!'

'Hush, Liddy. My mind is on a serious occasion not finery for an evening assembly in Saxmundham. Come, you can help me hang these out to air.'

As they were hanging up the garments in the garden, Richard passed. He looked first at the dress and then at Margery exclaiming, 'You surely do not intend to mourn for the old devil?'

'I must observe the proprieties, Richard, whatever I may feel for the person concerned.'

The light tone used by both of them did not escape Liddy, that added to what she had seen and heard in the last hour began to awake a dreadful suspicion in her mind. She was in a desperate state of indecision. She longed to be able to confide her fears in someone, but apart from Betty, who was there? And silly old Betty would huff and puff and be no help whatsoever. Of course she could try to speak to the master. He still treated her kindly, though she had to admit not with quite as much warmth as he once had. And what if she did speak? Would he not laugh or worse, be angry and dismiss her. And to be out of a place before Michaelmas, having to forfeit half a year's wages was not to be thought of.

The only other course open was to tackle Richard himself. Go straight to it and tell him she knew what he and the mistress were up to. Suppose she did do that – what then? Would not he too, laugh in her face as he had that day she had delivered the love letter. She could not – she would not, take that again, so let them get on with it – see if she cared if he was putting his head in a noose of his own making.

Best keep out of the way as much as possible, get on with her work and count the days until Michaelmas – two and a half months at most and then she could leave this place where there had been nothing but upset and misery since her coming. She would go and find a position where there were no children to bother with – or young menservants to lead her on. She considered going to a house where there were no men at all, perhaps as a companion to an old lady but she quickly changed that mental picture, old ladies could be very demanding without being particularly generous. She would settle instead for an old – though not too old – wealthy, childless widower, who was without mother, sisters or female relations of any sort, to whom she would make herself indispensable. That's what she would do. Forget about this lot here, just fix her thoughts on the future.

Whatever her dreams, the reality was that Liddy was to be very much caught up in the life at Sternfield over the next few weeks. The very next day, young Will Nunn came running from the fields to say that Master had been taken ill with the belly-ache and was asking for a dose of vomit mixture to be carried out to him.

'I'll get it,' Betty volunteered.

'No. I will attend to it.' Margery immediately stopped what she was doing. She took out a china cup and carried it to the locked cupboard where she kept such mixtures. With her back to the maids she carefully measured out the drops, calling over her shoulder, 'You get the hot water ready for me to mix this.'

A small quantity of steaming water was added and a clean white cloth was placed over and around it.

'Now Liddy, be careful as you go – don't spill a drop. I wouldn't want you to scald yourself. I will come myself in a little while to see how the master fares.'

There was a time, thought Liddy, when the mistress would have rushed out herself with the medicine. Why hadn't she done so now? She wasn't doing anything that would spoil for being left, so what was she waiting for?

The maid arrived in the hayfield to find John leaning against the cart, doubled up with pain.

'Here's the vomit mix, Master. Mistress said to say she be coming along presently.'

John took hold of the cup. Putting it to his lips he cried out as they touched the fiery contents.

'For God's sake, Richard, get some water from the stream to cool this.'

The man obeyed but with some difficulty, the prolonged summer heat having almost dried up the running water. The small amount of muddy liquid he managed to scoop up in an old ladle kept for the purpose was added to the cup.

John took a mouthful and promptly spat it out again.

'Good God! Are you trying to poison me?'

He threw the cup and its contents in Richard's direction. However, either the smell of the noxious potion or its fleeting presence in his mouth was sufficient to have the desired effect. By the time Margery reached the field, John had found relief from his symptoms and was already back at work.

She watched over him carefully for the next week, anxious that he ate nothing which might cause further upset to his digestive system. She gently cautioned him too, about drink, suggesting that might have been the root of the problem. Could that last bottle of rum, acquired from a friend of a friend who had connections with the illicit trade up the coast, have been of dubious quality?

John had dismissed such a notion with a laugh and told her

he no longer had need for such cossetting. It had been a simple belly-ache brought on, no doubt, by a bit of over ripe cheese and a touch of the sun.

'Don't you fear, my love, you'll not be rid of me yet. There's still a lot of life in me!' And he had given her a loving kiss to prove it, in front of all the household.

July was nearing its end when Margery had something new to worry about. Screams in the night from Pleasance brought her running from the parlour bedchamber into the adjoining room where the child shared the bed with Liddy. The maid had tried in vain to pacify the little girl who lay writhing in pain, one hand clapped to the side of her head. She refused to remove it even when Margery held her close, murmuring soothing words. Likewise she rejected the warm milk and honey that Liddy had crept downstairs to prepare for her. Eventually, worn out with crying, the child slept but in the morning it was discovered that a large abscess had formed behind her ear. It was difficult to treat such a swelling, especially as the child could not bear to have the area touched, so Margery had to agree, reluctantly, with Betty's advice to leave it alone until such time as Nature took her course and the abscess broke of its own accord.

Margery devoted herself that long day to the unremitting demands of the child. Intermittent bouts of screaming were punctuated by periods of heart-tearing whimpering which left Margery almost at her wits' end. The child would not have her leave her, even for a moment. In final weary desperation Margery carried her to bed, promising she would remain at her side. As she put her down, Pleasance let out a piercing scream, clapped her hand to her ear and then slowly held out the hand to Margery. The little fingers were covered in thick greenish yellow pus. The abscess had burst.

Liddy, who had come up with them was dispatched to the kitchen for warm water to wash the seeping wound. On her return she reported that the master had just arrived back from Saxmundham bringing Mr Scarlett with him.

'Of course! I had quite forgotten that he had taken an animal in to be slaughtered. Go back down, Liddy, and tell the master how things are here. Give my excuses to Mr Scarlett and make sure that he and the master have whatever refreshment they need.'

'Don't you worry. Betty's already making the punch for them. Shall I sit up and see master to bed?'

'No, Betty can do that. You need your sleep after last night. So come up as soon as you are finished below.'

Pleasance gave a little cry.

'It's all right, my little love, mother will not leave you. I will stay at your side all night long. Now be a good girl and close your eyes.'

Margery put on her nightgown and lay beside the child. By the time Liddy rejoined them, both were sleeping peacefully.

In the parlour, the two young men sat over the punchbowl. John leaned back in his chair possessed of a sense of total contentment. Now that Liddy had reassured him that Pleasance's dis-ease was at an end, he felt that all was well in his world. He had everything a man could wish for, as the butcher had just reminded him.

It had been a long time since John had entertained a friend in his house. It was very pleasant to sit like this, simply talking over old times or commenting on local affairs, with enough drink to oil their tongues but without the pressure to be over convivial as so often happened at larger gatherings.

James Scarlett had just made a reference to his celebration held earlier in the year saying how much had happened to John since then, when there was a hesitant knock at the parlour door. Richard entered to ask if there was anything further to be done that night or could he and the boys go to their beds.

John told him briefly what was to be done the following day and then dismissed him saying that he would see Mr Scarlett to his horse when the time came.

'That's a good man, you've got there.'

'Very true. A most trustworthy servant he's turned out. Though I had my doubts at first as to whether or not he'd take kindly to my service. Did you know that he once had expectations of being his own master? In fact, strange as it may seem, we were even at the same school. But he's never overstepped the mark. And I will confess that when I rather neglected things – and when I was ill – he proved well able to step into my shoes and run my affairs.'

'And wasn't it he who found you and brought you home that night after my celebrations?"

'Saving my life, so I'm told. Yes, I've a lot to thank Richard Ringe for. Let's drink his health.'

John refilled the glasses. Scarlett raised his.

'Here's to Ringe.'

'May he have a long life – and a happy one.'

Other toasts followed. To Margery, to Scarlett's intended bride, to Pleasance, even to the King, until the punch bowl was empty.

The host was all for calling for the bowl to be replenished but Scarlett insisted it was time he was on his way as it lacked but two hours to midnight.

John saw his visitor safely mounted, watched him until he was out of sight and then came back to the kitchen where Betty sat waiting to light him to bed. When the doors had been fastened, Betty took up the candle and led the way upstairs. They passed through the room where the curtains were drawn round the bed, to the door of the parlour bed-chamber. Betty paused at the threshold to allow John to enter, waiting for him to take the candle from her in order to light the one beside his bed. But he told her he had no need of it tonight, so wishing him a good night's rest, Betty took the candle to light the way to her own quarters.

John undressed quickly, shunning the nightgown which lay spread out on the foot of his side of the bed. Elated by the evening's entertainment he was not yet ready to sleep. He needed just one thing more to round off the day. He climbed into bed and edged towards where he expected Margery to be. Annoyed to find her place empty, he left the bed, threw on the nightgown and went into the other room.

Pulling aside the bed curtain, he roused his wife.

'I thought you would be there for me tonight.'

'Not tonight, my love. I'm so tired and the child needs me.'

'I need you too! I want you in my bed.'

His raised voice wakened Liddy who asked what was amiss. Margery told her to go back to sleep.

In a hoarse whisper John asked, 'Will you not come to me?'

'No. I cannot.'

Liddy listened as again he pleaded, 'Are you sure, you won't?'

'Please, my love, go back to bed. Tomorrow will be different, I promise. Goodnight.'

'Oh, very well.' A peevish note crept into his voice. He returned to the other room banging the door behind him. Frustrated, he fastened up his gown at the neck, swearing as his fingers fumbled with the buttons. He climbed back into bed, noisily closing the curtain beside him. Flat on his back he lay in the middle of the bed, tense, feelings of anger welling up inside him and nothing to do but listen to the noises of the night. The indefinable creaks of an old house, the distant bark of a vixen calling to her young, even the scratchings within the thatch were all familiar, there was nothing to disturb the calm of the summer night.

In the kitchen, the long spindly minute hand on the old clock left its stubby partner on the twelve to usher in the twenty seventh day of July. All the household were now sleeping, some more soundly than others.

Margery was having a nightmare. In it she was standing in her nightdress with the black shawl round her shoulders beside the pond in the middle of which was John sitting astride one of the farm horses. She called out to him that she had lost one of her beautiful jet earrings in the water. He slithered down from the horse to search and began to sink, deeper and deeper. She begged him to leave it and come out. But he was stuck fast. She stretched out her hand to him but he was too far off. Taking off the shawl she threw one end of it for him to catch. He grabbed it and slowly began to edge towards her. Then she saw his face and it was not John but her father who looked at her. Struck with fear, hatred and horror, she let go her hold of the shawl and the figure – now John again – sank beneath the murky water.

Her shriek of terror woke Liddy who found her sitting up trembling.

'Have you been having a nasty dream?' She spoke as she would to a child.

Margery mumbled she was sorry she had disturbed her and they both lay down again.

Once more the house slept, but not for long. John had also been dreaming and awoke violently as pain seared his chest. He felt as if he were being gripped tightly in red hot bands. Then his breath would not come, something was stuck and he was choking; he must relieve the pressure on his throat. He forced himself to sit up. Clutching at the neck of his nightgown, he tore at the buttons in an attempt to get free of the constriction. He must get up! With one hand still pulling at his neck, he made a grab with the other at the bed curtain, dragging it away from its fixings as he fell heavily, face downwards on the floor.

The noise of his fall penetrated Margery's sleep, drawing her into a consciousness which was still filled with the horrors of her nightmare. She shook Liddy into wakefulness,

'Something dreadful has happened to the master, Liddy. Go and get Richard.'

'You're only dreaming, Missis,' her voice was soothing.

'Something has happened – I know it.'

'Well, then, shouldn't we go and see for ourselves?'

'No!' Margery screamed. 'I can't bear it. Get Richard to look.'

Liddy scrambled out of bed and flung a shawl around her.

'Hurry, girl, hurry.'

'I haven't got a light, Missis.'

'Surely you can find your way without?'

The maid left the room progressing slowly until her eyes became used to the dim light of the passageways. She hammered on the door to Richard's room. When there was no response, she opened it and advanced on his sleeping form. Roughly she shook his shoulder until he opened his eyes.

'Liddy! Whatever are you thinking of? If you get caught here . . .'

'For goodness sake, Richard! You're to come at once. The mistress seems to think that something has happened to the master. I don't know what, for she wouldn't go to look nor let me go neither, but she says you're to come, at once.'

'Let me get some clothes on. Go back and say I'll be there in a minute.'

Liddy had barely reached the chamber before Richard caught her up.

Margery had not moved. She still sat in the bed, the covers drawn up to her chest, her hands clenched tightly together. Her voice, when it came, shook with fear.

'Go and look Richard. I think your master has fallen from his bed.'

He entered the darkened room. As far as he could see there was nothing amiss but as he felt his way round the end of the bed, his foot came up against an obstacle. He knelt down and could just make out the prone figure of John lying crooked, one arm tucked beneath him. As he turned the body over, the left hand fell away , releasing its grip from around the neck. With his own thumping heart echoing in his ears, Richard put a hand on the other's chest but his trembling fingers could not detect even a flutter. Still on his knees he moved towards the night table, his hands running over it in search of a candle. Finding none, he stood up and slowly walked round the body and then back to the doorway. Trying to control his voice he said, 'We need light. Have you a candle, Mistress?'

When Margery seemed not to hear, he addressed the question to Liddy and receiving the reply that there was none by, sent her to go down to the kitchen for both candle and tinder.

'He's dead, isn't he?' It was a statement rather than a question, the voice flat, bereft of emotion, as if from a very long way off.

'I fear so, Mistress.'

He had not expected the long deep sigh which issued from her breast. Confused, Richard interpreted it as an expression of relief, satisfaction almost.

Hardly knowing what he was doing he returned to the body.

He must get it up on the bed. He knelt again at John's head to try to raise him. Pictures of the last time he had done this crowded into his mind and with them all the hatred he felt for this man. He placed his hands about the shoulders and lifted them a fraction from the floor. Was it his imagination or did the body give a spasm? Was that a gurgling in the throat or not? Involuntarily, Richard's hands moved very slowly from the shoulders inwards, inwards towards the neck until his thumbs met and each pressed down heavily upon the throat of John Beddingfield.

How long he remained like this he could not afterwards remember but the sound of footsteps and a glow of light in the room brought him to his feet.

Liddy had called up the rest of the household and with the assistance of John Masterton and Will Nunn, the body was lifted upon the bed. Betty took it upon herself to attend to the corpse after dismissing the men from the room.

She rounded on Liddy who was sobbing quietly.

'You'd best attend to the mistress. Get her to come and see.'

'She won't get out of the bed. She's stuck there like a stone statue. I can't seem to make her understand.'

Betty pushed her aside and went to Margery.

'Shall I send for the doctor, Missis?'

Margery looked at her, eyes blank of all expression.

'What's the good? He is dead – and that is that. The doctor cannot bring him back.'

Betty was exasperated. She could not fathom Margery's reaction – or lack of one. Weeping and wailing or even a fainting fit would not have been unexpected but there was no understanding this total inaction.

'Well, then, shall I go for Master's mother?' Betty clearly felt that someone else should be involved.

Before she received an answer, Pleasance stirred, uttering little cries. Margery lay back down beside her, holding her close, murmuring words of comfort, oblivious of all else.

'Then what shall we do, Missis?' Betty's insistence continued.

In a flat weary tone, Margery answered her.

'Nothing. There is no more to be done. Wait for the morning. Go back to your bed – and Liddy with you. Leave me alone. It is all finished.'

Twelve

JULY – SEPTEMBER 1762

It was all very well for the mistress to lie in her bed but Betty was determined to take matters in her own hands. She had no intention of returning to her bed as if nothing had happened, – as if she would get any rest!

'You can do what you like,' she told Liddy, 'but I'm going across to old Mrs Beddingfield. She has a right to know before anyone else.'

As soon as day broke, she set out to carry the dreadful news.

When Mrs Beddingfield and Anne arrived they found Margery sitting huddled close to the kitchen fireside, still in her night clothes, clutching Pleasance tightly to her. She neither looked up when they entered nor did she respond in any way to their gentle words of condolence.

'She hasn't spoken to a soul.' Liddy whispered.

Pleasance, delighted to see her grandmother and aunt, struggled against her mother's enfolding arms. She pummelled her fists against Margery's chest, 'Let me down, let me down. I want Aunt Anne.'

Anne knelt beside Margery. 'Let her go, dear. I will take care of her while you go up with mother and dress. You will take cold if you remain like this.'

As if programmed to obey a command without question, Margery's hold on the child loosened and the little girl sprang at Anne with glee, her happy laughter and infant prattle providing a stark contrast to the sombre atmosphere in the room. Moving with the air of a sleepwalker, the young widow allowed her mother-in-law to lead her away.

Anne decided that it would be better for all, if she removed Pleasance from this gloomy place, so she requested Liddy to fetch such garments as the child would need, explaining to the little girl what was to happen.

'Going visiting again.' Pleasance clapped her hands and danced around Anne. 'I'm all better now. Can go visiting with Aunt Anne.' She ran to the door. 'Go now!' she commanded.

'When you are dressed, young madam.' Anne laughed, then stopped abruptly. She should not be merry at a time like this, when her brother, the child's father, was lying dead, but yet, for the child's sake she must appear bright.

Upstairs, Mrs Beddingfield had viewed her son's body. She had tried gently to persuade Margery to come in with her but when she saw the corpse she understood the girl's reluctance. She herself had recoiled as she gazed down at what once had been her beloved son. His face was bloated almost beyond recognition, hideous black marks covered the once slim neck. Her hands shook as she slowly replaced the sheet which covered him.

Recognising that Margery was incapable of making any decisions, the older woman took charge. Leaving the widow in the parlour with Liddy to watch over her, she gave her orders. Dr Edgar was to be called at once both to certify death and to look at Margery. The male members of the household were to carry on with the essential work of the farm. Even death could not stop the necessity to tend the stock, do the milking and bring in the final load of hay.

Subdued, but grateful for the opportunity to have something to take their minds off what had occurred, Richard and the boys went about their work.

The doctor came and announced that the coroner would have to be informed of the sudden death. As to Margery, he opined that her trance-like state was entirely consistent with the shock of losing her husband, particularly as she had borne so much strain earlier in the year. He had marvelled then at her resilience, but now her mind was unable to bear any more. He recommended sleep as the best cure and gave her a strong draught for that purpose. 'The longer she sleeps the better,' he said, giving Mrs Beddingfield a vial of drops for later use. 'It would be better if she were not present at the inquest.'

The hastily convened coroner's court was held the following day. Mr Wood, the coroner, was annoyed to be dragged out to Sternfield and wanted it over as quickly as possible. He hated these affairs, having to round up a jury in a rural area where people could ill afford time off from their labours, and then to have to sit in a crowded room on a hot day listening to long-winded and bumbling evidence. At the farm he, with Dr Sparham, an independent doctor, and Dr Edgar had viewed the body, having heard briefly how it had been found.

Wood took in the black marks on the neck of the corpse and asked Sparham for his opinion. The doctor looked closely, prodding the flesh.

'Come on, man, we haven't got all day. What do you think? Could he have throttled himself as he fell?'

The coroner gave a quick imitation of how it might have happened.

The doctor resented being hurried, he would have liked to make a more thorough examination.

'Well? Yes or no?'

'It is possible,' he said slowly.

'Good enough. Let's get on with it.'

First, Richard gave his account of finding the body with details of how it was lying with one hand under the neck. Then Betty was called to narrate the events of the evening leading up to the death. The coroner cut her short when she ventured her own opinions, reminding her that she was asked only for the facts.

Next, James Scarlett verified that the deceased had seemed in good spirits when they parted – and yes, they had been drinking, but neither of them to excess.

The only enlivening event of the occasion for the coroner was the pretty face of Liddy as she stood demurely before him. Gently, he encouraged her to speak up, her voice having dropped to a whisper as she gave her recital of the events. When he questioned her on the state of the bedroom of her master, she agreed that the curtains on the far side of the bed must have been dragged down as the master fell as they had been hanging securely enough earlier in the evening.

It was, the coroner decided, a simple case. The deceased had had some form of seizure, and everyone knew that such fits could cause the sufferer to clutch at his throat and so when he had fallen from the bed dying, he had inadvertently applied pressure to his throat, which probably speeded up the death. The jury would be quite right to record a verdict of accidental death and would join him in offering their deepest sympathy to the widow and family of the tragic young man.

The following day, the body of the twenty four year old John Beddingfield was laid to rest in the churchyard at Sternfield.

Life has to go on. That phrase which trips off the tongue so easily, was repeated over and over in the days that followed. With strong support from her mother-in-law, Margery regained her strength and assumed control of the household, even facing up to trying to sort out the involved financial state of his estate. Since John had not made a will, it was necessary for her to see the attorney to seek letters of administration in order to release money to settle outstanding accounts and provide for the day-to-day living expenses.

More and more she turned to Richard for assistance. She gave him the authority to run the farm as he wished, saying that at Michaelmas, they should look to hire someone to take on the position that he had held. In all but name, Richard was now master of Beddingfield's farm.

And more and more she turned to him for the companionship she had lost with her husband's death. She found comfort in his quiet presence as they sat together in the evenings, sometimes when they were alone they would share confidences, each telling the other of hopes and dreams never before revealed to another. Slowly, very slowly, it began to grow in Margery's mind that for the first time here was a man with whom she felt totally at ease. He neither excited her as John had done nor terrified her as had her father.

It was her father who was responsible for her behaving in a manner she was later to regret. Some six weeks after John's death, Richard returned from business in the neighbouring town which he had combined with a visit to Mrs Jollye. He waited until after the supper things had been cleared and the household dispersed to tell Margery that at last her father was dead. He added that he had, on her behalf, taken the liberty of putting the funeral arrangements in hand.

Relief overwhelmed her. Without thinking what she did she flung her arms about him and kissed him. Unnoticed in the doorway, the horrified Betty returned to the back kitchen where she banged down a saucepan, its resounding clatter startling the pair.

Again, without thinking of the consequences of her action, Margery whispered, 'We must talk more about this. We need to be undisturbed.' She thought for a moment. 'Come to my room when the others are abed and you can tell me what more needs to be done.'

The house rested. Stealthily, Richard slid past the curtained bed where the sleeping Liddy lay with Pleasance. The door to the parlour bedchamber was ajar but he closed it noiselessly behind him. Margery sat on the chest at the foot of the bed waiting for him. The room was lit for she was now unable to sleep without the comfort of a night light. He saw that she had changed into her nightgown over which she wore a large heavy woollen shawl that reached almost to her feet.

'Come, sit here beside me.' Her voice, of necessity, was low. To him it was seductive. He trembled as he did as she asked. Quiet and gentle as he appeared to her, he was inflamed by her proximity, the kiss she had given him earlier had roused all his former yearning for her.

'Now tell me.' She touched his hand as it lay on his knee and the folds of her shawl fell away on that side. Hardly able to control his voice, yet thankful for the need to keep his tone low, he told her that her father had expired in his sleep the previous day. Mrs Jollye was bearing up and he had seen the attorney and learned that Mr Rowe had, after all, made provision for his housekeeper. The house was left to Margery with Mrs Jollye having life tenancy.

'Thank God.' Margery breathed a sigh of satisfaction as he finished. 'And thank you, my friend. Thank you for all you have done for me. In this matter – and everything else. I don't know how I could have managed without you to rely upon. You have been so good.'

She stood up. The private discourse was at an end. He stood too, facing her. She smiled and held out a hand to him. Bemused, intoxicated, his head spinning he took the proffered hand and held it to his lips. Then his arms were round her waist, he held her very close and his lips found hers. The shawl slowly slithered to the floor where it lay unheeded. All Richard's pent-up passion erupted as he kissed her again and again – and she – she who had lost the one man she had loved, forgot that this was not he, and returned his kisses hungrily.

Burning desire filled both bodies, all rational thought was consumed and a fire, once alight, must rage until it burns itself out unless there is someone by to douse it. But there was no bystander ready to quench these flames. The fire of physical passion ran its course.

In the ashes of the early morning, Margery woke with a feeling of serene contentment which quickly changed to one of intense guilt when she realised that Richard lay sleeping at her side.

She roused him roughly. 'Quick, you must be gone. Betty will be here soon. She comes each morning now to see how I am.'

No time for honeyed words of endearment, no time for explanations or even recriminations, no time for anything except to pull on his breeches and shirt in hand make an escape. Too late! He reached the door at the same time as Betty. They faced each other from either side of the threshold but neither uttered a word. He edged past her, leaving her open-mouthed. Shocked to the very heart of her moral being, Betty was relieved that the curtains were still drawn around the bed. She could not bring herself to part them but stood at the foot to ask gruffly, 'I trust you had a good night, Missis.' Betty was incapable of the irony her words implied.

Barely waiting for Margery's muffled reply, she banged out of the room.

Grim-faced and tight-lipped, Betty went about her work. She spoke only when forced to, an occurrence so rare that it was inevitable that it would arouse comment.

'You're very quiet today. Have you got the belly-ache?' Liddy was solicitous but received no more than a grunt for her pains.

They continued to work in silence until Liddy, who rather looked forward to their daily exchanges, even if only to get a rise out of Betty, could stand it no longer.

'For goodness sake, girl! Tell me what's amiss. Have I done something to upset you? If I have, I'm wholly sorry, though I can't think what it can be.'

Betty gave a loud sniff. Liddy watched, mystified, as Betty left her churn, walked to the outer door of the dairy and made a great show of peering outside. From there she went to the other side of the dairy to the door which led to the back kitchen and again there was the elaborate show of looking up and down into the space beyond her. Then she came back to the churn, but her hands remained still.

'I don't know as how I ought to say. But it's so awful.' Huge tears rolled towards the edges of her nose hovering on her upper lip.

'You're not in trouble, are you? You're not . . .?'

The idea was so ludicrous, Liddy could not bring herself to say it.

'Course I aint! But the way things are going, there's someone in this house who might well find herself so. I tell you, Liddy, I'm not going to stay here after Michaelmas. I don't care if I haven't another job to go to, I'll take my luck at the Hiring and if nothing suits then I shall just have to go home to mother. I'd rather starve than stay in a house of shame.'

'Whatever's got into you? You'd best get it off your chest.'

Betty recounted what she had seen that morning ending with the opinion that the mistress intended to take Richard as her husband, 'and the master barely cold in his grave.'

'So, it has come to that, has it? I've had my suspicions for a long time that she was after him.'

'Oh no. I'm sure it's all his fault. Him being all nice to her as he is. And she did love the master.'

'Did she? I reckon she made out she did but I've seen the way she looked at Richard. Just you think back to that time before master died when she and Richard were always having little quiet talks together – making sure that they were alone – and then there was that letter.'

Betty had not heard about that. Now she listened to Liddy but still persisted in her belief that Margery had been led on by the man. 'He's only a servant, like us. He has no place to go making up to the mistress.'

'You can think what you like, but I know she egged him on.'

The sound of the latch being lifted on the outer door stopped further speech.

Richard walked in. He greeted both but neither responded. Betty glared at his back, mumbling, 'I should think certain people might be afeared to go into certain rooms. There's some who ought to be scared that master's spirit don't walk before them.'

If he heard her, he showed no reaction, merely looking at the unattended churn and remarking, 'The butter won't get made by itself while you stand gossiping.' Then he was gone.

'See! Thinks he's the master already.'

'We'll have to talk about this some more, Betty. I'll slip out to your room tonight and we'll decide what's to be done.'

With Pleasance insisting on dragging a basket almost as big as herself, Margery had gone into the meadow to pick blackberries from the hedgerow. She needed to get away from the house, away from accusing eyes, for she had no doubt that Betty would have confided to Liddy what she had seen. Her cheeks burned with shame. How could she have allowed herself to behave so badly?

Her thoughts raced as she wrestled with the brambles, each scratch across her face and arms became a scourge for her sin. Crushed berries stained her hands, the flowing juice making them as bloody as if she had killed someone – and she had – the memory of her beloved husband. Plunging deeper into the hedge she became entangled in the vicious runners and was held captive. If only she could stay like this and be done with life. Die and join John. But no, she had by one foolish action, destroyed herself for eternity.

She was roused from her morbid thoughts by Pleasance pleading with her to come. The child was bored by their inactivity. Struggling to get to the little girl, Margery ripped her dress, thorns gouging deeply into her flesh. Now she was forced to return and face the maids.

Her dishevelled state eased the tension with them. Liddy took Pleasance to empty her basket of the fruit while Betty insisted on attending to Margery's wounds before going with her to help her change her gown. Betty longed for her mistress to say something that would prove that she had been wrong in her thoughts. Perhaps, after all, Richard had only come into the room that morning a few seconds before she had. Maybe he was making an enquiry about some urgent business. He had been known to do that when the master was alive, there being no harm in such a conversation when the bed-curtains were closed. She tried desperately to think of some way of asking what she needed to know, but the right words would not come.

Taking out a clean gown from the press, Betty unthinkingly commented that the master's clothes were still there.

Equally without thought, Margery said, 'Oh, let Richard have them – he's about the same size.'

The damage was done. Betty was reminded of Richard's half dressed state that morning and now here was proof indeed that he was intended to supplant the former master.

Nothing could have been further from Margery's mind. In making the remark she was concerned only with being rid of these constant reminders of the one she had lost. But her practical nature would not countenance waste. She might well have said 'give them to Masterton', but she knew they would not fit him.

The mention of Richard's name reminded her that she had still to face him. Mercifully, he had absented himself most of the day, riding off to Aldeburgh on farm business. The man was in as much turmoil of emotion as Margery. The climax to their encounter of the night had exceeded his wildest fantasy, he had given vent to all his long restrained feeling for her, revelling in her complete surrender. Memories of the night stirred within him throughout the day, filling him with longing for what was yet to come. At last, he had achieved his goal.

Commonsense however, vied with passion. He was aware that they must be circumspect. Although it was often the case that widows and widowers, too, did not wait long before seeking another partner, yet he felt that it would be wise if they did not declare their intentions, at least until after Michaelmas. As he rode back, his heart high, just once, the thought crossed his mind that at last he was done with Liddy.

But it was she who was waiting for him on his return. He strode in, expecting to see Margery as eager to see him as he was her. Instead it was Liddy who slammed his supper plate down in front of him, with the words, 'I hope it chokes you to death, just like master was choked.'

He looked at her sharply. 'What do you mean by that?'

'I mean what I say. I hate you. Enough to wish you dead.'

She was standing by the loaf, bread knife in hand. 'If I had any sense, I'd use this on you. Then she won't have you either.'

His hand fastened round her wrist, holding it in a tightening grip until she let the knife fall.

'You're a fool, Liddy. You always were.'

'You usen't to think so. But I suppose I'm not good enough for you now you've got what I used freely to give from . . .her who pays you for it.'

Hatred sired by jealousy blazed from her eyes. 'You may think that you've got yourself a good deal, but mark my words, Richard Ringe, you'll rue the day you crossed me.'

'Go to bed, you stupid wench.' He turned from her.

'Oh aye, so you can go creeping again into the master's bed. Oh yes! I know all about that.'

She paused by the door. Like a card player who had nearly declared his hand too early in the game, Liddy had found a small trump which had lain hidden. 'Except you'll find you've got company tonight. She's taken the child in with her!'

The door closed behind her with a thud.

Alone, he picked at the food on his plate but all appetite had gone. The bubble of elation had burst, leaving him with the familiar black despair. He longed to go to Margery, to claim again the rights of a lover but he was not confident enough to make that move without invitation. And if Liddy had spoken the truth and Margery did have the child with her, then that was a clear statement that his presence was not welcome. He pulled the jug of beer towards him, paused a moment, then drained its contents almost in one gulp. He went back to the barrel several times more before he finally slumped across the table.

In Betty's room, the two girls sat crouched at either end of the narrow bed. Still raging with anger, Liddy confessed that she and Richard had been lovers long before they came to Sternfield, adding for the benefit of the shocked Betty, that he had of course, promised to marry her when the time was right. She accused him of being a faithless double-dealer who had robbed her of her innocence and now, when it looked as if he could better himself, he had cast her off like an outgrown garment. She finished by saying that he'd come back from Aldeburgh strutting in like a prize rooster.

'Aldeburgh, you say he's been? Last time I remember him going there, he brought back poison for the rats and . . .' her hand went up to her mouth in an expression of horror.

'What ever is it?' Liddy's voice shook with anticipation.

'Oh, my lor! I've just remembered what he said as I was preparing the poor master's rum and milk. He wanted me to put the poison in it! Said master was the biggest rat and we

169

needed to be rid of him. Course, I thought he was joking, but I told him nonetheless that it was wrong to even think such things . . . now I begin to wonder . . .'

For a time they both sat silent weighing the full impact of Betty's revelation. Then each recalled the more recent event when the mistress had been so quick to make up the master's vomit mixture and Liddy had heard those dreadful words he had shouted at Richard, 'Are you trying to poison me?'

Bit by bit they pieced it all together. All the secret meetings, Margery's mourning clothes brought out in blatant preparation for – now they knew what! And they dwelt on those awful marks round the master's throat. Had he really been dead when Richard entered his room? Was it not more likely that the man had taken the opportunity presented by the master's indisposition to do what they had not been able to achieve with poison? Most damning of all was Margery's behaviour. She had not been the loving, concerned wife that night, had she? She had made no attempt to go to help him. Now they knew why. It was only too obvious. She was a party to what was happening!

They called themselves fools for not realising before that they had stood by and watched a conspiracy to murder take place under their very noses.

'What ever shall we do now?' Betty breathed.

Liddy thought for a while, then decided, 'We must tell someone.'

'But who? Who's going to take our word against theirs? I suppose we could tell the old Mistress and Miss Anne . . .'

'No. That won't do. And I tell you, Betty, we're going to have to be very careful. If they find out we know, there's no knowing what they might do to us. You'd better watch her like a hawk to make sure she don't put something in our food.'

Betty looked aghast. 'She'd never!'

'If they've done it once and got away with it, who's to say they would think twice about doing away with us.'

Their talk became more wild as they let their imaginations rove over the possible fate that awaited them. Both were adamant they would leave the house at Michaelmas, unless sudden death came to them first.

Liddy's final words before they fell asleep were, 'Let's bide our time. Leave it to me.'

Thirteen

MID SEPTEMBER 1762

A strained air permeated the house as everyone kept their own counsel during the next two or three days. Work carried on but conversation was kept only for what was necessary.

Margery seemed unaware of the maids' unusual reticence, being much absorbed in her own problems. She had finally made the decision that Richard must be kept at a distance. She knew that she needed him to manage the farm but somehow their former relationship of mistress and servant had to be re-established. Thus she decided she would assume a more formal manner when talking to him, making sure that any discussions they had were only about business. And, she would take pains to see that they were never alone.

The day following his visit to Aldeburgh, Richard had suffered so much from his drinking bout that he had not wanted to speak to anyone, but the day after that, he had attempted a private interview with Margery. He came upon her when she was with Pleasance feeding the chickens. She looked up as he approached. They faced each other, then Margery quickly looked away, unable to bear the look in his eyes.

He took a step towards her. 'Mistress, I . . .'

To gain time, she threw a handful of grain at the hens clustered at her feet.

'Good day, Richard. I trust your transactions with the miller at Aldeburgh went well. Perhaps you will be so kind as to let me have the account books later.'

He was stunned by the very normality of her voice. How

could she behave so coldly towards him?

'Come, Pleasance. Time to go in. We have finished here.' She nodded at him, a gesture of dismissal, and turned away with the child.

Standing where she left him, he was nonplussed. Could she really have no feeling for him; had that night meant nothing to her? Rejection flooded through him – and yet, he told himself, maybe there was still reason to hope. After all, she had to be careful what she said or did in front of the child. Then excitement replaced his fears, she had asked for the account books, that surely was an invitation – the excuse to study the books together later – when they would be alone.

But when he did bring the ledger to her, she had young Will Nunn seated at her side. Casually, she said it would be good practice for the lad to learn to help with the accounting.

By the third day it weighed heavily on his mind that Margery did not see him as either a lover or a prospective husband. Like Liddy he was forced to realise that he would have to bide his time.

For Liddy that time came sooner than she had looked for. Margery had some urgent commissions in Saxmundham and sent the girl to carry them out, telling her that she might, if she cared to, call on her aunt when she had completed her errands.

Seizing this unlooked for opportunity, the girl almost ran into town, wasting not a moment on unnecessary gossip with those she met in the shops. Breathless with haste and anticipation she almost collapsed on arrival at her aunt's lodging. Surprised and delighted by this unexpected visit the aunt fussed about her to prepare some refreshment.

But Liddy was not interested in food and drink, she wanted only to share with an outsider the dreadful suspicions which had become firmly rooted in her mind. Her aunt had heard of Beddingfield's sudden death and naturally, she now looked for a first hand account of that sad occurrence. She sat down, eager to hear those little details which would enable her to gossip with authority to her neighbours, but she was entirely unprepared for the shocking catalogue of events which her niece now unfolded. Hardly able to take it all in, she begged Liddy to slow down and repeat it bit by bit.

After the third recital of the tale, the woman was in no doubt as to what must be done.

'Put on your bonnet and shawl, girl, while I get mine. We're going to the Constable.'

Liddy demurred. 'I couldn't. I'd be too frighted.'

'Nonsense. They must not be allowed to get away with this. It's your duty to inform on them. You've got nothing to fear. You just said you managed well before the coroner – it will be just like that. All you have to do is tell the Constable the way you've told me.'

'But . . .'

'No buts, if you please. Now come along with me. And it couldn't be a better time with the Sessions less than a fortnight away.'

Liddy was swept along by her aunt's determination and before the afternoon was out had made her deposition to the Constable. She was informed that it was likely a warrant for the arrest of Margery and Richard would be made out as soon as the Constable had reported to the magistrate. It was even possible, should that gentleman be at home, that the pair could be taken up that night, but almost certainly by the following day.

The girl was in high spirits as they walked through the crowded main street back to her aunt's home. There, her mood changed abruptly when she saw the shopping she had done for Margery lying on the table.

'I'll have to take these back.' her voice faltered. 'I forgot I'd have to go back there and face them.'

'They can't hurt you. Remember that. You've got the law with you now.'

All the way back she repeated this comforting phrase to herself. As she did so, her confidence grew. At last she had been able to get her own back on the faithless Richard and the woman who had stolen him from her. The thought obsessed her. She could not wait to see Richard's face when she told him what she had done. She laughed out loud, a maniacal sound that rent the tranquillity of the darkening countryside, as she imagined him begging her to say it was not true. In the scene she played out in her mind, she had him trying to persuade her that she had got it all wrong. He would be as gentle and loving to her as he once had been. He would ask her – no, implore her – on bended knees – to go back with him to the Constable and swear that it was all a mistake. But she would remain adamant. She had had enough of being a play-thing. They were done for – let them go hang!

She entered the house ready to face out her victims but in this she was thwarted. Margery had taken Pleasance to visit her grandmother and aunt and were, so Betty related, intending to spend the night there. Richard was also out and not expected back until late.

Some of her bravado evaporated as she told Betty what she had done. It was one thing to sit in bed and talk the night away planning what they ought to do, but to have taken the fatal step and set the course of law in motion put an altogether different aspect on the affair. Betty was thoroughly scared, doubting the wisdom of Liddy's action, fearful of the consequences to themselves. In all their wild imaginings neither had ever stopped to consider that they would become the chief witnesses in the court case that must inevitably follow Liddy's charges.

After Masterton and Nunn had gone to bed, the maids sat huddled by the fire, waiting. The room was unlit except for the flames from the hearth. It seemed better that way, not having to see clearly the face of the other and read there the mirrored expression of fear. They spoke little. Betty's hands twisted constantly in her lap, Liddy had her arms folded tightly across her chest. And so they waited. The slightest noise or movement from outside made them stiffen – waiting for the Constable to come.

Then they heard the sound of hooves clattering across the courtyard. They held their breath to hear, when it came, the summoning knock. Simultaneously, they stood up and drew closer together, drawing support from each other. Again they waited. Somewhere in the distance a door banged. Footsteps crossed the yard. The kitchen door slowly opened. Richard had returned.

Weary from the day's exertions, he took off his cloak and hung it on its accustomed peg by the door. With his back still towards them he gave them the usual evening greeting. The very mundane sound of the words pierced the girls like a red hot poker burning deep into their consciences. Betty crept to cower behind Liddy whose face became fixed in a fearful grimace.

Richard stepped towards them and instinctively they flinched and backed away. Puzzled, yet not over-concerned, he asked, 'What's amiss? Has something happened?'

Betty let out a strangled sob. 'For the Lord's sake, tell him, Liddy. Tell him and be done with it.' She would then have fled had she been able but she knew that her legs would never bear her even as far as the door.

She clutched Liddy's arm. 'Oh, God help us all.'

Now he too, was afraid. He sank down on the stool by the table, resting his head on his arms. In the course of a split second all the horrors imaginable flashed through his thoughts. At last he forced himself to look up and ask in a voice hoarse with terror, 'Is it the mistress? Has some terrible accident befallen her?'

This was the spark needed to flare Liddy into speech. 'To her!' She laughed hysterically. 'Aye, and to you too!'

No longer afraid, she confronted him. Like a witch possessed by demons, her voice rang out, shrill, unstoppable. With arm outstretched, a finger rigid, pointing, she reeled off her staccato list of accusations against him and Margery. The tirade continued reaching a crescendo as she announced his imminent arrest.

Throughout it all he had sat powerless to move, mesmerised by her voice like a frightened rabbit cornered by a stoat. It was like being in a hideous nightmare; words came and went, some immediately penetrating his conscious mind, others floating in air like bubbles, meaningless until they burst splattering their full impact of horror upon him.

The recital came to an end. On the hearth, a log shifted and a sudden spit of flame flared up and as quickly died away. Betty crouched in a corner, weeping noiselessly. Liddy, now exhausted of all emotion sank into a chair shivering from the icy chill that crept into every part of her body.

Whatever reaction she had anticipated from Richard she was not prepared for what came. Slowly he raised himself from the stool, carefully prepared his night candle and with measured steps walked towards the staircase door. There he spoke for the first time.

'So Liddy, you've done for me and I will hang! You have done your work well.' And then he was gone.

No recrimination. No pleas for forgiveness, no begging her to say she had made a terrible mistake, nothing – except total acceptance. It was too much for her to bear. She sobbed loudly and long, but the tears could not cleanse what she had done. There was to be no comfort for Liddy and Betty throughout that long sleepless night.

Richard's arrest took place early on Thursday morning. Such was the man's resignation to his fate that not only was he up, washed and dressed ready for his captors, but he had also made lists of what needed to be done about the farm over and above the routine work. These he entrusted to Will Nunn, being the only one among the rest who could read. Although he spoke to neither of the women who sensibly kept to the dairy and back kitchen as much as possible, he even ventured a joke with Will that it was a good thing he had mastered literacy, though he warned him that the ability to read and write would not necessarily guarantee he might not end on the gallows.

When Masterton and Will asked where he was going that required all these arrangements, he replied simply, 'A long journey.' Then he sent them about their respective tasks before the arrival of the Constables.

Having secured one of the parties, the problem was now to find the other. A trembling Betty told that her mistress would be found at the home of the older Mrs Beddingfield, so the horses were turned in that direction. Somewhat embarrassed at having to knock at the door of a respected member of local society on such an errand, the Constables were then thwarted in their mission. The maid who answered told them her mistress was not at home. She, Miss Anne, the young mistress and the child had driven off early that morning. She believed that her mistress was intending to stay for a few days at the home of her step-daughter, Mrs Burman, in Felixstowe.

Their quarry now turned fugitive, the Constables could do nothing except return to Saxmundham, lodge Richard in the Bridewell and start on the round of visits needed to secure the documents that would authorise their travelling out of the area.

It was nightfall before they managed to reach Ipswich where they rested at an inn before starting at daybreak for the little town on the estuary. Discreet enquiries among some fishermen led them to the home of Mr Burman where they interrupted the ladies at breakfast.

The Constable's breathless apologies, followed by his garbled account of his reason for disturbing them, turned into irritation at Mrs Beddingfield senior's snort of 'What nonsense is this?'

The officer refused to sit as she requested him. Standing firm against her, he repeated that he had a warrant for the arrest of one Margery Beddingfield.

The dowager merely laughed. 'Then I am afraid you have had a wasted journey. She is not here.'

The man became angry. Coldly he informed her that she was preventing him in the execution of his duty – as laid down by the King himself – and if she persisted in her conduct he might have to take her in charge too.

The lady was neither impressed nor daunted by his threat. Gently but firmly, she told him that she did not for a moment believe such a charge could be made against her daughter-in-law. That the word of an ignorant, vicious serving wench should be believed – and acted upon – without any proof whatsoever, was beyond the comprehension of any sensible person.

Stung by the slur, the man became more officious. He was now firmly convinced that the ladies were hiding Margery and declared he would search the house.

'Search away!' she replied, giving an inquiring glance at the mistress of the house who returned a nod of acquiescence. 'But you will not find her here. You could have spared yourselves a long, no doubt tedious – and expensive – journey. Mistress Beddingfield is not trying to elude your so-called justice. She will be found at Parham at the house of her late father where she had gone to visit his former housekeeper. We left her there yesterday morning on our way here. Far from running away, if I am any judge of her character, you will find her there, busy tending the needs of an infirm old woman. And now, perhaps you will be so good as to leave us to finish our breakfast.'

Thus they were dismissed. Frustrated of an arrest and enraged by the lady's off-hand manner, they made their way back.

Once the door was safely closed upon the intruders, the genteel calm within the breakfast parlour was broken as each lady voiced an opinion on the news. Anne had to be restrained from going immediately to change into her riding dress and taking off to warn Margery. She had already worked out that if she took a boat across the river, she could hire a horse, ride across country and reach Parham well ahead of the officers.

Her mother told her that such foolhardy action would be construed as confirming Margery's guilt and turn Anne into an accessory. Their hostess who was perplexed by the whole affair resorted to the suggestion that her husband be consulted.

'By all means let us hear what Mr Burman has to say. No doubt his advice will be sensible. However, I believe I should return home as soon as possible in order to engage an attorney to sort out this silly business.'

The quiet, self effacing Mr Burman agreed with his step-mamma, offering to accompany her should she wish it. She did not. Neither did she wish Anne to come. When the girl protested, she was silenced with a remark that her mother knew would have Anne totally compliant.

'Think of Pleasance, Anne. We cannot take her back with us.'

'No, indeed.' Mrs Burman shook with horror at the idea. 'Please let the child remain here. My children will welcome her continued company.'

'Thank you, my dear. That would certainly be the best solution. But,' she looked from Mrs Burman to Anne, 'poor Pleasance has had so many upsets in her short life and since she does so dote on her Aunt Anne, I think, if you will allow it, Anne should remain to help her settle.'

Anne capitulated at once. She loved the child dearly. At first she had merely delighted in the infant's prattle and pretty ways but as Pleasance grew Anne could unleash her natural high spirits in the childish romps with her niece which gave them so much pleasure. Now she was faced with playing a more serious role in the child's life. Already fatherless and about to be deprived of her mother until this frightful affair was sorted out, Pleasance would need her aunt to provide love and stability. Furthermore, Anne had to admit that her mother was more than capable of dealing with the authorities without any assistance from her.

Mrs Beddingfield was anxious to be on her way. Her maid was sent to pack, the coachman instructed to prepare the horses and by noon she was on her way home. She whiled away the tedious miles making lists of those she must see and rehearsing what must be said to them. Thoroughly weary by the time she reached the last few miles before Sternfield, she allowed herself to lean back and close her eyes. Not to sleep but for a parade of the events of the last four years to pass before her. So much had happened in that time; Anne's indiscretion of running off, her husband's death, John's marriage, the death of the baby, John's reckless behaviour and his ensuing illness and finally her son's sudden death. There, in the background of all these, was little Margery. Always ready to help, never pushing herself forward, yet they all had, at one time or another, relied on her strength. She was not the woman she would have chosen for her son yet she had proved to be what he needed. Her selfless, loving nature had tamed his wild spirit and given him much happiness. The mother was full of admiration for the way her son's wife had handled him. How then could anyone believe that such a gentle creature would even contemplate assisting another to murder? What wife has not, at some time, wished her husband dead? But who would go so far as to plan and execute such a deed – and with the hired help? Had John been a vile, drunken sot, three or four times Margery's age, then there might be some excuse for wishing him out of the way. But this was not the case. He had been a virile young man, barely a year or so older than Ringe who had been named as the perpetrator of the plot.

For the first time, Mrs Beddingfield considered Richard's part in the affair. On the occasions she had encountered him, she had been impressed by his quiet efficiency. He was always polite, as befitted his position, without being subservient. John had always spoken well of him and she knew that he was respected by other farmers and tradesmen. Quite rightly, Margery had relied on him to run the farm during John's illness – and after the death, it followed naturally that he should continue to do so. Could such a man have been plotting all the time to be rid of his master? Attempt to poison him and when that failed, strangle him? And to suggest that an unnatural liaison existed with Margery! The whole idea was preposterous.

It was very late when she reached home and there was nothing more she could do till morning.

At nine o'clock on Saturday morning, a smiling Margery answered the series of short raps on the door of the house in Parham. A look of puzzlement replaced the smile as she looked at the men standing there. Two advanced towards her, seizing her by the arms as another read out the charge against her.

An hour later Margery Beddingfield was safely locked up in Saxmundham Bridewell. The news quickly circulated the town. The rumour that she had vomited at the moment of capture was taken as a clear indication that she had taken poison to escape arrest.

Fourteen

SEPTEMBER 1762 – MARCH 1763

The Sessions at Saxmundham was over. Poachers and shoplifters, highway thieves and drunks and those in arrears with bastardy maintenance, all had appeared before the magistrates and most were bound over to appear at the next Assizes.

Among those to be taken to the jail in Ipswich were Margery and Richard. Their appearance at the Sessions had been brief. Neither had said anything apart from agreeing their names and entering a plea of innocence to the charges laid against them.

The magistrates, the local landowner and the rector of Saxmundham were embarrassed by the case, not least because of the earlier importuning of the older Mrs Beddingfield. They knew her socially and it had been difficult to turn their backs on her, as it were, by protesting they had a duty to perform. Whatever their personal belief on the matter, serious charges had been made and it was out of their hands. The law decreed that when there was the slightest doubt about a sudden death, then it had to be investigated.

As it already had been, she argued, at the coroner's court. Had not that returned a verdict of Accidental Death? All they could say to that was that evidence of which the coroner had not been apprised had since come to light.

'New evidence! Mere tittle tattle – maidservant's gossip.'

'Your loyalty to your daughter-in-law, does you credit Ma'am', the rector had said when she had called upon him. 'But surely, you of all people, would wish to know the full facts of your son's death.'

'Not at the expense of seeing an innocent young woman suffer. Quite apart from anything else, how long is she to bear the sheer indignity of being treated like a common criminal?'

The magistrate agreed that the Bridewell was not perhaps the best of places for a young woman who had known refined living, but, he assured his visitor, when Margery was moved to Ipswich to await her trial, Mrs Beddingfield could ensure that her lodging was more comfortable.

Stern-faced and erect of body, Mrs Beddingfield had sat at the back of the court, thus providing additional gossip for the local populace. She watched as Margery had faltered on entering the dock, willing her to stand firm against adversity. When the girl was led away again, she longed for her to look in her direction and know that she had her support, but Margery's eyes were only for the ground.

Before the prisoners were herded into their transport, Mrs Beddingfield was off ahead of them to Ipswich, to the jail in the West Gate, where she demanded an interview with Mr Hurst the jailer. Armed with gold in her purse, she inspected one of the small, private rooms that were available to prisoners with the means to hire them. Selecting the best of a poor lot, she gave orders for additional comforts to be made ready for Margery's reception. Further gold secured the services of a female attendant and the purchase of food supplies. The formidable lady made it very clear that her visits would be regular and that she expected to find her orders had been carried out.

Content that she had, for the moment, done all she could, she drove off to another part of the town where she had a friend she could trust who would give her lodging for a few days.

On an October day of relentless drizzle two heavy enclosed wagons bumped their human cargo over the long slow route to Ipswich to await an even longer incarceration before being called to stand trial at the Assizes.

Penned in the far corner of the leading vehicle, Richard crouched, trying to avoid contact with the rest of the rag-bag of men crammed inside the airless wagon. The stench of unwashed bodies and dirty clothes was nauseating. Added to this was the inner sickness, a combination of a lack of food but more especially, fear. Fear that he would be spending days, weeks, months even, with this ill assorted company. Little did he realise then that his fellows had even less desire to be close to him. Whatever crimes they had committed, none but he was branded as a murderer.

Yet over the next months when they were all herded together in the bare prison room, a kind of brotherhood would develop. In such close proximity from which there was no escape, they would find that they would come to depend on each other, listen to each other's life histories, sometimes even laugh together but more often try to comfort those who sank into deep despair. Richard had already accepted that he was doomed, he was resigned to his fate but there were those, even younger than himself for whom he could hope for the chance of a future. There would come a time when he would wrestle to understand a legal system which could as easily hang a lad of fourteen for stealing a rabbit or a game bird as the professional robber who had for years evaded justice and made a handsome living. But all that was still to come.

In the wagon that carried the women there were very different smells. Down on the straw-strewn floor, Margery sat cradling the head of a young woman of about her own age. The girl, she had learned, had been dismissed by her employer when she was found to be pregnant. After her departure from the house, a silver spoon had gone missing and it was assumed she was responsible. A search of her meagre lodging revealed not the spoon but an old dress belonging to her former mistress. That had been sufficient evidence to condemn her as a thief.

Now the girl was in the throes of a miscarriage. As her wasted body twisted in agony, Margery and a couple of the older women were doing what they could to help her through the ordeal. Margery had taken off her shawl to be used as a napkin to mop up the bloody mess which issued forth. She longed to be able to bathe the girl's face in some comforting balm but all she could do was moisten the bitten, swollen and cracked lips with a few drops of water from the leathern bottle which had been provided for the prisoners on the journey.

Throughout the ghastly trek, she continued to hold the girl, murmuring words of comfort, refusing to let go of her even when one of the other women whispered that it was all over. Only when the wagon finally drew up in the West Gate, did Margery allow the corpse to be taken from her.

While the rest of her companions, drawn together in the sisterhood of the travail of birth and death, were led away to the communal lodging, Margery was taken for an interview with the jailer.

Mr Hurst found it hard to reconcile the small figure in a blood-splattered gown with the lady he had expected. From the older Mrs Beddingfield's imperious demeanour he had anticipated that the accused woman would possess the same lofty manner. He had enjoyed a few moments before her arrival savouring her reception, divided between the idea of taunting her with what lay in store or, remembering the gold, being dutifully obsequious. But now that she stood before him, her face stained with the tears she had shed for the dead girl, he was overcome with pity. His years of keeping charge of all types of criminal had not entirely hardened him to the plight of his fellow creatures. Powerless to intervene, he had witnessed the dispatch of many of whose innocence he was convinced. Then he did the little he was able to ease their passage from this life to the next. Women troubled him the most; the old or infirm who had got themselves into scrapes which should never have demanded imprisonment; worse were the young ones whose lives, barring accidents, should have stretched happily before them; he had seen too many come and go, snuffed out by a careless twist of fate. Of course, there were others, the bold, hardened and immoral who deserved what they got. But this girl who stood before him – and she was no more than that, hardly as old as his own beloved daughter, for all that she was said to have done – she aroused his compassion.

Even if he had not been paid handsomely to look after her, his instinctive reaction to Margery's vulnerability would have been a desire to protect her from further hurt. After his initial scrutiny, he acted impulsively, leading her to a chair by his fire and insisting she take a glass of wine to revive her after the rigour of the journey.

Weary in mind as much as body, Margery accepted his offers without question. She pressed her spine against the hard panel of the chair conscious now of the racking pain that was the result of hours spent hunched over the dying girl. Memory of that most recent incident brought tears which she fought desperately to control.

Believing that his act of kindness was responsible, Mr Hurst permitted himself to place his hand upon her shoulder and murmur, 'It may not be so bad here, Ma'am, as you imagine. We will do all that is possible for your comfort.'

Margery raised her head to look at the speaker of the first gentle words she had received in days. The ghost of a smile briefly animated her pale drawn face.

'You are very kind, sir. But I do not look for any special treatment.' She began to rise. 'I thank you for these most welcome moments of respite, but surely, I should now join my fellows?'

'Indeed no, Ma'am. You are not to be accommodated with the hoi polloi.' His tone now changed to the obsequious. 'Your mamma-in-law,' he ran his tongue round the phrase and liking its taste, repeated it. 'Your mamma-in-law has already called upon me and given orders for your lodging. If you now feel sufficiently recovered, I will summon your attendant to take you. And rest assured, dear lady, you have but to command and I will do all I can for your comfort.'

The small room, lit only from a narrow window close to the ceiling beams, became her world. It was comfortable enough; a bed in one corner, two chairs and a small table placed close to the fire and a small chest to house her clothes and few personal belongings, in many ways it resembled the room she had occupied as a child. Here she whiled away the months before the trial. Her initial numbness of mind had given way to a time of fear and panic but as the days lengthened into weeks, she settled to a daily routine. Her meals were served by the motherly attendant who would, given the opportunity, linger to gossip. What she had to say was of little interest to Margery but it did bring the sound of another human voice. Most days, unless it rained heavily, she was permitted to walk with the attendant in the yard but she did not enjoy this time. The falling of the leaves from the trees which surrounded the yard, followed by the stark outlines of bare branches standing out against a white winter sky brought home only too forcibly the passage of time.

She felt much more secure, cocooned within her room, reading over and over from her limited store of books. She had her sewing too, carefully stitching garments to be given to less fortunate inmates. And as time went on, so her mind managed to blot out much of the past. Only in sleep did memory disturb her tranquillity.

That she could cope with but not, at first, the visits from Mrs Beddingfield. With her came too many reminders, not least of her child. In the beginning she had been eager to hear of Pleasance, anxious for her well-being, pleased to know that she was not pining for her, happy that she appeared to be enjoying being with her cousins in Felixstowe. But after one visit when her mother-in-law had given her a detailed account of the child's new life, Margery had cried bitterly for the daughter she had lost. Even if she should be cleared of this dreadful charge, how could she ever make a life for them together knowing that one day Pleasance might hear that her mother had been accused of being a party to her father's death. Pleasance, like all else that she had held dear, was lost to her forever.

When the tears were finally exhausted, it was as if they had washed Pleasance away with them, for Margery ceased to ask for news of her. If Mrs Beddingfield noticed the omission on her next visit, she very wisely made no comment. On that occasion she had other things on her mind and in any case, there was a third party present, the attorney who was to prepare Margery's case.

Both became a trifle exasperated by her seeming disinterest in her defence. Mrs Beddingfield had spent much time and energy, let alone money, in visiting those who might be called as witnesses to show that she and John had lived happily together. Now she was anxious to know if there was anyone she had missed.

'I can think of no one else.' Why could they not leave her in peace, she did not want to think back to . . . But it was too late, memories were beginning to escape. A picture edged into mental view, it was that drive to Lowestoft with Mr Starkey. She shuddered as she saw again, vividly, the body that had swung in chains at the Blythburgh crossroads.

'What is it, my dear?' Margery stared at her mother-in-law's concerned face.

'I just remembered John's friend, Mr.Starkey. You may recall that it was at his house that our little boy was born early.'

She bit her lip to stop the tears for the memory of that baby and his fate.

While Mrs Beddingfield wrote in her notebook, the attorney, fearful of an outburst of female weakness, said briskly, 'Now, Ma'am, I must ask you about your relations with Ringe.'

'Oh, poor Richard! I have not thought of him.' She turned quickly to Mrs Beddingfield. 'How will he have borne up? Do you know how he fares? Is he lodged with the common prisoners? He has no one to care for him as I have.'

Mrs Beddingfield and the attorney exchanged glances. This, the first sign of any animation they had seen in Margery and her very apparent concern for Ringe, did not bode well.

'I must remind you, Ma'am, that you and Ringe are charged as collaborators in this matter and that the feelings you have just expressed could well be taken as an indication of strong bonds existing between you.'

'Richard was a good friend to me – to us all,' she protested.

'A friend? Nothing more than a friend?'

Margery hesitated, for a second, no more. 'No! He was a trusted and loyal servant to my husband.'

'And to you?

'Yes. I relied on him when we were in trouble.'

'As a servant?' The attorney pressed the point.

September 1762 – March 1763

'And as a friend.'

'Are you friends with your other servants?'

'Yes – no. Not in quite the same way, perhaps.'

'And how would you describe that?'

Margery was struggling. She was aware of the innuendo in the attorney's questioning. For the first time in months her brain was being forced into thinking fast and clearly.

She turned to Mrs Beddingfield.

'You surely must understand. Richard was both servant and friend to us such as Chandler Cobb once was to you.'

The older woman nodded. She understood the comparison even if the lawyer did not. She would explain it to him later on the journey home.

The questions continued as the attorney tried to build up a picture of the household at Sternfield, the individual characters involved and the sequence of events which had led to the charges being made.

'Finally, Ma'am. Can you think of any reason why the maid Clebold should have made these allegations?'

'Liddy, you mean?' She shook her head. 'No, I know of nothing that could . . . except, maybe . . .'

'Well, Ma'am?'

'It is silly, I know, but I did once have occasion to think that she might be jealous.'

'Jealous? Of whom?'

'Me – and – my husband.'

This was not the reply the man had expected.

'What led you to think that?'

Margery did not want to talk about this particular episode but the inquisitor was insistent.

She chose her words carefully. 'Just after our son died, my husband was . . . very unhappy and during that time, I observed that Liddy was somewhat over-attentive in her duties to her master. And then when he was so very ill, she often tried to do things for him – of a very personal nature. When I chided her gently, she was resentful for a while but she soon recovered her spirits. Liddy is not one to hold a grudge, she's really a very kind soul. But I do believe that for a time, she fancied herself, as young girls often do, to be in love with my husband.

The attorney could not help an inward smile at this, not the idea of a maid servant in love with her master, that was commonplace enough, but at Margery talking with the wisdom of a middle-aged dowager about one who was so very close to her own age.

'So you would put her motive down to jealousy?'

'It sounds foolish to say that. Yet I can think of no other reason. I am certain I never gave her any cause to dislike me to this extent.'

'And Ringe? What cause did he give her?'

'None, I am sure. He treated her as he did Betty. With politeness and courtesy yet with a reserve which befitted his more refined upbringing.'

'So there was no understanding between them?'

'Understanding?' Margery brows drew in puzzlement.

'They were not having an affair? They were not lovers?'

'Good heavens, no!' She laughed. Such an idea was incomprehensible.

The interview drew to an end. Mrs Beddingfield gave her the parcels she had brought; some books, more sewing materials, wine and a few delicacies to eat. Embracing her as she was about to leave, she whispered, 'Keep up your spirits, my dear. And don't worry about Ringe, I have undertaken to make sure that he is adequately fed.'

The heavy snows of January blocked most of the roads to the town, so for a time Mrs Beddingfield was prevented from making further visits. February came with biting winds which howled round the prison house and crept in through every available crevice, chilling even those fortunate enough to have firing. Before the end of the month several of those awaiting trial had escaped from that ordeal, carried off by the disease of the lungs against which they had neither the physical stamina nor the will power to resist.

And so into March. As the days began to lengthen and out of

doors there were early signs of the new cycle of life, so activity stirred within the jail. The rumble of the heavy cartwheels over the cobbles told their own tale. The prisoners were being moved to Bury St.Edmunds ready for the Assizes. Soon it would be Margery's turn.

Fifteen

MARCH 1763

The Hon.Sir Richard Adams, Kt. opened the Spring Assizes at
Bury St.Edmunds on Monday, 21 March, 1763. The first three
days were taken up with the highway robbers, poachers, run-of-
the mill thieves, men and women whose names would feature
as little more than space-fillers in that week's copy of the Ipswich
Journal.

All interest was focused on the case which was set down for
Thursday. Annoyingly, this would be too late for full treatment
in the newspaper and would have to wait for the following week's
issue. In the packed courtroom, the reporter sat ready to take
down as much of the proceedings as he could for he knew that
this promised to be not just an interesting case but very likely,
for him, a lucrative one. Quite apart from the lines he would
write for the paper, which could well be cut through lack of space,
he expected to have a much more lengthy report printed privately
for the benefit of those readers who were not subscribers to the
Ipswich Journal. Even after he had deducted his printing costs, a
sale at sixpence a time would bring in a tidy sum. And unless he
had a rival in the courtroom, there was a strong likelihood that
he would be able to sell his story to the illustrious Gentleman's
Magazine. All in all, this particular trial would be one he would
remember.

He scarcely looked up when the prisoners were brought to the
bar to be arraigned. When he did, he received a shock. No one
had said how young they were. The man, possibly no more than
average height, looked taller, so thin was his frame. His clothes

192

hung off him making him resemble a scarecrow made from a thin bundle of twigs. His face had that cheese-like pallor common to those who have been shut away for long periods. Beside him stood the smaller figure of a young woman dressed in a simple gown of drab grey. An encompassing cap of a similar shade tied beneath the chin drained her face of any trace of colour it might once have had.

The pair stood rigid, apart from each other, yet joined in their common ordeal. They reminded the reporter of those carved alabaster effigies he had seen on tombs and commemorative tablets in local churches.

A hush fell on the court, the performance was about to begin. Bidding each of the accused to hold up a hand, the Clerk droned his way through the long arraignment while the journalist wrote down . . ."for that ye, not having God before your eyes, but being moved and seduced by the instigation of the devil, on the twenty seventh day of July, in the second year of the reign of our sovereign Lord, George III with force and arms . . . feloniously, traitorously, wilfully and of your malice aforethought, did make an assault upon the said John Beddingfield . . . you Richard, both hands about his neck . . . did choke and strangle him . . . and you Margery were present, aiding, abetting, assisting and maintaining the said Richard in the felony, treason and murder aforesaid . . ."

The reporter struggled to keep up, managing to use the time after the accused had entered pleas of not guilty and while the twelve men of the jury were being sworn, to fill in the blanks he had left.

The formalities completed, the prosecution called its main witness. The crowd of onlookers stirred at her entry, twisting their necks to gain a good look at what promised to be the star turn. As she stepped up to take the oath the contrast with the accused was startling. A bright neat dress showed off her well-rounded figure, wayward curls escaped from beneath her cap, framing a face that glowed with the flush of health and excitement. Her sparkling eyes, darting in all directions, widened as she took in the sea of faces before her.

Her confidence surprised the journalist. He was not sure what he had expected – a simple country girl overawed, perhaps, at having to make such an appearance – certainly not this poised young woman. But then, he was not to know that for nearly six months Liddy had very much enjoyed being the centre of attention.

The day after Margery's arrest, Mrs Beddingfield had visited the farm to make arrangements for its management. At the back of her mind lurked the idea of sending for Chandler Cobb to come. But that was for the future, something had to be done immediately. So she interviewed William Alston, a steady fellow who for years had been employed as a day worker at the farm and suggested that he and his wife might care to become managers until matters could be properly sorted. The two boys, Masterton and Nunn declared themselves quite happy to continue with their work.

Then Mrs Beddingfield had turned to the maids. What did they wish to do? Would they like to stay on to help Mrs Alston, Betty, in particular, knowing the ways of the dairy or would they rather seek employment elsewhere?

Mrs Beddingfield had been kindly and fair in her dealings with them, even though it cost her dearly to remain calm with Liddy. She concealed her loathing for the girl, determined to give her no further cause for wild accusations.

In spite of all she had said earlier, Betty decided to stay. A job, after all, was better than no job with only the possibility of Parish Relief and when all was said and done, she liked the place and she liked Mrs Alston with whom she had often gossiped.

It had been an uncomfortable interview for Liddy. Now that Richard and Margery were in custody she was a little less sure of the rightness of what she had done. Mrs Beddingfield's pleasant demeanour as she concentrated only on what was to be done with the farm unsettled the girl. Had the older woman made some allusion to what had occurred, had she even shown some antagonism towards her, accused her of lying, anything that would reveal what she really thought, that would have made

Liddy feel her action was justified. The girl liked everything to be black or white, she could not bear this grey area in between, not being perceptive enough to feel Mrs Beddingfield's underlying resentment.

Unwilling to look the woman in the eye, she had mumbled she would go. Mrs Beddingfield accepted her decision without comment, paid her the wages she was due, adding a little extra - but not enough to be construed as a bribe – to tied her over until she found new employment. Unable to cope with this unexpected act of generosity, Liddy had tossed her head defiantly, saying, 'There's really little reason for me to stay anyway, since I was employed to look after the child.'

The expression which crossed Mrs Beddingfield's face signalled that the interview was at an end.

So Liddy had packed her belongings and gone to her aunt in Saxmundham. That lady, being responsible for the predicament in which Liddy now found herself, felt duty bound to take her in. Another live-in post was out of the question – at least in the vicinity – for word had spread quickly that it was she who had brought charges against her former employer.

But she soon found work much more suitable to her temperament. The landlord of one of the inns was only too keen to take her on as a serving maid. Apart from her obvious physical attraction which led his customers to linger longer than they otherwise might, her notoriety drew many more from their usual drinking places.

Revelling in the attention, Liddy held regular court, telling her story over and over to eager listeners. The more she told it, the more vivid and detailed did the account become and she became expert at parrying any question which might hint at a discrepancy.

With this training behind her, it was small wonder that Liddy was now able to step into the courtroom at Bury St Edmunds with so much assurance.

The prosecutor started with mundane affairs, asking her how long she had been employed at Sternfield, what her duties had been and who else made up the household. Then he went straight to the hub, the relationship between the two accused.

Without hesitation Liddy replied that Ringe had been on very familiar terms with her mistress.

Immediately, Mr Sergeant Forster, Margery's defence counsel, leapt to his feet.

'My Lord, we object to any evidence of familiarities. It is not part of the question now.'

'Your objection does not stand,' the judge answered, 'they being circumstances tending to prove her consenting and abetting.'

The journalist made a margin note that it appeared the judge had already made up his mind on guilt.

Unshaken by the interruption, Liddy continued with her evidence, building up her picture of the liaison between the two. It was all there. The times they had lingered together after the meal time was over, sometimes using her to watch out for the master; the night she had sat up brewing and found Margery sitting on Richard's lap; how she had been forced to carry love letters for the mistress; the episode of the black dress and Richard's remark about not going into mourning for the devil – just before the master's death!

The prosecutor allowed her to run on with her damning catalogue of secret meetings, always when the master was absent, and her interpretation of words or looks that she had heard and seen pass between the accused.

Then he skillfully moved on to the events of the 27th July. Carefully and slowly, Liddy recited what had occurred, laying great emphasis on the fact that Margery had declined to sleep in her husband's room for at least two nights before the murder, choosing instead to share her bed.

As she began to describe the noises that had wakened her on that night, the journalist made another margin note. Where was the child while all this was going on? Had not the maid said earlier that she usually slept with her? He continued to listen as Liddy said,

'It appeared somebody was in great distress. It was a gory

shrieking noise. I heard it the moment I waked and it lasted a minute or two.'

'Then what happened?'

'After this I saw Richard. He came into the room. I saw him on that side of the bed where the mistress lay. There was no light but I knew it was him by his speech. When I saw him, I raised myself in bed and said, "Master?" And he said, "Hold your tongue; does anybody know of this but you two?"'

'To what did you think he was referring?'

'The noise we had heard.'

'Go on.'

'Then I think mistress answered "no". So Richard said, "He is dead and now I am easy."'

'Mistress then said, "Is he?" And I said, "How came you here?" And he answered "I was forced to it."'

An excited buzz ran through the spectators, they felt a great need to discuss the revelations they had heard but they were quickly silenced and the questioning continued.

'After Ringe had said he was "forced to it", what next occurred?'

'Richard stayed in the room till we had got some of our clothes on and then Richard said he would go back to his own chamber to wait to be called up and we went downstairs.'

'Did either you or the accused woman go into the parlour bedchamber?'

'No – not then.'

'Go on, please.'

'We went to the backhouse chamber where Betty Riches lay – across the landing place coming out of the kitchen chamber.'

'Did your mistress say anything to you?'

'Yes. She said, "Liddy never discover this to anyone" and I said "no." Then Mistress told Betty to call Richard.'

'Did you then return to your room?'

'Yes, we waited for Richard to come and go and look in the parlour chamber. He had a light with him and he came back and said the master was dead.'

'And what did your mistress do then?'

'She got back on the bed and lay there till morning. When the master's mother came she asked if the doctor had been sent for but the mistress said, "If he is dead, what signifies sending for the doctor?"

Finally Liddy was asked to describe the body as she had seen it laid out on the bed the following morning.

Why, the defence lawyer wanted to know in cross examination, had she not given all this information she possessed at the time of the inquest? At that time she had made no mention that Ringe had come out of the master's bedchamber on an earlier occasion. Had she not, he wondered, considered it, at that time, to be important?

Liddy was ready for that one. She answered pertly that she had not been asked about it. When she saw the counsel raise a quizzical eyebrow, she cast her gaze downward and said quietly that she was also afraid that if she had said anything she might be ill-used by her mistress.

So what had changed her mind? She paused before answering, a long hiatus that had the audience holding its breath, then came the one word – 'Conscience!' She followed this with, 'I could not live with myself knowing what I knew and what Betty Riches had told me.'

Plump, plain Betty did not command the same keen interest that Liddy had done, yet she had a spine-chilling tale to tell of the attempts to poison the master. Her recollections of the night of the murder were somewhat different from those of Liddy. She remembered the other maid calling her to inform Richard and finding the mistress in bed when she came to the room. She regaled the court with the important part she had played in organising events.

Under cross examination she agreed that on the whole her master and mistress had lived happily and that until Liddy had pointed it out to her she had been unaware there was anything going on between the mistress and Richard. That is, until . . . Betty's revelation that she had seen Richard coming out of the widow's bedchamber threw the court into uproar.

It was useless for the defence counsel to point out that this event had no relevance whatsoever to a supposed murder some two months earlier. The damage was done.

In vain, the defence tried to establish that the marks around the deceased's throat were caused by his own hand when he had fallen down in a fit. Useless, to call the two boys to describe that the bedclothes were turned back as they would be by the occupant of the bed getting out and that the state of the bed-curtains and their pole suggested they had been pulled down by someone falling against them. Both testified that John's nightshirt had been ripped as if the man himself had tried to loosen the constriction at his neck.

No one really listened as the two doctors who had examined the body gave their opinions as to the severe bruising at the neck. Dr Edgar stated that he had seen the marks of a thumb and four fingers on the neck of the corpse. Dr Sparham was forced into admitting that he had been hurried into making a decision, but he was quite certain that he had seen the imprint of a thumb and three fingers. The thumb was on one side of the neck, the fingers on the other. He had also seen scratch marks as if from fingernails on the throat.

Reluctantly he agreed that it was possible that the marks might have been caused by external pressure from the hands of another.

Margery's defending lawyer called a number of witnesses, including Starkey, to testify to the happy marital relationship of the Beddingfields.

This was dull stuff as far as the auditors in court were concerned. Who wanted to hear from an uncle who had visited only a week before the death that all was well in the household? And did it really count for anything that Mr Toller, the attorney in Saxmundham who had granted administration papers to the widow, said that he had never received any indication from his deceased client of any domestic discord neither, until Liddy's charge, had there been any hint from any quarter that John's death had been in the least suspicious. Liddy's evidence still held sway in the minds of most listeners

Mr Sergeant Forster did his very best for Margery. Having gone over the flimsy evidence against her, he then pointed out that had she been guilty, she had had ample opportunity to evade being taken up. The very fact that she had not done so, proved that she had nothing to hide. He concluded his address with the words, 'My Lord, two witnesses are necessary to convict a person of petty treason; not a witness has been examined in this case that affects Mrs Beddingfield but Liddy Clebold.'

His lordship replied, 'Both witnesses have given circumstantial evidence to affect her.'

Summing up, the judge solemnly directed the jury as to their duty. 'Your first inquiry should be as to Ringe, who is supposed to be the person who actually committed the fact. If you should think him not guilty, then you must of course acquit Beddingfield who does not appear, upon the evidence, to have been actually present in the same room at the time. But, if you should believe Ringe to be guilty, then your next inquiry should be as to the guilt of Beddingfield. Then the charge against her is as a principal in the murder in being present, aiding and abetting Ringe. If you are satisfied that she was previously apprised of Ringe's intention and knew of it and was consenting to it, then she too would be guilty.'

The jury retired, leaving the journalist time to catch up on the judge's closing words, stretch his fingers and rest his hand for a time.

The jury was not out for long. The foreman delivered their verdict. They found the accused guilty of felony, treason and murder.

The shouts and jeers which filled the courtroom were quelled as the Court Cryer intoned, 'My Lord the King's justices do strictly charge and command all manner of persons to keep silence while sentence of death is passing on the prisoners at the bar on pain of imprisonment.

'You, Richard Ringe, are to be taken from hence to the place from whence you came and from thence to be drawn to the place of execution on Saturday next where you will be hanged by the neck until you be dead and your body is to be dissected and anatomised; and the Lord have mercy upon your soul.

'You, Margery Beddingfield are likewise to be taken from hence to the place from whence you came and from thence to be drawn to the place of execution on Saturday next where you are to be burnt until you be dead; and the Lord have mercy upon your soul.'

Like a spark at the end of a fuse, a muted gasp of horror ran round the courtroom at the punishment meted out to Margery. Most of those present were unaware that a wife's murder of her husband was regarded as petty treason and that carried the penalty of burning.

Neither of the prisoners had spoken throughout the trial. They did not speak now, but for the first time they looked at each other.

Before he closed his notebook, the journalist added to his report that never before had he witnessed such despair.

Sixteen

APRIL 1763

Seven days. Each one slowly, steadily, crossing off the hours, minutes and seconds left to Margery and Richard. For them seven long days but for Mrs Beddingfield, just one short week to try to work a miracle. While the prisoners were returned to their former lodging in the jail in Ipswich, mentally immobilised by their sentence, she was dashing hither and thither, enlisting support for a reprieve. An interview with Mr Long, the major landowner in Saxmundham, resulted in letters of introduction to the Sheriff of the county and to the local member of parliament.

Then to London where, on the Tuesday, she met with the honourable gentleman who listened sympathetically to her plea. Having studied the papers on the case, he agreed that a petition should be made to the King. In the meantime he secured for her a stay of execution which she brought to the jail on Thursday afternoon.

Buoyed up with hope, she endeavoured to inspire the same feeling in Margery. She held the girl close in her strong arms for a long time, willing some of her own strength into the poor wasted body. At last, releasing her hold, she said, 'Do not despair, my dear. All is not lost.'

She recounted, without elaboration, the measures she had set in motion.

Margery seemed to be only half listening but when the petition to the King was mentioned, she looked astonished. 'The King! Why should he concern himself with me?'

'And why not? Are you not a true and loyal subject? Have you not as much right to his protection as any other?'

'But, if those who heard the case at Bury did not believe in my innocence, why should the King?'

Mrs Beddingfield snorted. 'Because the King and his advisers are sensible men. They will be able to see clearly what those stupid oafs who made up the jury could not. His Majesty will never allow such a grave miscarriage of justice to take place.'

In the silence that followed, Mrs Beddingfield could not suppress the nagging thought that she might be over confident in her expectations of the royal powers. It was as well that she was ignorant of the number of secretaries, officials and ministers who had to be consulted before her petition would reach the Sovereign – if it ever did. Fortunately, at that time she did not fully understand the workings of the political machine, did not know that personal prejudice could influence or jeopardise a career, that ministers were not always as supportive of each other or their monarch as they should be. Her trust was in a young King who would not fail her. And if he did? What else could she do? She pushed the thought to one side.

'Let us talk of other things. Is there anything you need?'

'Thank you, no. I have all I require for the time until . . .'

'Stop that!'

'There is one thing I would like.'

'Anything – you shall have it.'

Margery hesitated, almost afraid to make the request.

'If she will come, I would like to see Anne.'

This put Mrs Beddingfield in a quandary. It was quite in order for her to visit the jail; over the months she had become inured to it. The stench of the passageways and the wild cries of prisoners mixed with the sound of the clanking chains in which they were fettered had long ceased to assail her consciousness but should she inflict all that upon her daughter?

Margery instantly perceived her reluctance.

'Forgive me, I should not have asked.'

'Nonsense! Of course Anne will come. She has wished to on many occasions but I was not sure you wanted it.'

The seventh day came. Margery listened and Richard watched as the others who were to be executed were taken out of the jail. Two of the men who were confined with Richard had spent the night sleeping in the rough coffins that would accompany them to the execution ground. Wakeful, he had stared down on them as they lay in what appeared to be a rehearsal of that time, now less than twelve hours hence, when they would become permanent occupants of these wooden shells.

He became obsessed by the thought that when it came to his turn – for he pinned no hope on a reprieve – there would be no coffin for him. His head hammered with the words, "and your body be anatomised." They would not leave him and later in the day he was driven to ask his jailer what this really meant.

With relish the man told him.

'The surgeon slits you open to have a look at your innards. Takes 'em all out, just as you would a rabbit or fowl. Then he cuts your body all to pieces. All the flesh is then stripped off to get at the bones so as young gentlemen as are learning to be surgeons can see how they all fit together. As to your head, well he takes . . .'

Richard heard no more. He had fallen to the ground, unconscious. The jailer gave him a cursory examination, found he was still breathing and left him to it.

At six o'clock on the Tuesday of the second week, the London coach pulled into Ipswich bringing two important messengers. One hired a conveyance to carry him as speedily as possible to Sternfield, the other, after he had dined, made his way to the jail. There he handed a letter to Mr Hurst. His Majesty had not seen fit to grant a reprieve.

Mr Hurst informed Richard next morning but decided to wait until Mrs Beddingfield came before breaking the news to Margery.

The chaplain visited the male prisoner to prepare him for his meeting with the Almighty. Like most of the population Richard had never been more than a perfunctory attender at church; he had long since given up making private petitions to God, yet he had had sufficient religious instruction to have it ingrained upon him that the day would come when we "look for the resurrection of the body."

He took no comfort from the words the chaplain uttered. How, he cried, could he ever rise again and have life eternal when his body was to be mutilated by the surgeon? Valiantly, the minister embarked on an explanation, got thoroughly out of his depth and decided to try to change the subject.

'You will stand a much better chance of God's divine forgiveness if you now make a full and frank confession to the crime of which you have been accused. Do not go from this world with that guilt unpurged. Let the truth now pass your lips.'

Richard sank to his knees before the chaplain. It was all so muddled in his head. He had listened in court to Liddy and Betty and had recognised the truth of what they had seen and heard.

His brain tried to unravel the jumble of confusion that was stored there. Yes, he now cried, he had wanted to kill his master. He now believed he had tried to poison him, had indeed placed his hands around John's neck, squeezing every breath of life out of him. But it was all for Margery's sake. He loved her and he thought she loved him. He was sure that she had wanted him to rid her of her husband. She had encouraged him, led him on, shown him kindness and then rejected him.

'It was all her fault!' he screamed throwing himself forward to beat his fists against the hard earth floor.

The chaplain waited for his sobs to die and then congratulated him on a good confession. He would now be ready to face his execution with equanimity.

Mrs Beddingfield had been stunned by the news. All her activity, all her hopes, had come to naught. It was midnight before the messenger had left her and for a time she sat incapable of either lucid thought or even movement. She was utterly drained. Then Anne, who had at least wept, suggested her mother should try to sleep.

'Sleep! There will be time enough for that . . .later. Now we must go at once to Margery and remain with her as much as we are able.'

The indomitable spirit returned. She summoned members of her household, gave orders, and by dawn she and Anne were driving to Ipswich where she intended they should stay until the fatal day. She was glad of Anne's company, not only for her own support but it would help, she believed, to make the forthcoming meeting with Margery a fraction less difficult. She feared for the state of mind in which they would find Margery, not knowing that the girl was still ignorant of the outcome of the petition.

Just before noon on Wednesday, the two ladies entered Mr Hurst's private sitting room. Having offered his sympathy for the lost cause, he then imparted the information that he had waited for her to deliver the blow to Margery. Mrs Beddingfield was torn between relief that Margery had at least been spared an extra night of anguish and anger at the responsibility which had been foisted upon her. The mixed emotions, however, swiftly turned to seething fury when Hurst told her of Richard's confession.

'It would be better for her, Ma'am, if when she hears of it she too, admits her guilt. You will tell her? Or shall I ask the chaplain to do so when he prepares her for . . .'

Mrs Beddingfield wanted to scream, 'Do you own vile work! Don't expect that I should try to assuage your conscience.' But she kept command of herself.

'Leave it to me. I will judge when the time is right. And, I implore you to keep the chaplain from her for as long as possible. My daughter-in-law's experience with men of religion has been far from happy.'

Margery was overjoyed to see Anne. The sight of her friend brought animation to her face and speech. She talked volubly as she had not done for a very long time, recalling their schooldays and the carefree times they had shared. Anne, overcoming her initial qualms, responded in similar fashion. Mrs Beddingfield sitting a little apart from the two girls had the passing thought that to a casual onlooker, apart from the drab surroundings, this could be mistaken for an intimate social gathering. Her spirit failed her now. She could not destroy this fleeting moment of happiness for Margery. She did not tell her – because Margery did not ask – that the appeal had failed.

'I will tell her tomorrow,' Mrs Beddingfield told the governor. He looked grave.

'You are aware, Ma'am, that the execution will be carried out on Friday.'

'Then tomorrow will be soon enough.'

With Anne at her side, she entered the little prison room for the last time on Thursday afternoon. In an attempt to keep their minds occupied, they had spent the morning shopping. This was not mere feminine whim to while away the time; they had busied themselves in the purchase of food and wine to tempt Margery's appetite. A box of sweetmeats upon which to nibble as they talked and a huge bunch of early spring flowers to cheer the dingy room completed their purchases. Both were determined to do all they could to make her last hours as comfortable as possible.

Margery exclaimed with delight as the array of luxuries was spread on the small table.

'What a feast!' She savoured the taste of fresh new bread and sipped slowly from the glass of blood red wine.

'It must have been like this at the Last Supper.' Her mood was serious.

Mrs Beddingfield took her cue.

'And you, dear,' her voice trembled slightly, 'have also been betrayed.'

Quietly and as dispassionately as she was able, she told her that all hope was now gone.

Anne, tears flowing freely, moved close to the girl, placing her strong arms around her shoulders.

Margery listened intently. When the older woman had finished, she eased herself from Anne's encircling arm and knelt before Mrs Beddingfield. She took her hands in hers and looked into the strong face which was in danger of crumpling with emotion.

'Dear Mother – for so you have been to me – no words can express how grateful I am for all that you have done. I am truly sorry that I have brought so much turmoil and distress into your life. It would, perhaps, have been better for you all, if I had never been received into your home and yet, I would not wish that for myself, for you and Anne, and John too, gave me the only true love and happiness I have ever known. For that, I give my,' she faltered on the next word, 'undying thanks.'

She let go a hand to wipe the tears nestling below Mrs Beddingfield's eyes. Her fingers gently caressed the cheek, tracing a path to the lips as if trying to imprint their outline to carry back to her heart where she now placed her hand. Then she put her head in Mrs Beddingfield's lap and wept. For a time all three of them were drawn together in unrestrained emotion.

They had regained the semblance of composure by the time the attendant came in to mend the fire. Margery watched with morbid fascination as the thin logs were piled and the flames from the dying embers began to leap around them.

'I cannot imagine how it will feel.' Her flat statement sent an icy shiver through the others.

Then she laughed, not the light tone they had heard the previous day but a deep sardonic note.

'You know, my father must have been prophetic after all. He said I would burn.'

Mrs Beddingfield took a deep breath.

'Margery, I spoke earlier of betrayal. I think you should know that Ringe has made a full confession of his guilt.' Before Margery could put words to the look of astonishment that had crossed her face, she continued. 'And he insists that you were a party to his plans.'

'And you believe him?'

'That he did what he says, yes.'

'And me?'

'Of course not! How could we, knowing you as we do?'

'Then I am, as you say, betrayed. I believed in him. I looked to him as a friend. How could he have so misunderstood my feelings?'

She became angry. 'He had no right to say what he did. And yet . . .' she broke off, remembering the night she had allowed him to make love to her. Had she not betrayed the memory of John?

'Perhaps I am as guilty as he says and I deserve to die.'

'Do not say so. I refuse to believe that.' Anne cried out. 'You are the victim of circumstances. That wretched Liddy with her malicious slanders is the one who should pay for this.'

'Poor Liddy. Don't be angry with her. She could not help misunderstanding what she saw and heard.'

'Poor Liddy! How can you feel any thing for her after what she has done to you?'

'Dear Anne, do not be so angry.' She thought for a moment before continuing. 'Yes, I do feel sorry for her, truly I do. Remember, tomorrow will be the end for me, but Liddy has to live with herself for the rest of her days.'

There was a tap at the door, the attendant hovered to say that the chaplain wished to know if he might come in a few minutes.

It was time for the last leave-taking. Margery embraced them both in turn.

'I am quite calm now and ready to face the morrow. I know that I leave Pleasance to your loving protection. I can hardly bear to let myself think of her, but one day, should she ever ask about her dead mother, tell her I loved her dearly, as I loved her father. And if it is possible, never let her hear of how I met my end.'

Mrs Beddingfield and Anne did not join the multitude that assembled on the morning of the 8th April at the place of execution on Rushmere Heath. Hangings always drew a huge crowd not just from the peasantry and artisans but gentlemen too, who came on horseback or in their carriages to watch justice carried out. The gentlemen actively encouraged attendance by the general populace, being of the opinion that the spectacle would prove salutary to them – a dire warning of what could be their fate should they take to crime.

It was a busy and lucrative time for small traders; pedlars, ballad-song salesmen and sellers of refreshments plied their wares among those waiting. Regular attenders exchanged stories of the best and worst executions they had witnessed or regaled first-timers with the gory delights in store for them that day. For indeed, this promised to be an exceptionally good day. Hangings were, when all said and done, a mere two-a-penny but few could remember when they had last had a burning.

It was a sense of macabre horror that had drawn so many to stand and gaze as the wooden post was hammered into the ground and the pile of dry faggots was heaped up round its base.

The representative of the Ipswich Journal skirted the throng noting down which of the gentry were in attendance. The faces of a group of men who had set themselves apart from the main body of bystanders seemed vaguely familiar. Then he realised that he had seen them in the courtroom at Bury. They must have come from Saxmundham. As he looked in their direction he wondered for a moment if that pretty maidservant was with them. His eyes scanned the crowd for her. Would she, with all her confidence, come to witness the conclusion to the drama to which she had been the Chorus.

For a long time he had been unable to get her out of his mind. After the trial he had, by chance, found himself at an inn where some of the witnesses had gathered. With the trained ear of the reporter he had eavesdropped on a snatch of conversation.

"Tis my belief that Liddy Clebold was just downright jealous. Betty Riches, herself, told my wife that the girl was in love with Ringe. So it's plain to see that when he didn't want her, she set out to ruin him.'

'More than likely,' his comrade replied. 'She's a flighty piece by all accounts. Eggs men on too, so I'm told. Likes to be the centre of things. But, for all that, would she have made up all them things she said? She'd have to be mad to want a man to die just because she couldn't have him.'

Others passing between the reporter and the speakers meant

that he heard no more but he was unable to forget that snatch of conversation. His impartial judgement of the case had been that it was possible that Ringe had murdered, but he was not convinced of Margery's guilt in the affair – and now here was a motive for the accusations against her that had not even been considered at the trial.

A sudden movement in the crowd put an end to further thought on that subject. The carriage bearing the dignitaries who would supervise the executions had entered the arena. Then a shout went up from a short distance off – the procession from the jail was nearing its destination.

The sledges bearing the prisoners came to rest. Loosed from their bonds, they had to be helped to stand, their bodies already bruised and jolted from the long haul over nearly three miles of stony road. They had been dragged first through the streets of the town where residents had leaned from upper storey windows to hurl abuse. Below them, bystanders had added to the cacophony, women in particular shouting obscenities at Margery. Only very few averted their gaze as they considered the fate which awaited the poor wretches.

A brief respite from the deafening roars had come as they passed into the countryside but neither was in any condition to appreciate the clean, crisp air whipping against their faces, or the first spring leaves bursting on the overhanging trees and a sky, so bright and clear that its radiance blinded eyes which had so long been accustomed to gloom. There was no space for thought as they endured the uphill drag over jagged flints and uneven stones, flung this way and that by ruts, bumped out of potholes to be banged against the hard boards against which they lay inclined. It had seemed a blessed relief when at last they stopped.

And now they stood facing a seething mass of onlookers. Neither of them had ever seen so many people gathered in one place. As if by some unseen and unheard signal, the crowd was instantly silenced. A thrill of expectation hung in the air, the audience was waiting for the curtain to go up on the last act.

The actors took their places. Mr Hurst formally presented the prisoners to Mr Clarke, the under Sheriff who had the painful duty of making sure that his Majesty's justice was carried out. Waiting, to one side, the hangman and the man who would fasten Margery to the post and put the tinder to the faggots. The chaplain stood between Richard and Margery.

'Are they prepared?' Mr Clarke inquired of the chaplain. He nodded, finding it difficult to control himself for Margery had refused to admit her guilt when he had prayed with her.

In his experience those facing execution usually made a clean breast of all their sins but this woman, while acknowledging that she had not perhaps been a dutiful daughter and that she might inadvertently have hurt the feelings of others during her short life, steadfastly denied that she had been implicated in her husband's death. The reverend gentleman had wrestled long with her conscience. Now it was his own that troubled him.

'Do you wish to say anything to either the prisoners or the assembly at large? You will rarely have such an opportunity to sermonise to so many.'

The chaplain shook his head. 'There is nothing I wish to say that can be of any use now.'

'Very well. Let us deal with it as speedily as possible. I have little taste for such business as this.'

He turned his attention to the male prisoner and read out the formal charge in ringing tones concluding with ,'Richard Ringe, have you anything to say before you leave this world?'

Richard raised his haggard face. Few of the onlookers would have been aware that this bedraggled creature had once been a healthy, good looking young man. Scarcely twenty two, his years hung on him like a man of thrice that age. His now lustreless eyes were sunk deep into the pinched sickly face. Slowly, as if his neck was already encased in rope, he turned his head towards Margery and whispered, 'Forgive.'

Then he faced the under Sheriff. 'I am ready.'

He was led away to the gallows. While he mounted the cart to have the noose placed round his neck, Mr Clarke repeated the charge to Margery.

He found it repugnant to have to carry out sentence on a woman. Having read the formal words, he allowed himself to look at her. She was dressed all in white save for a band of black crepe upon her arm. Her head, from which most of the hair had been cut that morning, was enclosed in a white cap. For all that she had endured, she possessed a dignity he had not before witnessed on such an occasion.

He could barely bring himself to ask her if she wished to say anything.

Even at this moment, Margery was capable of compassion. She felt the man's uneasiness. Just the hint of a smile touched the corner of her mouth.

'Nothing, sir, except to thank those, like Mr Hurst who have used me kindly.'

Clarke could not bear it. 'Take her to the place of execution.'

Now an excited murmur ran through the crowd as they watched her being placed against the stake, tied by hands and feet. The clamour grew as those in the front ranks saw Mr Clarke pull out a large kerchief and hand it to Margery's executioner. They could not hear what words were exchanged but as the signal was given for the cart to be pulled away from Richard's feet, leaving him suspended, his neck broken, the kerchief was put round Margery's throat and drawn tight, ever tighter, until all breath was gone. Then the tinder was applied to the faggots and the flames licked their way upwards to encircle her body.

The fire burned well. Very soon the air hung heavy with the smell of charred flesh, acrid smoke stinging the eyes of the crowd. Many of those who had watched unmoved, now found themselves weeping as the flames drew closer to the already blackened head. Women screamed, hiding their faces from the horror which would haunt their nights for years to come.

Richard's body was cut down and placed in the cart which would carry it to be dissected by the surgeon. The crowd began to melt away, subdued by the spectacle they had witnessed.

With the fickleness of April, the day which had been so bright, clouded over and slow drops of rain began to fall.

Those who stayed to gaze at what was now but a pile of ashes with a few glowing embers were suddenly disturbed as a figure pushed through them. A young woman came to a halt by the charred remains. She stood as if transfixed – then let out a scream that ripped at the hearts of those who heard it.

'What have I done?'

In a frenzy she turned to appeal to the bystanders. 'Who will ever forgive me?'

Lost and demented, she cried again, 'What is to become of me?'

Then Liddy threw herself down upon the ashes. The drama was finished.